Work in Progress

and other stories

The Caine Prize for African Writing
2009

Work in Progress

and other stories

The Caine Prize for African Writing
2009

The Caine Prize for African Writing 2009

First published in the UK in 2009 by
New Internationalist™ Publications Ltd
Oxford OX4 1BW
www.newint.org
New Internationalist is a registered trademark.

First published in 2009 in southern Africa by
Jacana Media (Pty) Ltd
10 Orange Street
Sunnyside
Auckland Park 2092
South Africa
+27 11 628 3200
www.jacana.co.za

Cover illustration: 'Tears' by David Tettey Charway, Ghana.

Design by New Internationalist.

Printed on recycled paper by TJ International Limited, Cornwall, UK,
who hold environmental accreditation ISO 14001.

British Library Cataloguing-in-Publication Data.
A catalogue record for this book is available from the British Library.

Library of Congress Cataloguing-in-Publication Data.
A catalogue record for this book is available from the Library of Congress.

New Internationalist ISBN: 978-1-906523-14-5
Jacana Media ISBN: 978-1-77009-750-6

Contents

Caine Prize Sponsors

The Council of the Caine Prize for African Writers is immensely grateful to all who have helped the Prize and the Workshop in 2009. The principal sponsor of the Prize has been the Oppenheimer Memorial Trust, and the principal sponsor of this year's workshop Zain Africa BV. Grants have also been received from the Booker Prize Foundation, the Gibbs Trust, the Beit Trust, the British Council and a number of generous private donors; and valuable help in kind has been given by the Royal Over-Seas League, the Bodleian Library, Kenya Airways, the Rector of Exeter College, Oxford, and the Institute of English Studies, University of London.

Introduction

Ten Years of the Caine Prize

THIS YEAR, 2009, we celebrate the Caine Prize's Tenth Anniversary. The Prize's tenth winner will be chosen from among the five shortlisted stories that appear below, and announced at the Award Dinner in Oxford at which this anthology will be launched.

What is there to celebrate? Quite an achievement. Shortly before he died in 1999, Sir Michael Caine was working on the idea of a prize to encourage the growing recognition of the worth of African writing in English, its richness and diversity, by bringing it to a wider audience. Today we can say this has been steadily happening. Most of the Caine Prize winners to date – and many of the shortlisted candidates – have since had novels or collections of their short stories published by mainstream publishers in the UK and US, publishers such as Jonathan Cape, Bloomsbury, Hamish Hamilton, Fourth Estate, WW Norton, Algonquin and Massachusetts University Press. Their books have been widely reviewed and seriously promoted, no longer relegated to some hidden shelf of exotica in the bookshops. There is no doubt that African writing has achieved far greater prominence than it enjoyed ten years ago.

At the same time it has become much easier for African writers to get their short stories published in the first place – entries for the Caine Prize in recent years have been running at levels two or three times as high as in the earliest years. The internet has been a very valuable new vehicle. But there, as elsewhere, the very existence of the Caine Prize, and the profile it has acquired, has been a key stimulus. And the Caine Prize has also contributed directly: we have published the stories written at our workshops alongside the shortlisted stories each year, a total of almost a hundred new stories to date.

Of course there have been other factors at play. A real hunger for good news out of Africa. And a feeling among a new African generation that it was time to recover the literary vitality of the 1950s and 1960s, and in particular that the image of Africa in the rest of the world should no longer be left to be defined by whimsical, self-absorbed, alien expatriates. This feeling was notably strong in Kenya, where the Minister for Education upbraided young Kenyan writers for the fact that there was not a single Kenyan entry for the Caine Prize in 2001, spurring Binyavanga Wainaina to write the story that won the Prize in 2002 and gave him the space to devote his time to a new literary magazine, *Kwani?*. This magazine then published the next year's winning story, by Yvonne Adhiambo Owuor. *Kwani?* has continued to be a rich source of Caine Prize entries and of participants in Caine Prize workshops.

Entries and shortlist for the Tenth Prize

The urge for self-expression is often born out of adversity. Astonishingly, the country with the highest number of entries for the Prize this year was Zimbabwe, the first time the list has not been dominated by Nigeria and South Africa, thanks to the weight of population in the one and the publishing opportunities in the other. And almost all of the Zimbabwean entries were from anthologies published in 2008 by the courageous independent publishers there.

The overall quality of entries for the 2009 Prize was high and it took the Judges a whole day to decide on a shortlist – a task that has previously only taken half a day.

They deserve our special thanks. In the Chair was Nana Yaa Mensah, Chief Sub-Editor of the *New Statesman*; and she was assisted by Professor Jon Cook of the University of East Anglia, award-winning novelist and Georgetown University professor Jennifer Natalya Fink, *Guardian* journalist and author Hannah Pool, and Mohammed Umar, the Nigerian novelist, journalist and bookseller.

The Judges eventually chose for the shortlist Mamle Kabu (Ghana) *The End of Skill*, from *Dreams, Miracles and Jazz*, published by Picador Africa, Johannesburg 2008; Parselelo Kantai (Kenya) *You Wreck Her*, from the *St Petersburg Review*, New York 2008; Alistair Morgan (South Africa) *Icebergs*, from the *Paris Review* 183, New York 2008; EC Osondu (Nigeria) *Waiting*, from the internet magazine *Guernica*; and Mukoma wa Ngugi (Kenya) *How Kamau wa Mwangi Escaped into Exile*, from *Wasafiri* 54, Summer 2008, London. Parselelo Kantai and EC Osondu have both been shortlisted for the Prize before, in 2004 and 2007 respectively. *Icebergs* is Alistair Morgan's first published story.

The 2009 Workshop and other publications
by Caine Prize writers in the year

The 2009 Zain Caine Prize Workshop for African Writers was held in Ghana – its first time in West Africa. Acting in a tutorial role were Jamal Mahjoub and Aminatta Forna, who have both served as Caine Prize Judges in the past. There were four participants from Ghana, two from Sierra Leone, two from Nigeria, two from Zimbabwe and one from South Africa. I thought the stories – published in this volume – were the best from a Caine Prize workshop yet. (I am teased for saying this every year, but that does not mean it is not true!)

2009 has seen a quite exceptional crop of books by Caine Prize writers. A first novel by Brian Chikwava (Caine Prize Winner, 2004), *Harare North*, was published by Jonathan Cape, to widespread acclaim. Cape also published *Fatta Morgana* by Chika Unigwe (Nigeria, who was shortlisted in 2004). Laila Lalami (Morocco, shortlisted 2006) had her first novel, *Secret Son*, published by Algonquin Books of Chapel Hill. Binyavanga Wainaina (Kenya) and Monica Arac de Nyeko (Uganda), winners in 2002 and 2007 respectively, have both delivered first novels to their publishers. Petina Gappah (Zimbabwe) had her first collection of short stories, bearing the name of a story she wrote at the Caine Prize workshop in 2007, *An Elegy for Easterly*, published by Faber and Faber. Another workshop participant, Sulaiman Addonia (Eritrea) had his first novel, *The Consequences of Love*, published by Chatto and Windus late in 2008.

The 2008 Caine Prize anthology, *The Jambula Tree*, was the first to be published in Nigeria, by Cassava Republic, and our thanks go to them and our regular publishers, New Internationalist (Oxford) and Jacana Media (Johannesburg).

Nick Elam
Administrator of The Caine Prize for African Writing

Caine Prize Stories 2009:
Shortlist

The End of Skill

Mamle Kabu

THE SECOND TIME JIMMY had a soul exchange with his father was the day they talked about the fate of the Adweneasa cloth. It was exactly what Jimmy had hoped to avoid, for he knew that if it happened, his father would speak to that part of him over which he had no control. When their eyes locked in that inexpressible way, he heard the word come out of his lips. The one he had promised himself he would not say. His father's reaction shattered his daze.

"He did what?"

There was a painful silence.

"Speak up boy, and let me open my ears well this time because I didn't hear you right."

Jimmy looked into his father's face again and knew he had heard him very well. He could not stand the burning gaze, full of pain and angry questions. He dropped his eyes.

"I said he put it on the..."

"Silence!"

Obediently, he swallowed the last word. He dared not protest against being ordered to speak and to shut up at the same time. He might be a grown man now – a 'guy' in town, a hero to his younger brothers, a success story – but when his father spoke to him like this, he might as well be five years old again. He kept his eyes on the floor and his hands behind his back.

"Let us not offend the ancestors with this talk."

His father put down the shuttle he had been gripping tightly throughout their conversation and climbed out of the loom. For an angry man, his movements were gentle, contained, and even graceful.

They walked out into the compound. After the inner sanctuary of the old man's weaving room, the heat and glare of the dry-season March day were like a blow to the senses. They walked past the fragrant cooking fire and the main weaving shed where 12 boys and young men were engrossed in their work, pretending not to notice the troubled pair pass by. As he skirted the line of warp threads stretched out before the looms, Jimmy caught the eye of his younger brother. Kwabena kept his fingers moving so that their father would not catch the look that passed between them. "You fool," it said. "You went and told him, didn't you?"

The sound of clicking shuttles receded as they stepped over the little gutter that circled the compound, stopping finally at a disused weaving shed. Jimmy quickly pulled out the weaver's stool, dusted it off with his hands and set it down for his father. He shooed away a hen and her chicks and perched on a rusty tin trunk.

"Kweku."

"Yes, Da."

His father never called him Jimmy. That was the name he had given himself after he had left home. But it had taken over so much now that he only remembered 'Kweku' on his trips back home. His father had never given any indication that he was aware Kweku had any other name.

"What did the white man do with our *Adweneasa* cloth?"

"Father, he treasures the cloth so much. If only you could understand."

On their short walk between his father's weaving room and the old shed, Jimmy had racked his brains for a way to convey to his father that foreigners simply had different ways of expressing their admiration. Jimmy had never doubted the ambassador's profound appreciation of the cloth. "Ah, what a masterpiece," he had said the day Jimmy brought it to him. As he unfolded the great cloth, Jimmy saw the same awe in his eyes that lit them up every time he brought him a piece. "Ken-tay is so beautiful," he said, shaking his head with the mystery of it as he stroked the perfect web and traced the colourful geometry with his fingers. "You really are a master."

Jimmy did not bother to explain that he had not woven any of it. It made no difference anyway, because he could have done so. But why waste time explaining that it would take one man four months to weave such a cloth on his own, and that all his father's apprentices had worked on it. What mattered to the ambassador was that he had his cloth and it was beautiful. What mattered to Jimmy was that he would be paid. But the ambassador was not ready. He wanted to know more about the cloth. Its name, the meanings of its motifs. Jimmy was impatient for his money but he was no fool. He would not be standing in a cool, plush ambassador's residence in Accra, about to receive several crisp bills of a coveted foreign currency, if he had not learned that there was more to a good sale than the exchange of goods and money. That was what set him apart from other young kente weavers. They slaved away in villages under their masters, in crowded city craft markets and in the dusty din of urban roadsides, making a pittance. Jimmy had carved a niche for himself. He had "made connections" and was now the envy of them all.

It all started when he met Cassie at the Golden Sands Hotel. That was three months after he had arrived in Accra to seek his fortune. Jimmy had big dreams and he was smart. He had kept quiet as his father poured libation to invoke the blessings of the weaving forefathers on the loom he would carry to Accra. He had friends who had gone to Accra and found work as waiters, gardeners and security men. Some of them worked for white people and earned far more than a village weaver could dream about. His friend Boateng had grown dreadlocks and found a white girl at the beach who had taken him to America. Jimmy had heard that he had become a taxi driver there and earned more than a bank manager back home. Someone who could barely speak English when he left Adanwomase!

Jimmy knew he could make it too. After all, he had a primary school education, which was more than many of the others had. With his quick brain and flair for languages, he often gave the impression of being more educated than he was. He was also blessed with good looks and natural charisma. He was what people called 'a free man' – good natured, ready to see the humour in everything. This combination of attributes made him popular with people in general, and women in particular.

At first, he had squeezed into the stuffy chamber-and-hall in a suburb of Accra, which was shared by his friend Jonas, his brother and another friend. Jonas worked as a waiter in a fast-food restaurant and he tried, unsuccessfully, to help Jimmy get a job there. Jimmy would walk around town, asking in shops and restaurants and even at some private houses, but everyone seemed to be suspicious of a footloose new arrival. What he needed was a 'connection', but how to get it was a problem. He also started weaving. He had brought his loom to Accra mainly so that he did not have to explain to his father that he had no intention of weaving. However, he soon realised that kente cloth had taken on a new life in the big city. The roadside weavers were not wrestling with the problem of trying to sell 12-yard pieces of cloth for chiefs and rich men to wear to festivals. They were selling single 'letterstrips' with messages like 'I Miss You' woven into them, which were snapped up by tourists and passers-by.

He went to the central craft market in Accra and saw an astonishing variety of modern fashion items made or trimmed with kente cloth. He bumped into Nana, one of his father's former apprentices. He was making things that Jimmy had never seen, like sets of table place-mats composed of a few strips sewn together and cut into pieces.

"You can sell a set of six like these to a rich tourist for the price of a full cloth back in Adanwomase," Nana told him. "And you don't even have to be as careful with the quality as when you are with your master back home."

Jimmy did not need any further encouragement. He was in debt now and hardly eating properly any more. He was also excited by the challenge of making something so different. He set up his loom under a tree in the crowded compound. Nana had agreed to sell something for him if he could take a share of the sale. Jimmy's father had given him some yarns to take to Accra, which he had secretly planned to sell. Now he brought them out and began weaving a strip, which he planned to turn into a set of place-mats.

It was good to be weaving again. He had always loved it and had clearly been a born master from the time that his father began to teach him at the age of seven. He started creating new patterns as soon as he had mastered the old ones. By the time he was 14, his father would boast, "As for Kweku, my first born, I can sell his work to a chief and tell him I wove it myself. And all he will say is 'Egya Kwame Mensah, you've done it again'."

In his loom, Jimmy found an inner peace, which he never found anywhere else. It was another world in which he and his art became one and did not need anyone or anything else. The design flowed out of him and into the cloth. He worked for hours, feeling neither hunger nor thirst. The disappointment of not finding a job and the tension over his uncertain future were lulled to sleep by the rhythm of the loom as the heddles parted the warp threads and the shuttles flew through, trailing their colours behind them.

He had often secretly watched his father at work. Even before he ever wove himself, he knew that otherworldly look on his father's face and understood that stopping work and climbing out of the loom was a transition from one world to another. The closest comparison he could think of was waking from sleep. He knew that not all weavers felt this way. Back home in Adanwomase, weaving was an occupation which all young boys were expected to follow, and many did so simply because it was the family tradition. They learned the technique and produced acceptable pieces of cloth, but they never became masters. True kente masterpieces were made by weavers who entered another world when they climbed into their looms.

It was not a topic one ever heard discussed. He always knew which of his father's apprentices were destined to become masters simply by watching their faces as they wove. He knew his father had seen it in him too, but they never talked about it until the day of his thanksgiving ceremony. It was a great day when Egya Kwame Mensah, bursting with pride, officially declared his first son a competent weaver. After Kweku had presented the customary drinks and a fat white ram to his father, and the requisite libation had been poured for a prosperous weaving career, they sat down to discuss his future. That was when the old man first realised that his son did not want to be a weaver. He could not take it seriously.

"Kweku, I have always been so proud of you. You are my first-born and the best weaver in the family. Yes, one day you will be even better than me. I know it already and I thank God for it. What more could a father ask?"

Kweku was ready. He had rehearsed this scene in his head dozens of times, made a mental catalogue of all his father's possible protestations and prepared answers for each one of them. He was deeply sorry to spoil his father's joy on such a day, but he knew this discussion could not be postponed any further. He was certain it would not end acrimoniously, for the two of them had an understanding beyond the usual filial relationship, which hinged mainly on respect from the son. Although he was not altogether conscious of it, this special understanding was not unrelated to their mutual belonging to that other realm, which they entered through the loom.

It was also due to this special understanding that Kweku knew he could no longer keep up the pretence of wanting to be a weaver. If he was dishonest about it on such a momentous day, it would be even more difficult for his father to forgive him later on. He had never actually misled the old man on this point. However, the assumption that he would become a weaver was so strong that nothing short of a direct refutation would shake it. Kweku's silence on the issue had never been interpreted in any way as ominous. Now, finally, it was time to speak.

"Father, I know that in the olden days weavers rubbed shoulders with royalty, and that our great-grandfather wove for the King himself, but how many weavers today can make a living only from weaving?"

If it would not have been disrespectful to his father, Kweku would simply have come out and said that he did not want to be like most weavers today – a poor man. That he did not just want to be a respected village master-weaver. He wanted to live in the city, own a car and a beautiful house, travel abroad... He wanted a completely different life from his father. He was talented and driven and it showed in his weaving, but he knew he could apply that talent to other things and be successful. He could never realise his dreams through weaving, much as he loved it. However, it was precisely this love that complicated things. Even as he argued, as respectfully as he could, against his father's objections, Kweku felt guilty in doing so. He did not intend to admit it, but he fully sympathised with the old man's failure to comprehend that he should want to give up something he clearly loved so much. Still, he was not prepared for what his father said next. What he had prepared for was something like: "But Kweku, you enjoy weaving so much, how can you talk about giving it up?"

And his response would have been: "Yes, Father, I do enjoy it, but times are just too hard now. If I get a good job and make money, it will benefit all of us."

Instead, his father said something so simply and quietly that Kweku would not have been sure he had heard him correctly if his meaning had not been unmistakable:

"My son, I have seen the look in your eyes when you weave."

Kweku looked up to meet his father's direct gaze. They had never exchanged a look like that before. In the interminable few seconds that it lasted, it completed the conversation. For the first time in his life, Kweku realised that he had participated in an exchange between souls that was far more eloquent than the language of spoken words. And he knew that he could discard the rest of his set responses. His eyes had given his father the answer he wanted, and it came directly from his soul. But they had given it involuntarily, startling him in the process. He was uncomfortable with what had happened. It was as if his father had spoken to a part of him that he did not fully know himself and that had betrayed the Kweku with whom he was more familiar. The one whose dreams he was determined to pursue.

Now he tried to rally that person and focus on his ambition. One day, when he was rich and could buy the whole family everything they had ever longed for, cushioning his father in health and wealth for the rest of his life, the old man would forgive him for leaving their secret world. In the meantime, there would be no need for him to know that Kweku was not weaving. After all, he could not check up on him in Accra. It was pointless to cause any further pain now. Kweku wanted to end the conversation but he could not find the words to respond to the look that had just passed between them. As if in recognition of this, his father picked up the spoken part of the conversation.

"Kweku, the way you feel when you weave, it is not just an accident. Not all weavers feel that way. Do you know where that feeling comes from?"

Kweku felt his scalp tingle. His father's hushed tones and direct gaze did not frighten him, but they conveyed a sense of something beyond the ordinary, which he had sensed but never consciously investigated.

"Your gift for weaving is God-given and is guided by the ancestral spirits. When you settle in the loom, they invite you into their world, in which you find the peace, inspiration and perfection that make you a great weaver. These things do not belong to the ordinary world. You may not have realised it, but I am telling you now that the spirits of our great weaving ancestors are with you when you work. When you enter the loom and lose yourself in the web, you cross over to their world. It is not all weavers who can go there. Only those with a special gift, like you and I."

These words echoed in Jimmy's head now as he wove under the tree in the squalid little compound. He had thought about them a great deal since that day. They had made certain things clearer to him. Once when he was a child, his father

16

had caught him 'practising' on the loom in his weaving room. In his confusion at being caught and his haste to vacate his father's seat, he had tripped and fallen. He knew he was in trouble, but had not been prepared for his father's degree of horror and agitation, for which he naturally blamed himself. It was only much later that he learned it was a taboo to fall in a loom and that special rites and sacrifices had to be performed to save the person who had fallen from the curse of the offended spirits. Jimmy also knew that the fixed loom in his father's weaving room was special. Although his father often wove on the mobile looms outside, it was only on the indoor one that he created new designs. Jimmy had watched him pour libation and sacrifice fowls there before. With advancing maturity, he also came to understand that it was their menstrual periods that barred his mother and sisters from that room at certain times, and even barred them from speaking to his father while he sat there. Jimmy knew that not all weavers of his father's generation were so traditional. It was their proud history as descendants of royal weavers that made the old traditions so important to his father.

The day Jimmy met Cassie, his fortunes changed forever. He and Nana were selling their place-mats and table-runners at a craft bazaar at the Golden Sands Hotel. He had brought along his loom. He knew the 22 hotel staff and the other vendors would find it odd, but he had thought about it and decided that it would probably attract people to their stall.

He was right.

"Oh look, a kente weaver," people exclaimed excitedly, hurrying over to watch him at work.

Their goods sold out long before they had anticipated, and they even had difficulty holding back a few to serve as samples. Jimmy continued to weave while Nana took orders. Nana had to admit that it had been a good idea to bring the loom, although he would never have tried such a thing himself. That was the difference between Jimmy and other people.

He always thought of that little extra that made the difference between mediocrity and excellence. What really set him apart, though, was that he had the courage to match the boldness of his ideas and translate them into action.

Cassie was the first person who asked if she could have a go on the loom. Nana smiled and was about to explain that it was too complicated for a beginner and that even weavers did not start learning on proper looms. But Jimmy stopped him with a look that said, "Of course", and stepped out of the loom and beckoned her into it with an engaging smile. Nana knew that Jimmy's father would never have allowed a woman to sit at a loom or to touch a weaving instrument, but he was beginning to realise that Jimmy, the obedient son and apple of his father's eye, had his own set of rules. Jimmy guided the heddle toeholds between Cassie's toes, placed a shuttle in her hand and showed her what to do. She was extremely eager but, predictably, was confounded by the complexity of it. He placed his hands over hers and guided them as well as he could from behind. It was an agreeable sensation, enveloping her small, beautifully manicured white hands in his. He sensed immediately that he was not alone in enjoying the feeling. Perhaps that was why she was having trouble co-ordinating her hands and feet.

On an impulse, he suggested that she sit on his lap, so that he could help her with the footwork. He knew it was an audacious proposition and did not bother to apprise himself of Nana's reaction. Following bold impulses could be dangerous, but he often felt that it was the only way to pull oneself out of a rut and force new opportunities to open up. The look Cassie gave him affirmed that audacity was not alien to her nature either. They felt this common trait pull them towards each other across the many gulfs of difference that lay between them. It was a tight fit in the loom but Jimmy would not have suggested it if Cassie had not been a slim, small woman. He acted as a full-body puppet-master, not pulling strings, but matching his body to hers and guiding her with his movements. He folded his arms around hers and moved his legs underneath her as a prompt. After a few bumpy beginnings, they found perfect rhythm. She clasped the heddle toeholds tightly between her bare toes and pumped them up and down in tandem with Jimmy, parting the warp threads to create a space for the shuttle, which he guided into place with his fingers – manipulating hers.

They became lovers the next day. Cassie was spending her summer vacation with a friend, Margaret, whose husband worked for a multinational company in Ghana. Margaret was well connected in the Accra expatriate social scene and soon became Jimmy's most important client and promoter. She had money to spend, time on her hands, and friends with whom to share her new discoveries. Within weeks, Jimmy was receiving a flurry of orders, being invited to coffee mornings where he could display, sell and take new orders; he was frequently receiving foreign currency as payment. He gained a foothold as an exciting young local artisan in many expatriate households and his 'free' character made him so popular that he even started receiving party invitations. By the time Cassie left, he was quite the flavour of the month, and was well on his way to his new, exclusive niche at the top of the kente-trading ladder. Margaret and her friends would ask, "Oh, is that a 'Jimmy'?" every time they saw a beautiful piece of kente, so that his name became synonymous with the textile within the narrow but powerful confines of the expatriate community.

Of course, charisma alone was not enough to sustain this kind of success. Underpinning Jimmy's comet-like rise to artisanal fame and glory, was the outstanding quality of his work. However, it did not take long for the volume of his orders to exceed his capacity. The time had come to enlist help from home. Jimmy made his first trip home nine months after he had left, taking along money, gifts and a stack of weaving orders. It was a sweet return, for he had fulfilled his father's dreams in spite of himself. He rejoiced quietly in the knowledge that his father would never have to find out that he had attempted to be anything but a weaver since he left home. The old man was quite beside himself with joy to see his beloved Kweku again. Although he had expected his son to be successful in the city, he was amazed by the number of orders he brought back home and was speechless when Jimmy showed him the first dollar and euro bills he had ever seen.

For Jimmy's brothers and the other apprentices, his fashionable clothes, new slang expressions and sharp 'American Gigolo' haircut were the clearest signs of success. It had the desired effect when Jimmy asked them to weave letterstrips for him with the messages 'My Sweet Tanja' and 'Vanessa my African Queen'. He told them offhandedly that he did not have the time to do them himself as he had to focus on the main orders, but the truth was that he knew the foreign names and sugary messages would convey the requisite information about his new lifestyle to the boys at home without him having to brag about it. He was right, because when he approached the busy line of looms the following morning, a football match-like chant of "Ji-mmy! Ji-mmy!" went up. He grinned conspiratorially and told them to shut up.

The message for Vanessa showed his growing awareness of the issue of African-American heritage and its value on the kente market. Vanessa had been his greatest education on this topic so far. Thrilled to meet a kente weaver, she was effusive about what kente meant to her and the sisters and brothers back home. She already owned several kente-patterned items, which she had bought in America, including a backpack, a head tie and a dressing-gown. On the day she took him to the beach and stripped off to reveal a kente-patterned thong bikini, however, the expression, "Now I have seen everything" came to his mind. Even as he enjoyed the rear view of the tiny kente triangle pointing like an arrow to the shapely cheeks of Vanessa's bottom, he could not shake a niggling feeling of discomfiture.

"How d'you like my kin-tay bikini, Jimmy?" she asked.

"It's very sexy," he said evasively and then added in what he hoped was a casual tone, "So you like wearing kente like this?"

"Are you kidding me? Man, you know what it means to us. I feel so African when I wear it. I love it, can't you see that? I want it around me all the time. You know Jimmy, I could wear it all day long – day and night."

Jimmy had perfected the art of keeping his father out of his mind on such occasions, but this time the spectre of the old man rose unbidden before he could stop it. If he could see and hear Vanessa now... what would he say to the idea of a kente thong bikini making someone feel 'African'? The cloth of kings worn day and night, a kente arrow pointing to the cheeks of a woman's bottom... Jimmy shuddered. How could love and esteem be expressed in such different ways? He knew his father would never understand that a person who used kente in such ways could genuinely love and esteem the cloth. Vanessa, on the other hand, would never be able to understand that surrounding herself with something and making it a part of her everyday life could show anything but love. She had big plans to help Jimmy break into the American market, and had promised to explore export opportunities for him when she returned home. She assured him that there were many African-American companies that would snap up his cloth for graduation gowns, designer clothes and all sorts of 'heritage' goods.

Jimmy showered her with kente gifts. This fulfilled the multiple role of expressing affection, promoting his weaving for future marketing opportunities and compensating for his periodic blunders with regard to her racial sensitivities.

It took an exquisite stole, originally ordered by an ambassador's wife, to appease her the day his friend Nana called her white. Vanessa was one of those African-Americans who had more white blood than black.

In Ghana, far darker people were called 'white'. Even Ghanaians of mixed parentage were often called white. Jimmy had actually laughed aloud the first time he had heard her call herself a black woman. He was astonished by the degree of anger and pain this caused her, and was cowed by her scathing attack on him for his failure to recognise his own brothers and sisters from the Diaspora. Jimmy quickly realised that not taking her seriously on this topic would be the quickest way to end their friendship. Although he could not fully comprehend her point of view, he resolved not to make any other careless slips about her colour. He also came to realise that racial sensitivity and an awareness of the issue of heritage gained him incalculable goodwill with his African-American clients, which naturally translated into excellent profits.

However, keeping up his guard with Vanessa was harder than he had imagined, especially as it also meant worrying about his friends' blunders. The day he introduced her to Nana at the craft centre he was nervous. He had warned Nana in advance but was still fearful because he could see that Nana could not take it seriously. Nana gave Vanessa an effusive welcome, which delighted her, and when he teased Jimmy in Twi, "So this is your black woman," and laughed heartily, Vanessa assumed that they were simply exchanging some guy gossip. Jimmy laughed too but warned him again not to slip up. Nana assured him that there was no need to worry. Everything went extremely well at first, and Vanessa took a liking to the talkative Nana. She admired his kente goods and asked about some of the patterns. Jimmy knew that Nana would be surprised by her knowledge of kente designs. She had read a book about kente and, through her persistent questions and discussions, had even taught Jimmy some new things about the cloth.

"Oh, that's 'Fathia is right for Nkrumah'," she exclaimed, pointing at the cloth named for the Egyptian wife of Ghana's first president. "And this must be 'Family is strength'." Nana nodded in open-mouthed admiration and asked if she also knew the names of the newer designs.

She had no idea but was eager to learn. He picked out the ones he thought she would find most interesting. "This one, for your former president – is named 'Clinton'."

She was duly intrigued. Jimmy explained to her that it was of the same pattern as the one that had been presented to President Clinton on his visit to Ghana.

"And this one call 'Hippic'," continued Nana, thoroughly enjoying himself, "for people who can't afford."

Vanessa looked puzzled. Jimmy did not actually know the full term 'Highly Indebted Poor Countries', but he explained as best he could that the cloth had been jokingly named to mark "Ghana going HIPC". To their joint relief, Vanessa understood and found it extremely witty. While Nana cast about for another interesting cloth, she glimpsed a heavy rayon piece with a dazzling variety of patterns.

"Is this the Adwi... Adwen... I mean, the one that means 'the end of designs' or something like that?"

"*Adweneasa* – My skill is exhausted," supplied Nana in garbled English, impressed again.

"Oh, is that how you translate it?" Vanessa looked confused. "So what does it mean, literally?"

Jimmy sighed. Naming kente cloths was a complicated business. His father was one of the few people he knew who could name most cloths with confidence. Young city-based weavers often referred to a popular chart of kente names and meanings when questioned by their clients. That was where Nana's version of Adweneasa had come from. It was a particularly challenging example with a variety of different interpretations.

"Adwen..." he mused. "Nana, how do you explain Adwen?" he asked in Twi. They discussed it for a few seconds and Jimmy said:

"Something like 'ideas' or 'intelligence'."

"Wisdom," chimed in Nana.

"Art... creativity, skill," mused Jimmy.

"I thought it meant 'designs' or 'motifs'," said Vanessa.

"Yes, it does," said Jimmy, and Nana nodded emphatically.

Jimmy tried to explain that the motifs woven into the cloth represented the inspiration and skill of the weaver, hence the use of the same word for them. "And 'asa' means 'finished'," he concluded. "They say that the Asante King for whom this design was first woven admired it so much that he said... er, how can I put it?"

"That the limits of weaving skill had been reached," provided Vanessa, who had read about it.

"Yes," said Jimmy, relieved for this succinct explanation. "So it means, 'the end of skill'."

"But there's another version," said Vanessa, "that the weaver who created it used all the designs known at the time in one cloth, so it means 'all designs have been used up'."

Although Nana was not able to follow Vanessa's American English with any degree of accuracy, the fact that she was displaying an impressive knowledge of kente nomenclature did not escape him. He could not contain his admiration.

"Ei sister, you have tried! You know kente proper!"

Vanessa was delighted. She liked being called 'sister' and had enough experience with Ghanaian English to know that "you have tried" actually meant, "you have excelled". She thanked him for the compliment.

Shaking his head in wonder, Nana gushed, "In fact, this is my first time to see a white who knows kente more than me."

Vanessa's face froze. Jimmy's froze a split second later. It took Nana a few seconds to realise what he had done. With great alarm, he apologised to Jimmy first, making it obvious to Vanessa that they had discussed her sensitivities before. This did not improve things.

She said stiffly, "I'm not white, OK, I'm black! Just because I come from America doesn't make me white. Man, don't you guys understand anything about our history? How can you say that shit when you're our brothers? I'm an African, like you!"

She stopped there because Nana was losing the battle against laughter. Jimmy was horrified. He knew exactly how Nana felt and fully understood that he had no intention of causing offence. Jimmy was slowly coming to understand that this now familiar scenario was simply a glimpse of the sea of cultural divergence, historical erosion and plain misunderstanding that churned between home Africans and their Diaspora kin. To compound his horror, he was irresistibly infected by Nana's helpless mirth. His face betrayed his own struggle between

Vanessa's anguish and Nana's artless incredulity.

Vanessa was beside herself. She rounded on him, but before she could formulate any coherent words, her face crumpled and she dissolved into tears. She ran out, hailed a taxi and was gone before Jimmy could catch up with her.

Although he was able to make amends to some extent with the beautiful 'Gold Dust' stole, things were never quite the same between them again. Their relationship eventually petered out, taking along with it Jimmy's dreams of a lucrative export business and his secret hope of being taken to America one day by Vanessa. Although he was not short of other girls to take her place and gradually to reconstruct his ambitions, he did miss her. The lessons she had taught him about African-American heritage, her struggles with her racial identity and her amazing way of loving kente had somehow touched him, and they earned her more space in his heart and memory than any woman had ever claimed.

The day he saw the Adweneasa cloth on the floor of the ambassador's living room, he heard the echo of Vanessa's voice. "I love it, can't you see that?"

It had been spread out carefully, lovingly, displaying every inch of its 12-yard length. Few applications could have shown it off so effectively. Exhibited thus in its entirety, it proclaimed the toil, skill and creative ecstasy that had worked miles of plain thread into a spectacular web of colour and art. Its predominant tones of maroon, green and yellow denoted the royal Oyokoman warp pattern and its myriad of tiny motifs symbolised a wealth of cultural and historical meaning. In the centre of the cloth stood an exquisitely carved Asante stool upon which had been placed a collection of antique brass-cast gold weights.

"Do you like my arrangement?" asked the ambassador proudly.

Jimmy stammered out a polite response, keeping his back to the ambassador. He could indeed appreciate the beauty of the artistic arrangement, but it took a while to recover from the shock of seeing the magnificent textile, of which his father had been so proud, used in such a manner. The room was so large that the space allocated to the cloth did not impede free movement and Jimmy hoped this meant it would not be trodden upon.

He had become used to seeing kente cloth used in all manner of new ways and had learned to harden himself to it because of the profits involved.

As Nana said, "Once they have paid, you can't tell them what to do with it. Just take your money and shut up."

But this time, Jimmy felt a strange, indefinable pain. It was one thing to see a made-in-America nylon triangle, machine stamped with the approximation of a kente pattern, sandwiched between the cheeks of a woman's bottom. It was another thing to see a full piece of Oyokoman Adweneasa kente cloth, hand-woven in his father's workshop, on the floor. The ambassador wanted to order an identical piece as a wall hanging to complete his 'Asante kingdom' display. The thought of another generous payment helped Jimmy recover from his shock.

However, he knew his father would be curious about an identical order of such magnitude so soon after the first. He knew the old man was already uneasy about the ways in which the foreigners who were buying it were using their kente. He had asked questions before, but after his reaction to the tablecloth and bedspread orders, Jimmy had passed most subsequent orders off as wall-hangings or bodily attire.

As long as the cloth was assigned a decorative rather than utilitarian function, his father could accept it. However, the idea of kente cloth having things placed on top of it was definitely unacceptable. Jimmy did not allow the cutting of strips into small items like place-mats in his father's workshop. That could be done in Accra to save awkward questions. Naturally, the old man suspected that Jimmy was not always telling the whole truth. However, he realised, in the cold light of economic reality, that there was not necessarily much to be gained by questioning his son too closely. That year, Jimmy had paid for him to have a critical operation and for the expensive medication he had been taking ever since. Jimmy knew that his father could turn a blind eye to some things but would never forgive the use of his kente as a floor-rug.

He decided that it was not necessary for him to know this particular detail. He would think of a way to handle his questions. Before his trip home, Jimmy mentally prepared himself for their conversation, building up a stock of responses for the various different turns it might take.

The silence in the old shed lasted so long that the hen and her chicks wandered back to see if their rusty tin home had been vacated at last.

"Kweku," the old man said finally. "I have only ever heard of one other instance of kente being put on the ground. Do you know when that was?"

Jimmy shook his head.

"In 1931, when our king returned from his long exile in the Seychelles, where he had been sent by the colonial British government, he came here to Adanwomase to see his chief weaver, your great-grandfather. They wove three special cloths in preparation for his visit, and when he arrived, they spread them on the ground like a red carpet for him to walk upon. The people wept for joy. It was a wonderful tribute. You see, only a mighty king could tread upon the king of textiles."

Jimmy understood what his father was saying, but he felt torn. Conflicting thoughts buzzed around in his head. Several samples from his repertoire of responses should have been of help to him now but they suddenly all seemed inappropriate. His father saw the struggle on his face and said gently: "I know, my son, we have made a lot of money but we have also paid a price."

With that, Egya Kwame Mensah rose and walked silently back to his weaving room. Jimmy followed at a respectful distance. His father sat back in his loom. He pulled down a short strip of Oyokoman Adweneasa cloth draped on the loom frame. It was a leftover piece from the long strip he himself had woven for that magnificent cloth. He looked at it for a long moment. "Adweneasa," he murmured softly to no-one in particular, shaking his head sadly.

Jimmy closed the door and walked away. He had never seen his father cry, and he suspected the old man would rather keep it that way.

Mamle Kabu was born and raised in Ghana, where she now lives, having studied in the UK. In addition to writing fiction she does research consultancy in development issues. Her short stories have been published in anthologies, including one, 'Human Mathematics', in *Mixed: An Anthology of Short Fiction on the Multi-racial Experience*, WW Norton, 2006. 'The End of Skill' was first published in *Dreams, Miracles and Jazz*, Picador Africa, Johannesburg, 2008.

You Wreck Her

Parselelo Kantai

YOU DO NOT KNOW how far you have fallen down in this world until you see yourself crawling up a *karao*'s face on a Friday night. You are slobbering and gagging over your short-time, ignoring the after-taste of condom coming into your nostrils from the back of your throat, like Goort's coffee bubbling in the machine on a Sunday morning a long time ago. You lather and stroke. Your head bobs like a bar of soap in bathwater. You can feel he is getting close. There is a commotion far away, beyond the squeak of rubber screaming in your ears, and your short-time is fumbling around you like he lost something important in your pubic hair. He finds your breast. He is clutching you like a handbag thief on Moi Avenue. His thing grows larger in your mouth, then trembles and the thing in your mouth grows soft and your jaws are aching and there is a tap on the window. And right there, on the uniformed policeman's face you see yourself.

The clock dial on the dashboard of the Land Rover Discovery says it is 2.35am. This car park is empty, save for the junkery and wreckage of old government vehicles – the lorries sitting on stones because nobody could find a spare part for the alternator. The grey shells of military Land Rovers with hibiscuses and bougainvilleas growing in them because they have not been moved since the attempted coup in 1982. Up Harry Thuku Road is the Central Police Station, which is right now bursting with street-girls like yourself unlucky enough to have been caught tonight. They will do what you have just done *and* pay the policemen for it. Across the road is the Norfolk Hotel, where you have just been with the *mzungu*, where your eyes met across the Delamere Terrace. In the old days *mzungus* used to shoot Africans passing by for sport from the Delamere Terrace.

Now you suck on their penises for 500 shillings per half hour. The fruits of independence came in strange ways.

This is the short-time car park. It is guarded by the police.

In the dimness, the *karao* looks like a phone booth with a moustache. He glistens like he has just been dipped in oil. The light bounces off his dark face, his cap low so that the whites of his eyes startle you when you see them. He is wearing one of those luminous green police coats and he is looking straight at you, making you cover your breasts with your hands.

The *mzungu* rolls down his window a little way. He had switched on the radio. It blares news of a war in a place with an unpronounceable name. The *mzungu* told you he liked to listen to the BBC, "during". He had said it with a shy smile. His voice was that of a boy, his face with the rabbit's teeth and the beaky nose and the bushy eyebrows over eyes that learned somewhere long ago that the best way to look straight at a man is to squint, his face was that of a man of this world. And world news turns him on.

"Terribly sorry, officer. I'm afraid we got rather carried away." The *mzungu*'s voice is imported from England, cough syrup and charcoal crackling – a half-laugh that sounds like a wheeze. You want to giggle. His trousers are around his ankles, his shirt halfway up his belly. He still has his jacket and tie on and he says "carried away" like it was a boardroom meeting that got a little heated. He gropes in the dark looking for something in his trouser pockets. In the dimness you make out his wallet. He picks out two notes and passes them through the crack in the window without looking.

He is not prepared for the gunshot.

The bullet goes in through the driver's window and out through yours. You hear the gunshot from one side and the ping and spark of metal on the rusted rim of the Nissan Urvan parked next to you. One moment you are behind the safety of tinted windows and in a blink you are covered in glass. You are relieved to find that you are not hurt.

You are not sure whether the voice with a hoarse scream is yours saying shut up, shut up, but you can make out the charcoal-syrup voice of a man who only hears about violence on the radio and is saying what the fuck, what the fuck in university English.

It is a mistake to argue with a man with a gun. It is a mistake to listen to the bubble and knot of your small intestines, the rise of panic in your throat forcing you to say without thinking do you know who I am, do you know who I am, you can't touch me. It is a mistake to pull out your passport from your jacket and hold it up as if it is a weapon. And to keep saying over and over again, do you know what this, is as if a piece of paper can be your shield and defender at a time like this. To keep saying "Di-plo-ma-tic I-mmu-ni-ty" as if you are a schoolteacher in a village class and the children want to share those words with you like roast kidney and *ugali* on Easter Sunday. It is a mistake that ignorant white men in Africa cannot hear often enough.

"How old are you, sir?" asks the *karao*, as if it is very important that he knows. The barrel of his pistol rests against the *mzungu*'s head. The *karao* has a torch in his other hand. His head is halfway inside the car, close enough for you and the *mzungu* to smell the smoky aroma of a recent cigarette on his breath. You find that you are staring into the *karao*'s moustache and the torchlight is almost blinding. So you get cross-eyed from the staring and find yourself back in your father's house. He is sitting in his old chair, pulling off his shoes and you are a little girl standing before him with his dinner, waiting and silent and wondering whether the food sometimes gets trapped in his moustache.

The light moves from your face and you can finally exhale. You find yourself travelling with the light, down your face, your breasts and stomach, so yellow and blotched and bloated that they feel like they belong to somebody else. The light circles your groin, licks your thighs. It rests briefly on your g-string on the floor next to a bunch of tissues, the torn condom wrapping. It pans across the leather seats, the music system, the dashboard with its wood panelling. You spot your earring in the gear-stick pouch, the one you bought that Tuesday at Maasai Market when you went shopping for your new life with Goort. The stall woman was charging 800 bob for it and you brought her down to 400 or you would move with your *mzungu* tourist to another stall, you were so confident then. And now your earring is trapped in the gear-stick pouch. It is making a bulge, making you think of lip-plates and those women in one of Goort's coffee table books on African beauty.

"How old are you, sir?"

"None of your business. I have diplomatic immunity!"

You have travelled with the torchlight to the *mzungu*'s thing. You are a spectator peering into the wreckage of a bus accident. The scene has been evacuated. The thing lies lifeless beneath the mountain of his belly. You watch the condom sliding off. It falls silently between the *mzungu*'s legs. You notice idly how white his legs are, like something on an X-ray sheet. The *karao* does not shift the light of the torch even when the condom begins to ooze, even when a slow trickle of fluid begins making its way towards the *mzungu*'s buttocks.

All you hear is that the *mzungu* has fallen silent. Then there is the sound of another trickle when you hear a click from the pistol and the *mzungu* starts babbling again.

"How-old-are-you-sir?" The *karao* emphasizes every word.

"I… 45 years old." He falls back into the leather and runs a hand through his hair.

The torchlight stops moving.

"How old are you?" He is talking to you.

"Sixteen," you say automatically.

He shines the torch in your face again. He laughs for the first time, a dry, heaving sound.

"Sitaulisa tena." His Kiswahili sounds like it was manufactured in your village, but it doesn't hide the threat. "I won't ask you again."

The *mzungu* glances at you quickly, curiously. He was telling you before at the Delamere Terrace what he liked doing with little girls. You said 2,000 bob for short-time, 5,000 for the night. The love left his eyes and he said for a girl like you, nothing more than 500. You said okay, you knew a place.

"Ishirini na sita," you find yourself saying. Your teeth are chattering. You think it's from the cold coming through the windows. You are 26 years old, past your 'sell by' date, Goort had said. You laughed with him. *Je pons kill fo ko tu ai.* You thought it was a birthday joke.

By this time other *karaos* would have already walked away, a thousand bob richer, two if they talked nicely. They would have peered in on the scene, gently tapped on the window and stretched out a hand. The man in the car with the trousers around his ankles would have cough-laughed. His fingers would pick out some notes, pass them through the half-opened window. The *karao* would walk away, nodding vigorously, his eyes agreeing with the stupid grin playing on his mouth like a JamboAfrica band at a tourist hotel. But the way this one looked at you! And he didn't know you had seen him watching as you mouthed off the *mzungu*. He had a look of an insect that had burrowed itself underneath his skin and was crawling up his face, and you, not the *mzungu* with the thing the size of a flea-bite, you were that insect.

That is why you know somebody is going to die.

"When you get out of Kamiti prison you will be 60 years old, sir."

You can feel the rumble of panic rising from the *mzungu*.

"There is no diplomatic immunity for child molesters in Kenya."

And even now the *karao* has not blown your cover. You are 16 again.

You are 16 and out on the town. Friday night on Koinange Street in downtown Nairobi and all you can see are red lights of cars soundlessly gliding, windows tinted. *Malayas* with handkerchiefs for skirts, ostriches in heels clattering after red lights – tail-lights, brake-lights – and up and down the street the calls of *"Hanee! Hanee!"* will echo in the darkness until it becomes grey and the sounds of other birds take over.

You have been here among the ostriches for two weeks, maybe less, and every night you learn how there is nothing new under the sun. They cackle and blow smoke in your face when you speak of a lost and painful childhood where you became your mother after she died, washing and cleaning and carrying the house during the day and carrying the weight of your father between your legs at night because he said you were now old enough to carry the family flag. They tell you to save it; everybody has a copy of that story. You can sell it for an extra 500 bob to a sad man in the short-time car park. They tell you that you in particular need every little extra that you can get. That you are too tall, too skinny and too dark, you don't stand a chance against a long line of short, plump and brown ostriches. They tell you to soak in Jik, to use Ambi and Oil of Ulay or those little tablets from China that the Congolese girls like because in two weeks the men will be asking if your father was a German tourist. They call you Marabou. They say it is because you are tall and skinny and dark. That all you can expect from the street is garbage, like the Marabou Stork.

And it is true. You only get lucky towards the end of the night, when the good girls have gone off with the men in the soundless cars and the prices have dropped. You become a specialist in sad men with straggly beards and creaky cars that smell of sleep, sweaty socks and half-smoked cigarettes.

During the day, you live in a hole in the wall just off Kirinyaga Road, among the refugees and illegals – the Congolese, Rwandese and others; some Beninois who can never fully explain how and why they came halfway across a continent to idle around and plait each other's hair and cook pounded banana and cassava in three different peppery sauces. But you like them, these people who talk about Brussels as if it is their village. And when you ask them who has ever been there they do something complicated with their mouths, roll their eyes and turn away. They say, with their mouths drooping and their wrists limp and their palms asking a question, you are Kenyan girl, you know notin'.

They tell you how much you will have to save to buy the Chinese pills, and you despair.

But Lingala is music to your ears. An endless succession of Franco and Kofi Olomide and Wenge Musica streamed through tinny cassette players at all hours of day and night. You want to know what "Bolingo" means, or "Motema na ngai." On the stairs at the entrance of the tenement where everybody sits around after lunch talking about nothing in particular because they are really listening to the music and waiting for the night, you learn how to move your waist and your inner-thigh muscles while holding your shoulders completely still, your face communicating that you are appalled at what your buttocks are doing. And everyone rolls about and laughs until they are crying and saying "Marabou, Kenyan girl, *arrêt, arrêt, s'il vous plaît*! You kill os! You know notin', notin' at all!"

You grasp at a French that floats along the dim, narrow corridors of the tenement, snatch the last ends of sentences bouncing against your plywood partition. You learn it the way people learn songs from radios playing in the upstairs room. *Je pons kill fo ko tu ai.* And always you will hear those words and see men leaving, tucking in their shirts and doing their belt-buckles in the corridor, and a formidable Congolese woman standing by a door, a flowery lesso tucked under her armpits, looking ready for war if he dared show his face here again.

"It means, ah tink you should get di fok out," somebody tells you one day after you have heard it a million times and don't care that you will look stupid if you ask. Then you meet Goort.

Stop, your Rwandese friend who is almost your height and yellow like a mango in season, has told you no work, tonight we go party like regular people. She likes you, she says, because of the way you refused to laugh when she told you the story of her name. She tells the story as if she is still annoyed by the whole business, that she is the eighth child in her family and when her mother was in labour having her, she screamed "Stop!" in English and so loudly that her father heard her from the village bar a kilometre away. Stop must have also heard because it took her a day and a half to make her way down the birth canal. It was only then that her father, who did not understand English and her mother, who did not speak the language either and is still puzzled where the word came from, it was only then that they knew that this was to be their last child.

You have put on jeans and a t-shirt and a New York Knicks basketball cap that you bought for 50 shillings on the street. You are at Madhouse discotheque on Koinange Street with all the ostriches who have made the step up from chasing red lights on the street downstairs. You have been told but you have never seen that this work of yours is a ladder. The street ostriches all want to climb up the stairs to Madhouse and the ostriches already up the stairs want to dance into a *mzungu*'s life because a *mzungu* has wings that will carry you over the hills and far away to Europe.

Stop is at the counter buying another round of cold Pilsners and a second packet of Sweet Menthols because you already have your habit of smoking too much when you drink. You are alone at the table, so intent on the two ostriches in the middle of the dance-floor flicking each other with their tongues that you do not even sense that there is a man staring at you. It is only when the ostriches slowly turn away from their kiss and start watching you that you come back to yourself and see him. He has an eye patch over his left eye and is supporting himself with a crutch. He is wearing a bush green jacket, a black shirt and trousers that cannot possibly be purple; it must be the disco lights. You see that his hair flops over his ears and that if he wasn't so bent and angry, he would look exactly like one of those cute little dogs in the foreign magazines. You also see that he was young a long time ago.

That is how you were discovered. It was only years later that it occurred to you that Stop never returned from the counter with the Pilsners and cigarettes, but by that time you were a different person, surrounded by flashing cameras and fashion journalists in New York and London and Paris and Milan. What you remember from that night, as clearly as if it were yesterday, was Goort exclaiming over and over, "You wreck her! You wreck her!"

You became in a very short time a new person. Goort made arrangements for you to obtain a new wardrobe and a new identity. He was not in favour of your New York Knicks basketball cap and your jeans and t-shirt. He said you needed to look more African. So you went with him to the Maasai Market on a Tuesday afternoon and bought an armful of jewellery and the red and blue wraps and shawls, the *shukas* that made you so famous. You were surprised when at his house in Runda where he was boasting that one of his neighbours was a Cabinet Minister and another a European ambassador, he whipped out his bush-knife and began ripping up the *shukas*, because what was the point of buying new things only to destroy them. You were not happy when he told you to strip down to nothing and to put on the torn *shukas*. Or when he gave you a rusty old rifle and told you to stand under a tree and next to an old Mercedes whose tyres had been replaced with stones so that he could take an endless round of photographs. This is why in those early photographs of yourself in the fashion magazines, you are looking as if your mother has just died in a war-torn country.

You were surprised when at the point of his crisis that first time you made love Goort called you my Sudanese girl. You told him you were not Sudanese but he said not to worry, that people can be whatever they want to be. He told you that Sudan was 'hot' at the moment and that if you behaved yourself you could be the new Alek Wek. He laughed when you asked him what Alek Wek was.

"Not vaat darleenk, who. Alek Vek is very famous African model in Europe and America. You are beautiful like her." Then he kissed you very gently at the exact moment that you understood that you were in love for the first time, he kissed you on the forehead and said: "You can *be* her."

Goort told you that he used to be a soldier of fortune.

"I shoot ze war in Congo, ze war in Sudan Sud, even ze genocide in Rwanda. After I take ze pictures, I sell to ze one who pay ze most. Zere are so many magazines in Europe that vant zis kind of image. I am, how you say, a soldier of fortune." It was from all those places that he collected the old guns. He put them in a cabinet in his sitting room. "But it is oggly beezness, very oggly. So much blood. Ze African he slaughters ze ozzer African. Like, like les animaux, ze animal. And to take zese pictures, it is to spread ze sadness, ze oggliness in the world. So I go back 'ome to Brussels and tink what I am going to do. But I love Africa. It is in ze blood. So I must return."

Then another night when you had exhausted each other in his bed and he was smoking a triumphant cigarette, he told you how he had discovered his life's mission after his motorcycle accident in the streets of Brussels, how he would change himself and bring beauty to the world.

"Ven I am lying in ze hospital vizout ze leg, vizout ze eye, I say to myself zere iz no drama in motorcycle accident in Brussels so how I give myself ze drama. So I tink zat if I say zat I stepped on a landmine in eastern Congo, zen zere is ze drama in zat. And I tink again zat now I must come back to Africa looking for ze African beauty. How it can be so easy to put ze drama in ze beauty because in Europe zere is no drama any more. It is all pouff!" And he made that complicated expression of the illegals on Kirinyaga Road, of rolling his eyes and blowing out his cheeks.

"So I come back and for tree months, *rien*, nothing. Every night I am going out and ze girls, zey look like, how you say, ostrich. Zey have tin legs, very tin. And zey vear high heels, and lipstick and zey are yellow, not dark like true African woman. Not like you." And he kissed you on the forehead and stared lovingly into your eyes.

"So zat night when I see you in ze disco I say to myself, 'You wreck her!' *Mais oui*. I have found it."

Goort was alarmed by your second-hand knowledge of Brussels, about how you talked about the market in Matongé, which he insisted was called Ixelles, with the smells of frying fish and roasted cassava and Congolese music in the air, and about "Le Manneken-Pis," the silly little boy who urinates in public near Le Grand Place. He said we can't have you talking about that, you must remember that you are a child soldier from Sudan whom I discovered resting under a tree in Yei County, near the border and not having eaten in three days. He said you have to remember that. Also do not forget that your mother was raped by soldiers and got pregnant with you only to die in a hail of bullets at childbirth. He said drama was what would make the world love you, such a beautiful creature rescued from such ugliness.

You remember when you were on the aeroplane going to Europe thinking how true it was when the ostriches said that the *mzungu* had wings. You remember seeing your photograph of a rusty gun and a tattered *shuka* from Maasai Market on the cover of a magazine in Europe, and how Goort said this was your plane ticket to success. You were surprised about how all these *mzungus* would get out their handkerchiefs and tissues every time you repeated your story of a child soldier.

Later, when you were so busy and the name Marabou was on everybody's lips and on the sides of buses and the covers of magazines, you started telling Goort that it was very kind of him to buy you all these nice clothes and to pay the rent and take you wherever you wanted to go but could he also pay for you to improve your English for the times you would wake up in London, and maybe your French for when you were in Paris at a fashion show. And he told you that bubbles would burst if we did that and your plane ticket to success would be taken away if you started talking like a professor. The world loved you, silent and sad with your African beauty.

And you still do not know why the world woke up one morning and stopped loving you. All that you know is that nobody was making phone calls to Goort any more so that you could get on the metro to go for a shoot. You were no longer on the sides of buses. Instead you were a student at the market in Matongé. You were learning economics and history and the mathematics of how far you can fall when your country goes to war from the Rwandese and Congolese and all those other professors who masquerade as second-hand clothes sellers, fishmongers and market women. It felt as if you were back on Kirinyaga Road. So you can say that at least you were happy like in those days of your hole in the wall.

Then Goort disappeared. When he returned all those difficult weeks later when you had almost given up on this love of your life, he was saying "You wreck her!" There was a girl with him as yellow as Stop and she was smiling and clutching his arm as if she was a yellow version of you when you first arrived. Goort said that Sudan was not hot any more. "Ze drama" was now in Angola. Then he talked to you as if you were a man doing up his belt buckle in a corridor on Kirinyaga Road. He said to you *je pense qu'il faut que tu ailles*.

That was the day you knew you needed to become a new person again.

The market women in Matongé were very helpful. They gave you the Chinese pills on credit. They said that now you will be transformed into a real African beauty.

They say that if you wish for something too much you should also worry about how you will receive it. Maybe that is why when you were living in some unspeakable tenement in Matongé with the Congolese women and you were so ill that you thought you were going to die, they were kind enough to raise the money for your plane ticket back to Kenya.

You are certain that this is why you are back in the short-time parking after all these years, a plump, yellow ostrich whose skin did not take to hydroquinone, with a *mzungu* who is yelling about diplomatic immunity. You want to tell him to shut up, that if he could shut up he would only lose the mask that he wears. You try to tell him that life is a masquerade and there are wars being fought everywhere.

But the *mzungu* refuses to be quiet. And Rafiq, your new partner in this work of stripping people of what they have because nothing is ever given for free, he is still looking at you with that strange expression when the gun goes off and the world falls silent.

Parselelo Kantai is a Kenyan writer and investigative journalist whose short fiction has been published in *Kwani?* and several anthologies. His debut short story, 'Comrade Lemma and the Black Jerusalem Boys' Band' was shortlisted for the Caine Prize in 2004. 'You Wreck Her' appeared first in *St Petersburg Review*, New York, 2008.

Icebergs

Alistair Morgan

TOWARD THE END OF last summer, when I was combating a bout of loneliness after the death of my wife, a new neighbour moved in next door. He arrived at number 16 – I'm number 14 – late one night. I had seen the colour advertisement for the house in the property section of the *Cape Times*: panoramic views of the Atlantic; three-minute walk from the beach; twenty-minute drive from the centre of Cape Town; six bedrooms en suite; swimming pool; double garage; price on application.

The FOR SALE signs went down the same day he moved in. Although when I say 'moved in', I don't mean that he was accompanied by a moving van and stream of brown boxes; he came only with his driver, who, I would later discover, was also his bodyguard. If there were any suitcases I never saw them. I was sitting on my pool deck, having a final cigarette before bed, when I heard him step out onto the balcony of what I imagined was the master bedroom. Even at such a late hour he was formally dressed in a suit and tie. His face was in shadow but I could still make out the glint of his glasses. He stood with one hand in his trouser pocket and stared into the darkness for several minutes.

There was no sound apart from the waves throwing themselves onto the rocks below us. We couldn't have been more than 10 or 15 yards from one another, and the cool Atlantic breeze was carrying the smoke from my cigarette up toward him. He cleared his throat, and from out of the shadows around his head I heard a crisp, well-spoken voice say, "Good evening."

"Evening," I replied. "Welcome to Llandudno."

"Thank you. It's very pleasant out here."

"You can feel that autumn's on its way, though."

Whatever he said in reply was lost in the pounding of the waves. After a few moments he said, "Well, good night," and as he turned back toward the light of the curtainless bedroom I caught a brief glimpse of a slender, greying man with dark skin. He stayed for only two days and then I didn't see him for nearly a month. While he was away several vans delivered furniture, still wrapped in plastic, and later I noticed that curtains had been fitted in the master bedroom. I had recently

37

retired and so had plenty of time to watch these comings and goings.

Mostly I am on my own. Three years ago my wife was taken from me in pieces: first her right breast went; then her left breast; then her will to fight; until, finally, what remained of her was wheeled away down a corridor. My two boys are in London, and my daughter still insists on living in Johannesburg, in the same house in which we were all once a family.

For many years I ran an advertising agency in Johannesburg. When I sold my shares in it my wife and I bought the house in which I now live. We were lucky because that was just before the property market erupted and I doubt that I could afford the house today. My wife did most of the interior decorating and oversaw the renovations, but toward the end she became too ill to leave Johannesburg and she never did get to live here. She made me promise to move in after she was gone, as she didn't want strangers living in the dream house we had worked so hard for together. So I spend my days alone, although I am constantly surrounded by her.

Most of the houses here are holiday homes. They stand empty for long periods of the year, and in the summer they fill with tourists – those that can afford the ridiculous weekly rates for a rental – and local people who have either had the houses in their families for decades or were fortunate enough to buy at the right time. Few people move in permanently. Because of this there isn't any sense of community and people rarely acknowledge their neighbours. And so for company I have to make do with the echoes of my wife's voice.

I suppose it was company I was looking for when I invited my new neighbour over for a drink one afternoon. He was just getting out of his car in the driveway as I was walking back from the beach. As usual he was dressed formally in a suit. He nodded at me, and I walked over and stretched my hand out to him.

"Dennis Moorcraft," I said, feeling his smooth fingers tentatively squeeze my hand.

"Bradshaw."

Later I would read in the newspapers that this was his Christian name. He seemed slightly surprised when I suggested he join me for a sundowner or two, and he glanced at his driver, who was scrutizing me with heavy-lidded eyes, before politely accepting my offer.

From my pool deck there is an unrestricted view of the Atlantic. My wife had designed it so that it would be the ideal spot to watch the sun setting over the sea. With the ocean so near, and the sounds of the waves as constant as a heartbeat, it sometimes feels as though I'm sitting aboard an ocean liner. As my brother, who now lives in Canada, once said when he came out on a visit, "It's like standing on the upper deck of the *Titanic*."

Bradshaw and I sat side by side, facing out to sea, he in a linen suit and tie, me in a golf shirt and Bermuda shorts. My eyes were drawn to his hands, which seemed to hang in the air in front of him as he spoke, as though they were wet and he was waiting for someone to pass him a hand towel. From time to time he would straighten and bend his wrists to emphasize certain points of his conversation. His fingers were long and thin, like the teeth of a comb, and the nails were in immaculate condition. In fact, everything about him and his clothing was precise and carefully measured. Before speaking, and between sentences, he would suck in his lips and it almost looked as if he were checking the words in his mouth, rolling them over with his tongue, before letting them out.

He appeared to be about my age, but his face did not bear the creases and folds that mine had. We made cautious inquiries about one another's background, as strangers do, and how we had come to be living where we were. He kept his questions vague and circumspect, and I got the impression that he wished me to do the same.

It turned out he was not from South Africa. He was, he said, a businessman from a neighbouring country. From what I could gather he was involved in imports and exports. However he was gradually phasing himself out of his work and he hoped to be fully retired within three months. When I asked him about his family he shrugged and said, "They may visit from time to time." I thought it odd that he would move all this way on his own, particularly when he had such a large house, but then I realized that I was in a similar position and I ushered the conversation on to a less personal subject.

We discovered that we had both spent some time in England. He had studied at the London School of Economics, and I had spent several years working in advertising in London before coming home to start up my own agency. We were drinking Scotch on the rocks, and by the time I'd refreshed our glasses for the third time we were both sitting a little lower in our chairs. Bradshaw's hands became more animated as he spoke.

"A few months ago," he said, "I had to entertain some English businessmen. At the end of their stay I asked them how they liked my country and one of them said, 'Well, it's not England', and I replied, 'Oh, so you like it then?'"

We both laughed out loud at this, and he reached over and squeezed my forearm. After reminiscing about our experiences in England, we fell into a contented silence. Perhaps it was the Scotch, but I hoped that Bradshaw and I might become friends. We seemed to share a lot of common ground and, although neither of us mentioned it, I think we both realised that, on the whole, life had been good to us, and we shared a sense of common relief at having got to where we were. No doubt we had very different lives to look back on, but somehow we had ended up together, as neighbours, each retired and alone in a cavernous house.

Later, as I walked him back to the front door, he stopped to study some of the paintings hanging in the hallway. There were seven in total, and they ranged in size from two feet by four feet to six feet by eight feet. They were mostly abstract, although they were composed around natural forms – the rings of a seashell, the bark of a tree, the veins of a leaf. Sometimes parts of the actual objects were mixed into the oils to give the paintings added texture. The lines of the shape were then repeated over and over again, like ripples in water, and by the time these ripples reached the edge of the canvas the original form had evolved into a series of reverberations of itself.

With his glasses in his hand Bradshaw pointed to the largest canvas, which depicted an intricate series of lines around the skull of a rat, and asked, "This is an original?"

"Yes, my daughter is a painter. They're all hers."

He squinted at the signature in the bottom right-hand corner and nodded. "Ah, Melissa Moorcraft. Her name is familiar, actually."

"She has done quite well for herself. Do you like art, then?"

"Oh yes. I have a little collection. You should come over one night this week and have a look."

"Thank you. Melissa is going to be coming down from Johannesburg soon, so perhaps we could also get together then. I'm sure she'd be interested to meet you."

"I'd be honoured to meet such a talented artist."

We said our good nights and he repeated his invitation for me to come over to his house. But after that evening his house stood dark and silent, with curtains drawn, for three or four weeks, and I presumed he'd been called away on some urgent business.

Melissa arrived during Bradshaw's absence. Ever since the death of my wife, I'd been campaigning for her to move down to Cape Town. But already, at the age of 31, she was set in her ways, and she was determined to keep on living in the house in Johannesburg. It was as if she could not live beyond the walls of the house and its foundations, which were firmly embedded in the past. Perhaps it was because she felt she was closer than the rest of us to her mother and that she was therefore duty-bound to preserve her memory in bricks and mortar.

Two years ago, she had the house converted into a gallery for her work, though her brothers and I had asked her to move out so that we could sell it. I did not impose any time limits on my children with regards to the mourning of their mother, particularly with Melissa, as she was the youngest; but after three years I felt that it was time for us all to close that chapter in our lives and to start looking ahead again. Melissa's visits to Cape Town were constantly shadowed by these issues.

As always, she had come to paint. Two or three times a year she liked to escape her day-to-day surroundings, come to Cape Town, and work on a new series of paintings. She used one of the spare rooms as a studio and after breakfast she'd excuse herself and disappear until I called her for lunch. That was our routine. In the afternoons we'd walk on the beach or take a drive. She always had her Polaroid camera with her and I was used to having to slam on the brakes and pull over whenever we passed something – a rock, a farmhouse, a horizon line – which she thought she could use in a painting.

We had parked on the edge of a forest so that she could capture the texture of the arthritic-looking limb of a pine tree when I mentioned my new neighbour.

"He sounds a bit weird," she said as she waited for a Polaroid of the tree to develop. "Why do you think he's on his own?"

"Don't know. Maybe his family will move down when he's fully retired. Or perhaps he's divorced. Anyway, I'm sure you'll have a chance to meet him one of these days."

That evening was unusually warm, and Melissa and I ate dinner out on the deck. Afterward we drank red wine and smoked as the sea played its usual symphony on the rocks below. Occasionally, Melissa liked to smoke a joint. Although I disapproved I preferred her to do it in front of me rather than sneak around behind my back. She also became very chatty when she smoked, and I enjoyed our after-dinner conversations.

"Uncle Bruce might be coming out for Christmas," I said, referring to my brother in Canada.

"Well, don't expect me to be here if he does," she said. Her knees were pulled up under her chin and she was hugging her shins. "He's never got a good word to say about this country, but he's only too happy to come back once a year and sponge off you."

"He's my brother. I don't consider it sponging. And he's got plenty of good things to say. Why do you think he comes back almost every December?"

"Have you ever experienced a Canadian winter?"

"You're just cynical."

"I'm cynical? He's the one who stood out here last time and said it was like the upper bloody deck of the *Titanic*. If people want to emigrate that's fine. But they shouldn't be allowed back into the country afterward. It's like leaving your husband or wife and only popping back now and again for a quick shag." She plucked a piece of weed from her tongue and flicked it away.

We were silent for a few minutes and then I asked, "How is Jo'burg? Are you still happy up there? There's plenty of room here if you ever –"

"Dad... I wish you wouldn't bring this up every time. There's a fat fucking chance of me moving to Cape Town. All my friends are in Jo'burg, my work is there, I love the old house and, anyway, we'd drive each other nuts. And this place feels like an abandoned holiday resort for most of the year – all these houses like empty seashells."

I must have looked hurt, because she said sorry and leaned over to kiss me. She smoked the rest of the joint and I finished off the wine. And then she cleared the table and I carried in the cushions from the chairs. As I walked inside I looked up to Bradshaw's bedroom window and thought I saw the curtain moving.

The next day, after Melissa had emerged from her morning in the makeshift studio, we decided to take a picnic down to the beach. Although it wasn't a particularly warm day the sky was clear and the air was still. I think it was the last fair day we had before the winter clouds rolled in. As it was a weekday, we practically had the beach to ourselves. While I unpacked the picnic basket Melissa stripped down to her bikini and briefly endured the sharp Atlantic water. For a moment, as she trotted back to her towel, she could have been her mother. She had the same springy rust-coloured hair and pale skin; I could clearly see the blue highways of veins that transported her mother's remaining blood along the contours of her spindly legs. It was only in the eyes that Melissa differed greatly from her mother: her mother's were a life-giving green, whereas Melissa's were the colour of an overcast sky.

We ate some ham-and-cheese rolls and then settled down on our towels. I had brought the newspaper with me and Melissa had her iPod. She placed the headphones over her ears, removed her bikini top, and lay back to gather what sun she could. I hid behind my newspaper.

I suppose I must have fallen asleep. When I surfaced again my face was in shadow. A familiar voice floated in over the waves breaking on the beach: "Good afternoon, Dennis." It was Bradshaw.

I blinked, then stood up and shook his hand. He was wearing a long-sleeved collared shirt with no tie and formal trousers, which he'd carefully rolled up over his ankles to reveal his elegant feet.

"You've been away some time."

"Yes," said Bradshaw, his eyes skimming over Melissa's body. "I had to attend to some matters at home. I'm looking forward to some rest now."

"I'm afraid you may have missed the last of the good weather."

"Oh, I don't mind. The beach doesn't really appeal to me."

"Well, when you've had some rest you should come over again. My daughter, Melissa, is staying with me." I pointed to Melissa, but as I did so I remembered that she was topless and I dropped my hand to my side.

"Yes, I noticed. The artist."

"She's been quite busy with some new work, actually."

"Really? I'd be very interested to meet her. I'm looking to add to my collection."

"Perhaps tomorrow night then?"

"I look forward to it."

He wandered off down the beach, and I lit a cigarette. And all the while Melissa lay on her back, with a T-shirt covering her face and the iPod shouting in her ears.

"You should have said something to me," she said later, as we prepared supper in the kitchen.

"How? You were listening to music. And it was awkward with you topless and everything."

"Oh, don't be such a prude, Dad."

"I think he was probably more embarrassed than I was. He didn't stick around for too long."

"I'm sure he's seen plenty of breasts before."

"Maybe," I said, although for some reason it was hard to imagine Bradshaw having been with a woman.

Bradshaw came by as arranged the next evening, and I introduced him to Melissa. They were still shaking hands when Bradshaw began to speak about her paintings.

"I find your work very charming," he said. "Have you ever worked in just pencil or charcoal?"

"Not since I was an undergrad. People know me more for my textured layers than anything else."

And as she spoke I could see the young Melissa emerging from within the invisible layers in which she had repeatedly wrapped herself since her mother's death. I was startled at how easily Bradshaw had pierced this armour. Melissa stood with one leg behind the other, just as she used to do as a teenager when she wanted pocket money or some other favour from me.

"Well, it's easy to see why you're so well known."

"Dad says you have a collection of your own."

"Just a small one," he said with a thin smile. "I don't like to keep too many

43

pieces down here in the sea air: it can be a very corrupting influence."

We went through to the lounge where I had managed to get the first fire of the winter going in the fireplace. Bradshaw sat next to Melissa on the sofa facing the fireplace, and I sat in an armchair to the side. We made small talk about other local artists, where to eat out in Cape Town, wine estates that Bradshaw was curious to visit, books, and generally anything that didn't involve politics or religion. The conversation eventually came round to family. Up until then Bradshaw had divulged little about his personal life, but now, with the help of three or four glasses of wine, he gradually began to let down his defences.

"My children are working in America," he said. After a pause he added, "It's good for them to travel."

"Are they going to stay there?" asked Melissa.

"Well, they were schooled there and afterward they came back to stay with me. But they had started to see the world differently and struggled to adjust to our African ways. I try to visit them once or twice a year."

"And your wife?"

"We're divorced. She never adapted to life here. America is her home. Atlanta. It's funny, don't you think? I sometimes meet American businessmen... sorry, African-American businessmen, who tell me how much they love coming back 'home' to Africa. And then I tell them that my wife and children have chosen to leave Africa and live in America. In the South. I can't imagine what their ancestors must think!"

"That is pretty ironic," said Melissa, topping up Bradshaw's glass.

"It is harder these days to try and keep a family together. Geographically anyway," I said.

"Every family is different though, Dad. Some work better when they're split up all over the place. Like ours."

"I don't think we're better off than when we were under one roof."

Turning to Bradshaw, Melissa said, "Dad keeps wanting me to move down to Cape Town to live here with him."

"And you don't want to?"

"I have my reasons."

"In my culture the children are expected to look after their parents when they get old."

"So what about your children?"

"Are you saying I'm old?"

For once Melissa was lost for words.

Bradshaw smiled and then his face went serious again. "I'm not sure if they ever considered themselves to be a part of my culture. They were always closer to their mother."

"God, families can be so complicated," said Melissa.

"From the outside," said Bradshaw, "they appear simple enough: two parents and children. Or sometimes one parent," he added with a glance in my direction. "But it's only once you've been invited inside the family that you get an understanding of all the little intricacies. It's like going backstage at a theatre. Only then are you aware of all the ropes and struts that hold the different scenes in place, and how thin and flimsy the painted houses appear, when from the stalls they seemed as solid as brick and cement. I've always enjoyed going backstage. It teaches you about deception."

Then Bradshaw looked at his watch and drained his glass. "I'm terribly sorry, I've been jabbering on without realising how late it is."

He thanked us and we walked him to the front door. After complimenting Melissa once more on her work, he wished us good night. When he was gone Melissa joined me on the deck for one of her 'cigarettes'.

"What a nice man," she said.

"He is. There's something very sad about him though."

"Why, because he's all alone with no family to share his big house?"

"You know what I mean."

"He seems happy enough to me."

We smoked in silence until Bradshaw's bedroom light came on. "Come," I said, "let's go inside before he thinks we're spying on him."

"Don't you think it's him who's spying on us?"

"No. But I do think you smoke too much of that stuff."

"Another reason why I'm not going to move to Cape Town."

When the doorbell rang just after ten o'clock the next morning, it took me a moment to recognise Bradshaw's driver, as he was wearing dark shades.

"Is Melissa in?" he asked.

"Yes. What is this about?"

"I have an invitation for her."

"From Bradshaw?"

"He would like Melissa to accompany him to look at some vineyards."

"He would? Oh, well, I'm not sure. You see, she's very busy right now. Painting."

The driver showed no sign of comprehending this information, or perhaps he sensed in my reply a thinly veiled tone of suspicion.

"If you don't mind, I would rather she declined the invitation herself."

We stood and stared at one another for several seconds as I tried to think of a plausible reason why Melissa couldn't accept. But my mind was too occupied with the possible consequences of Bradshaw's invitation, and no convincing excuses were forthcoming. Eventually I muttered a feeble, "Right, right. Of course."

I knocked on the door of the room Melissa painted in and repeated the invitation to her.

"What the hell do I know about wine?" she said from the other side of the door.

"Exactly. Shall I tell him you're too busy?"

"Uh. No. It's OK – I'm not being very productive today anyway. It might be fun to do some wine tasting."

"You sure? Don't feel obliged. Your work should come first."

She opened the door. "It's fine, Dad. Tell him I'll be five minutes."

As I walked back down to the front door I wondered why Bradshaw had sent his driver over for Melissa. Was he embarrassed to invite my daughter out face-to-face? Was it less awkward for him like this? Did he think that this was the best way to explain that I wasn't invited?

When Melissa came down the stairs I saw that she had put on some make-up, something she hadn't done in all the time she had been here with me. She was wearing perfume, too. She kissed me on the cheek and then walked away with the driver.

I spent the day trying to convince myself that there was nothing disturbing about Bradshaw's invitation to Melissa. After all, he was a respectable man. It didn't matter that he was a stranger from another country and old enough to be her father: he simply needed someone to buy wine with, someone who knew something about the local estates. But obviously not me. Of course I realized I was thinking like a paranoid parent. If I was to prove to Melissa that we were capable of living together like two adults, I would have to show some restraint by not interfering in her personal life. But I couldn't ignore the parent in me.

At four in the afternoon I tried phoning Melissa to find out where she was, only to hear her cellphone ringing in the bedroom where she'd left it. I pretended to take a stroll down to the beach, even though it was cool and cloudy, just so that I could walk past Bradshaw's house to look for signs of life. Nothing. I didn't have Bradshaw's cellphone number, in fact I didn't even know if he had one, and his home number was not listed in the book. Already I had begun to regret introducing him to my daughter. I wondered what my wife would have done. She and Melissa had been very close. Two girls against three boys. She had dealt with Melissa during her difficult teenage years, while I had spent my days and most of the evenings at the office, working for a comfortable retirement. For this.

It had been dark for some time when I heard the front door open and close.

Melissa appeared in the lounge as if she'd only been out for five minutes. Her cheeks were flushed.

"So? How was it?" I asked as nonchalantly as I could.

"Cool! I feel like I've been on a grand tour of the Western Cape though. He bought a shitload of wine. And then we had dinner and he's just shown me around his house. Did you know that he has three original Chagalls?"

"Oh? Wow. Where did you have dinner?"

"La Colombe. Pretentious as all hell. But at least he insisted on paying."

"That's nice."

She flopped down on the couch next to me. I noticed that her teeth were tinted purple from wine. Then: "Guess what?"

"I don't know, what?"

"Bradshaw asked me to paint his portrait."

"Portraits aren't really your thing, are they?"

"For 120,000 rand they fucking well are."

"You're kidding. He's going to pay you that for a picture?"

"Why do you sound so surprised? I've sold paintings for more than that before."

"I know, I know. I'm just… when does he want it by?"

"He says I can take as long as I like. So, if it's OK with you, I may extend my stay a bit."

"That's great. Stay as long as you need. That's really good news, Mel. Well done."

And so the next morning, instead of going off to the spare room to paint, Melissa took a sketch pad, pencils, and her camera over to Bradshaw's house. She returned at midday with rough compositions and a series of close-up photographs of Bradshaw's polished hands. That's where you capture the essence of a person, she said, in their hands. She spent several days working out a composition and she repeatedly tried to convince Bradshaw to consider wearing something other than a suit and tie for the painting. In the end they compromised on a white, long-sleeved collared shirt and navy suit pants. I was not privy to any of these sittings or discussions. Often they would go into the city for dinner and to talk about the portrait, and I would be in bed long before Melissa returned home. But she was excited about the project and it made me proud to see how professional and thorough she was. And who knew, perhaps a stint of work in Cape Town would make her feel differently about living here.

For two weeks I hardly saw Melissa. I found signs of her in the kitchen – breadcrumbs on the table and soggy teabags in the sink – and sometimes she'd leave notes asking me to take her laundry out of the washing machine and put it in the dryer, or to buy more groceries. It was clear that our holiday time together was over. The studio she had set up in one of the spare rooms had been transplanted into Bradshaw's house, and it was there that she spent her days, often working deep into the night.

Late one evening I went out onto the deck for a cigarette before bed. I had eaten alone and tried unsuccessfully to watch an old Ingmar Bergman movie on television, but my concentration span had somehow shrunk or been tampered with by the sea air. The wind was gusting up from the ocean and it took four matches to light my cigarette. There was music on the wind: a woman's melancholic voice accompanied by a piano. It was coming from Bradshaw's house. His bedroom light was on and the curtains were drawn. Probably the old boy's lullaby music, I thought to myself. And then the door leading onto the bedroom balcony opened and Melissa stepped out into the night. Whether she saw me or not I can't say, but she turned to go back inside almost immediately and the music was silenced and the bedroom darkened. From my deck it was hard to say what she had been wearing, however, as she'd turned to go back inside, I thought I'd seen, in silhouette, a clear profile of her breasts.

The next morning Melissa's bedroom gave no clue as to whether or not she'd spent the night there. Her bed hadn't been made in days, and her clothes were scattered around the room. After breakfast I went over to Bradshaw's house. Bradshaw's driver answered the door, and I was asked to wait in the marmoreal foyer as he went off to find Melissa. A painting on the wall, presumably one of the Chagalls, depicted a woman floating upside down in a starry night sky. Melissa eventually came down the stairs, barefoot and wearing an oversize paisley-patterned dressing gown.

"Is this what you paint in these days?" I said.

"I worked late and decided to stay over. In a guest room. There's no need to get all excited."

"I came to see how you were doing. If you needed any supplies of new paint or brushes."

"Dad, I'm fine, honestly. I've just got to finish up something and then I'll come over. OK?"

She gave me a hug and pressed her face against my chest. Her hair was oily.

Later, after she'd returned to my house, I asked her how the portrait was going and how soon she expected to complete it.

"I don't know. Probably a week or two more. I've made a couple of false starts but I think the one I'm doing now is working well."

"Is Bradshaw pleased with it?"

"He's not allowed to see it until the end. Neither are you."

"And outside of the painting?"

"What do you mean?"

"I mean what else is going on over there? I hardly see you any more."

"Dad, I've been working. You see, this is why I could never live here with you: you're constantly watching over me."

"I'm not watching over you. But what am I meant to think when you spend all day and night next door?"

"That I'm working bloody hard!"

And then she was gone again for several more days.

I first noticed the man when I was returning from Hout Bay one afternoon. I had gone down to the harbour to buy some yellowtail for dinner and as I pulled into my driveway I saw a small Japanese hatchback parked a little way up the street. He was sitting in the driver's seat, sipping from a Coke can. It looked like he was waiting for someone. I didn't think much of it at first, and even when I saw him in the same place the next morning I wasn't too concerned. It was only when I saw him again that evening, sitting alone in the car, staring down the street, that I became suspicious and started to look at him a little closer. He didn't seem to care that I was beginning to take an interest in him.

The passage outside my bedroom has a window facing out onto the street, and from up there I had a clear view of the man. He wore a T-shirt and jeans, and his face and head were cleanly shaven. I watched as he answered a call on his cellphone and I noticed that there was a camera on the dashboard. After a lengthy conversation he put the phone down and adjusted his seat so that he was almost in a horizontal position. That was when he saw me. I pulled my head back and felt my face flush with blood. Fool! What did I think I was doing, spying on someone in the street just because he didn't look like the kind of person who would own a house here? I had become like the other people in the neighbourhood: people Melissa criticized for living insulated lives behind high walls and security fences.

Feeling like a child caught out, I turned to go downstairs. But then the doorbell rang. I went back to the window and looked out at the car. It was empty. The doorbell rang again. And then there was a loud rapping on the front door. Hard knuckles, I thought. I stayed where I was, thinking how ridiculous I was being, yet at the same time just wanting to be left alone. The doorbell rang twice more and then there was silence. After a minute I heard a car door close. The engine started and I heard what sounded like a can being crushed under a wheel as the car drove off. When I looked out the window again the hatchback was gone. Only a small puddle of oil and a flattened Coke can remained.

The next morning there was no sign of the hatchback and its lone driver. I put it down to one of those strange occurrences that happens daily in cities. Melissa was already over at Bradshaw's house, and I drank coffee on my own in the kitchen. There was no rush for me to do anything – a feeling I wasn't yet sure I was comfortable with in my retirement. I showered and dressed and decided to take a drive into Camps Bay to pick up a newspaper. The ocean was grey, and a southwesterly wind was beginning to push a bank of low clouds in over the sea toward the rocky shoreline. Large clumps of kelp, looking like nests of glistening eels, were washing up in the breakers. As I approached Bakoven, I passed the Japanese hatchback heading in the opposite direction. There were two passengers with the driver.

When I returned home with the newspaper the hatchback was parked outside Bradshaw's house. The three occupants of the car were standing outside having a discussion. One of the men had what looked like a television news camera mounted on his shoulder, and the shaven-headed man was now wearing a suit. As I pulled into my driveway the shaven-headed man approached me. He indicated for me to lower my window. I opened it a couple of inches and he leaned forward and asked, "Do you know the owner of this house?"

He pointed at Bradshaw's house.

"No," I said without hesitation, even though I knew my daughter was inside painting Bradshaw at that very moment.

"When did you last see him?"

"I don't keep track of my neighbour's activities."

The man looked back at his two companions and shook his head. It was only when I sat down in the lounge and opened the newspaper that I realized what was going on. An article on the second page reported that Bradshaw Muchabaiwa, 65, brother of his homeland's finance minister, Gideon Muchabaiwa, was under investigation for charges of corruption and illegal dealings in foreign currency. Gideon Muchabaiwa had also been implicated, but through his lawyer he had released a statement defending the dealings as "family investments", adding that he had "nothing to hide" as all of his and his brother's financial dealings were "above board." There was no comment from Bradshaw as he was "currently out of the country on business". The investigations would be continuing, the article concluded.

No doubt Bradshaw had already heard the news. Would he have mentioned anything to Melissa? I went upstairs and looked out the window onto the street. One of the passengers from the hatchback was filming Bradshaw's house while the shaven-headed man stood in front of the camera and spoke into a microphone. I tried phoning Melissa but her cellphone was off. She had to get out of the house before it was besieged by the media. But the last thing I wanted was to be filmed knocking on Bradshaw's front door and asking for my daughter back. And I was sure Melissa didn't need that kind of publicity. Within an hour four more news crews were setting up outside Bradshaw's house.

Melissa phoned me and told me not to worry.

"It's just a political thing," she said. "There's an election coming up and there's a whole lot of mudslinging going on. It'll die down in a day or two when they can't find any evidence. Bradshaw's not that kind of man, Dad."

"Whether he's innocent or not doesn't really matter to me. But you're getting caught up in something that has nothing to do with you. Come home and we'll go away somewhere for a few days. Take a break."

"I'm not leaving Bradshaw on his own."

"He has his driver."

"You don't understand. I want to stay with him."

"What?"

"I'll explain later. Although I doubt you'll understand. But I'm happy, Dad. I'm happy with Bradshaw."

"Happy in what sense? A relationship? Is that what you're trying to tell me?"

"Yes."

"Since when?"

"Not long. But I know it's what I want."

"He could be gone tomorrow, back in his home country, standing trial. I mean, you hardly know him, for Christ's sake!"

"This isn't about what the newspapers say, is it. Come on, Dad. Is it his age? His colour? What?"

"I'm just worried, Melissa. Can you understand that? Can you understand someone else's feelings for once?"

"Fuck you."

"Please. Melissa. Why don't you come over and we can talk about this properly?"

"I've made up my mind already. This thing will pass in a day or two. It's just rumours. You'll see."

That night the rumours were on television. Bradshaw's house and its worth were displayed across the screen for all the world to see. There were scenes of people queuing for bread and petrol in his homeland, juxtaposed with the sea views from his house next door to mine. A crowd bristling with sticks and placards was demonstrating outside his brother's house in the capital city. Another house, alleged to belong to Bradshaw, was shown being ransacked and looted. I switched off the television and poured myself a drink. Melissa had left several Polaroids of

Bradshaw's hands on the dining-room table. The knuckles on his fingers bulged out like full pockets. Once again I noted how well kept the nails were. How, I thought, could a man who paid such close attention to small details get himself into a situation like this? And then I thought of the fingers working loose the buttons on my daughter's clothing and I turned the Polaroids face down on the table and went to bed.

The English reporter who knocked on my car window the next day said he was from the BBC. He wanted to know if I knew the woman in Bradshaw's house. I had just returned from buying three different newspapers – two English, one Afrikaans – and had noted that all of them were leading with a story on Bradshaw. One of them had a picture of Bradshaw and Melissa eating out at an expensive restaurant and the caption identified her as "acclaimed local artist, Melissa Moorcraft (31)."

"I'm not aware of what goes on next door," I said.

"Isn't your name Dennis Moorcraft?"

"Why?"

"The woman's name is Melissa Moorcraft. I thought you might know her."

"I'm sorry, I have nothing to tell you."

"No! No, you can't do that!" Bradshaw's driver was striding out from the house toward the reporter and me. Before the reporter could say anything the driver took him by the collar of his shirt and pushed him up against my car. By the time I'd stepped out to try to intervene the driver had turned back to the house and the reporter was kneeling on the driveway, blood streaming from both nostrils.

"Bloody hell," he said. His colleagues came over and helped him back to their car. Someone had filmed the whole thing.

I went over the papers in my lounge. There were calls for Bradshaw to be extradited to face the charges against him. An "unidentifed but reliable source" had come forward with new evidence and his brother was said to be "assisting" the police with their inquiries. As I had said to Melissa, it was of no concern to me whether Bradshaw was innocent or guilty; but he had, quite literally, brought trouble to my doorstep and he was involving my daughter in his affairs, even if it was by her own will, and I felt that sooner or later I would have to confront him and ask him what he planned to do next and, more to the point, what his intentions were with my daughter.

The police arrived that afternoon. Two bored-looking constables took a statement from me regarding the assault on the journalist, and I told them exactly what I had seen. I had to lend them a pen as their ballpoint had run out of ink. And then they went and knocked – rather optimistically I thought – on Bradshaw's front door. There was no reply. After a brief discussion between themselves they drove away.

That night was the turning point in the whole matter.

Melissa phoned me a short while before the evening news. Something had happened to Gideon, Bradshaw's brother. He had been returning from a police station, where he had been questioned with his lawyer, when his car was attacked by a mob. The car had been set alight and Gideon had tried to run away. He hadn't stood a chance. His smouldering body was flashed briefly on the news later that evening. Bradshaw was obviously deeply upset, said Melissa, and his driver had not been seen for some hours.

"What now?" I said.

"I'm not sure."

"Come home. This has gone too far."

"I can't just leave him."

"Dammit, Melissa. It's not your business. Let him sort it out. Otherwise you'll be in more trouble than you know."

"We'll think of something."

"Like what?"

"I don't know yet."

I suppose that was the last chance I had to speak some sense to her – when we spoke again there just wasn't enough time. But I'm not sure I could have made any difference. It was like watching a glass topple at the edge of a table and knowing that you will not reach it in time to stop it from falling and shattering. That night I went to bed knowing that I would have to live with whatever happened, and I did not sleep very deeply. As a result the phone call at three-thirty in the morning didn't disrupt any dreams. It was Melissa. She was outside my front door. When I went downstairs I saw Bradshaw's car in the road with the engine running. Bradshaw was behind the wheel. He did not look at me. There were no other cars, no television crews or journalists. They would be back at first light.

"We're leaving," said Melissa. "I need to get some of my stuff."

I followed her up to her bedroom. "Where are you going?"

"I'll let you know when we're there."

"You don't have to do this. Do you realise what you're giving up for this man?"

"I've told you. This is what I want."

"I'm going to speak to him then," I said.

"It won't help. He has asked me to stay behind too. It's not his decision that I'm going."

She was picking up dirty clothing off the floor and stuffing it into a tote bag.

"Please tell me where you're going."

"I can't, Dad. I'll email you."

"They'll find you. You're not exactly an inconspicuous couple."

"We'll sort it out."

"They'll freeze Bradshaw's bank account, if they haven't already done so. You won't survive long."

Melissa zipped up the bag. "We've already thought about that."

I followed her out the front door and to the car, which was still idling in the road. Melissa hugged me then and I felt my throat close up and my eyes start to sting.

"Come back," I said.

"Don't worry."

She climbed in next to Bradshaw and I bent over to speak to him. But as Melissa closed the door the car pulled away and I was left standing in the street in my underwear.

That was all last year. I get the occasional email from Melissa. It's impossible to tell if she's in Africa, America or Australia. She mentions a villa near the ocean. Is it the same ocean I stare out at from my deck?

She says she is healthy and happy and painting many pictures. In the end, I suppose, we have to make our own choices, take what we can while we can, so that our final years are comfortable. Isn't that the aim: to build up as much padding as possible in order to soften the impact of death?

After sending Melissa a reply (regards to Bradshaw) I switch off the computer and leave the study. My house is the envy of many people, I'm sure. But my life echoes back at me when I walk through it. I stand in the doorways of the spare rooms and look at the bare beds, their stiff mattresses not yet patterned by archipelagos of stains from spilt bodily fluids. In the lounge I pass the huge yellowwood dining table, a desert plain. I make tea in the kitchen, feeling like a priest pouring wine in an empty cathedral. And then I step out onto my deck and scan the vast horizon.

Alistair Morgan was born in Johannesburg and lives in Cape Town. 'Icebergs' is his first story to appear in print and was first published in *The Paris Review* 183, New York, 2008.

Waiting

EC Osondu

MY NAME IS ORLANDO ZAKI. *Orlando* is taken from Orlando, Florida, which is what is written on the t-shirt given to me by the Red Cross. *Zaki* is the name of the town where I was found and from which I was brought to this refugee camp. My friends in the camp are known by the inscriptions written on their t-shirts. *Acapulco* wears a t-shirt with the inscription, Acapulco. Sexy's t-shirt has the inscription *Tell Me I'm Sexy*. Paris's t-shirt says *See Paris And Die*. When she is coming toward me, I close my eyes because I don't want to die.

Even when one gets a new t-shirt, your old name stays with you. Paris just got a new t-shirt that says *Ask Me About Jesus*, but we still call her Paris and we are not asking her about anybody. There was a girl in the camp once whose t-shirt said *Got Milk?* She threw the t-shirt away because some of the boys in the camp were always pressing her breasts forcefully to see if they had milk. You cannot know what will be written on your t-shirt. We struggle and fight for them and count ourselves lucky that we get anything at all. Take Lousy, for instance; his t-shirt says *My Dad Went To Yellowstone And Got Me This Lousy T-shirt*. He cannot fight, so he's not been able to get another one and has been wearing the same t-shirt since he came to the camp. Though what is written on it is now faded, the name has stuck. Some people are lucky: London had a t-shirt that said *London* and is now in London. He's been adopted by a family over there. Maybe I will find a family in Orlando, Florida that will adopt me.

Sister Nora is the one who told me to start writing this book, she says *the best way to forget is to remember and the best way to remember is to forget*. That is the way Sister Nora talks, in a roundabout way. I think because she is a Reverend Sister she likes to speak in parables like Jesus. She is the one who has been giving me books to read. She says I have a gift for telling stories. This is why she thinks I will become a writer one day.

The first book she gave me to read was *Waiting For Godot*. She says the people in the book are waiting for God to come and help them. Here in the camp, we wait and wait and then wait some more. It is the only thing we do. We wait for the food trucks to come and then we form a straight line and then we wait a few minutes for the line to scatter, then we wait for the fight to begin, and then we fight and struggle and bite and kick and curse and tear and grab and run. And then we begin to watch the road and wait to see if the water trucks are coming, we watch for the dust trail, and then we go and fetch our containers and start waiting and then the trucks come and the first few containers are filled and the fight and struggle and tearing and scratching begin because someone has whispered to someone that the water tanker only has little water in it. That is, if we are lucky and the water tanker comes; oftentimes, we just bring out our containers and start waiting and praying for rain to fall.

Today we are waiting for the photographer to come and take our pictures. It is these pictures that the Red Cross people send to their people abroad who show them to different people in foreign countries and, after looking at them, the foreign families will choose those they like to come and live with them. This is the third week we have been waiting for the photographer, but he has to pass through the war zone so he may not even make it today. After taking the photographs, we have to wait for him to print it and bring it back. We then give it to the Red Cross people and start waiting for a response from abroad.

I want to go and join my friend under the only tree still standing in the camp. Acapulco is raising a handful of red dust into the air to test for breeze; the air is stagnant and the red earth falls back in a straight line.

"Orlando, do you think the photographer will come today?" he asks.

"Maybe he will come."

"Do you think an American family will adopt me?"

"Maybe, if you are lucky."

"Will they find a cure for my bedwetting?"

"There is a tablet for every sickness in America."

"I am not sick, I only wet myself in my sleep because I always dream that I am urinating outside and then I wake up and my knickers are wet because it was only a dream, but the piss is real."

"The same dream every night?"

"Yes."

"Do you think that if I go to America, my parents will hear about me and write to me and I will write to them and tell my new family to let them come over and join me?"

"When the war ends, your parents will find you."

"When will the war end?"

"I don't know, but it will end soon."

"If the war will end soon, why are the Red Cross people sending us to

America?"

"Because they don't want us to join the Youth Brigade and shoot and kill and rape and loot and burn and steal and destroy and fight to the finish and die and not go to school."

This was why Acapulco was always sitting alone under the tree: because he always asked a lot of questions. Sister Nora says it is good to ask questions, that if you ask questions you will never get lost. Acapulco begins to throw the sand once more, testing for breeze. Pus is coming out of his ears and this gives him the smell of an egg that is a little rotten. This was another reason people kept away from him. A fly is buzzing around his ear; he ignores it for some time and at the exact moment the fly is about to perch, he waves it away furiously.

"I wish I had a dog," he said.

"What do you want to do with the dog?"

"I will pose with the dog in my photograph that they are sending to America because white people love dogs."

"But they also like people."

"Yes, but they like people who like dogs."

"London did not take a picture with a dog."

"Yes, London is now in London."

"Maybe you will soon be in Acapulco," I said laughing.

"Where is Acapulco?"

"They have a big ocean there, it is blue and beautiful."

"I don't like the ocean, I don't know how to swim, I want to go to America."

"Everyone in America knows how to swim; all the houses have swimming pools."

"I will like to swim in a swimming pool, not the ocean. I hear swimming pool water is sweet and clean and blue and is good for the skin."

We are silent. We can hear the sound of the aluminium sheets with which the houses are built. They make an angry noise like pin-sized bullets when going off. The houses built with tarpaulin and plastic sheets are fluttering in the breeze like a thousand plastic kites going off. Acapulco raises a handful of dust in the air. The breeze carries it away. Some of it blows into our faces and Acapulco smiles.

"God is not asleep," he says. I say nothing.

"There used to be dogs here in the camp." He had been in the camp before me. He is one of the oldest people in the camp.

There were lots of black dogs. They were our friends, they were our protectors. Even though food was scarce, the dogs never went hungry. The women would call them whenever a child squatted down to shit and the dogs would come running. They would wait for the child to finish and lick the child's buttocks clean before they ate the shit. People threw them scraps of food. The dogs were useful in other ways too. In those days, the enemy still used to raid the camp frequently. We would bury ourselves in a hole and the dogs would gather leaves and other stuff and spread it atop the hole where we hid. The enemy would pass by the hole and not know we were hiding there.

But there was a time the Red Cross people could not bring food to the camp for two weeks because the enemy would not let their plane land. We were so hungry we killed a few of the dogs and used them to make pepper-soup. A few days later, the Red Cross people were let through and food came. The dogs were a bit wary, but they seemed to understand it was not our fault.

And then, for the second time, there was no food for a very long time. We were only able to catch some of the dogs this time. Some of them ran away as we approached, but we still caught some and cooked and ate them. After that we did not see the dogs again; the ones that ran away kept off. One day, a little child was squatting and having a shit. When the mother looked up, half a dozen of the dogs that had disappeared emerged from nowhere and attacked the little child. While the mother screamed, they tore the child to pieces and fled with parts of the child's body dangling between their jaws. Some of the men began to lay ambush for the dogs and killed a few of them. They say the dogs had become as tough as lions. We don't see the dogs any more. People say it is the war.

I decided I was going to ask Sister Nora. As if reading my mind, Acapulco told me not to mention it to anyone. He said people in the camp did not like talking about the dogs.

"I am not sure the photographer will still come today," I said.

"Sometimes I think there is a bullet lodged in my brain," Acapulco said.

"If you had a bullet in your brain, you would be dead."

"It went in through my bad ear. I hear explosions in my head, bullets popping, voices screaming, *banza, banza bastard, come out we will drink your blood today,* and then I smell carbide, gun-smoke, burning thatch. I don't like smelling smoke from fires when the women are cooking with firewood; it makes the bullets in my brain begin to go off."

"You will be fine when you get to America. They don't cook with firewood; they use electricity."

"You know everything, Zaki. How do you know all these things though you have never been to these places?"

"I read a lot of books, books contain a lot of information, sometimes they tell stories too," I say.

"I don't like books without pictures; I like books with big, beautiful, colourful pictures."

"Not all books have pictures. Only books for children have pictures."

"I am tired of taking pictures and sending them abroad to families that don't want me, almost all the people I came to the camp with have found families and are now living abroad. One of my friends sent me a letter from a place called Dakota. Why have no family adopted me? Do you think they don't like my face?"

"It is luck; you have not found your luck yet."

"Sometimes I want to join the Youth Brigade but I am afraid; they say they give them *we-we* to smoke and they drink blood and swear an oath to have no mercy on any soul, including their parents."

"Sister Nora will be angry with you if she hears you talking like that. You know she is doing her best for us, and the Red Cross people too, they are trying to get a family for you."

"That place called Dakota must be full of rocks."

"Why do you say that?"

"Just from the way it sounds, like many giant pieces of rock falling on each other at once."

"I'd like to go to that place with angels."

"You mean Los Angeles."

"They killed most of my people who could not pronounce the name of the rebel leader properly, they said we could not say *Tsofo*, we kept saying *Tofo* and they kept shooting us. My friend here in the camp taught me to say *Tsofo*, he said I should say it like there is sand in my mouth. Like there is gravel on my tongue. Now I can say it either way."

"That's good. When you get to America, you will learn to speak like them. You will try to swallow your tongue with every word, you will say *larer, berrer, merre, ferre, herrer.*"

"We should go. It is getting to lunch time."

"I don't have the power to fight. Whenever it is time for food, I get scared. If only my mother was here, then I would not be *Displaced*. She would be cooking for me; I wouldn't have to fight to eat all the time."

We both looked up at the smoke curling upwards from shacks where some of the women were cooking *dawa*. You could tell the people that had mothers because smoke always rose from their shacks in the afternoon. I wondered if Acapulco and I were yet to find people to adopt us because we were displaced and did not have families. Most of the people that have gone abroad are people with families. I did not mention this to Acapulco; I did not want him to start thinking of his parents who could not say *Tsofo*. I had once heard someone in the camp say that if God wanted us to say *Tsofo* he would have given us tongues that could say *Tsofo*.

"Come with me, I will help you fight for food," I say to Acapulco.

"You don't need to fight, Orlando. All the other kids respect you, they say you are not afraid of anybody or anything and they say Sister Nora likes you and they say you have a book where you record all the bad, bad, things that people do and you give it to Sister Nora to read and when you are both reading the book both of you will be shaking your heads and laughing like *amariya* and *ango*, like husband and wife."

We stood up and started walking towards the corrugated-sheet shack where we got our lunch. I could smell the *dawa*, it was always the same *dawa*, and the same green-bottle flies and the same bent and half-crumpled aluminium plates and yet we still fought over it.

Kimono saw me first and began to call out to me, he was soon joined by Aruba and Jerusalem and Lousy and I'm Loving It and Majorca and the rest. Chief Cook was standing in front of the plates of *dawa* and green soup. She had that look on her face, the face of a man about to witness two beautiful women disgrace themselves by fighting and stripping themselves naked over him. She wagged her finger at us and said: No fighting today, boys. That was the signal we needed to go at it; we dived. *Dawa* and soup were spilling on the floor. Some tried to grab some into their mouth as they fought to grab a plate in case they did not get anything to eat at the end of the fight. I grabbed a lump of *dawa* and tossed it to Acapulco and made for a plate of soup but as my fingers grabbed it, Lousy kicked it away and the soup poured on the floor. He laughed his crazy hyena laugh and hissed saying: the leper may not know how to milk a cow, but he sure knows how to spill the milk in the pail. Chief Cook kept screaming, hey no fighting, one by one, form a line, the *dawa* is enough to go round. I managed to grab a half-spilled plate of soup and began to weave my way out as I signalled to Acapulco to head out. We squatted behind the food shack and began dipping our fingers into the food, driving away large flies with our free hand. We had two hard lumps of *dawa* and very little soup. I ate a few handfuls and wiped my hands on my shorts, leaving the rest for Acapulco. He was having a hard time driving away the flies from his bad ear and from the plate of food, and he thanked me with his eyes.

I remembered a book Sister Nora once gave me to read about a poor boy living in England in the olden days who asked for more from his chief cook. From the picture of the boy in the book, he did not look so poor to me. The boys in the book all wore coats and caps and they were even served. We had to fight, and if you asked the chief cook for more, she would point at the lumps of *dawa* and the spilled soup on the floor and say we loved to waste food. I once spoke to Sister Nora about the food and fights but she said she did not want to get involved. It was the first time I had seen her refuse to find a solution to any problem. She explained that she did not work for the Red Cross and was their guest like me.

I was wondering how to get away from Acapulco. I needed some time alone but I did not want to hurt his feelings. I told him to take the plates back to the food shack. We did not need to wash them because we had already licked them clean with our tongues.

As Acapulco walked away to the food shack with the plates, I slipped away quietly.

EC Osondu was born in Nigeria. He worked as an advertising copywriter for many years before moving to New York to attend Syracuse University, where he gained an MFA for Creative Writing and is now a Fellow. He has won the Nirelle Galson Prize for Fiction and was also shortlisted for the 2007 Caine Prize.

How Kamau wa Mwangi Escaped into Exile

Mukoma wa Ngugi

I

HE HAD BEEN RUNNING for hours. His lungs were about to implode. Each heartbeat, a resounding thud of pure will, sounded spaced out, lonely even, as if at some point the distance between each beat would grow larger and larger until only his body would be left running. He was wheezing and heaving for breath. He had been running for hours through small gardens, then larger farms, tea plantations and now through a dense forest trying to make it to the meeting point. Earlier he had had to abandon his rucksack, his survival kit of two books, roasted goat meat, a pair of expensive black dress pants, white shirt and newly polished black leather Prefect shoes. Before abandoning it, he crumpled a brand new passport (but not before in the moonlight quickly looking at the passport photo with a bemused look as one does at the airport before handing it to the customs officer) in the back pocket of his jeans. Into his left front pocket he tacked in a few thousand shillings and in the other school transcripts which looked out of place in his large sweaty hands in the middle of a forest.

Besides what was in his pockets, his other possession was an army flask. With its strap broken, he had to carry it in his hand. Earlier, the sound of water hitting its insides had seemed louder than it actually was. Now, even though empty, it was getting heavier and heavier. His temples were throbbing and his body felt as if his blood was going to break its banks and he would bleed to death. Before, to take his mind off things, he had become fascinated by how quickly the rings of smoke he spurted out dissipated into the cold air but now the only thought in him was to make it to the meeting point. Moonlight was folding back into the night. The early sun, peering underneath the earth's plate, was beginning to heat the soil and more smoke appeared to be rising from under the forest canopy. It was almost daybreak.

Feeling his t-shirt and jeans clinging uncomfortably to his body like they were made out of wet rubber, he realised just how unprepared he had been for this moment. He would have been better off running in his nice trousers and shirt – they were lighter. He had thought of running without a shirt but a quick look at his bare arms, sliced in a thousand places by thorns and dry branches, had convinced him not to take it off. He did not mind the pain as sweat-drops rolled into the razor-thin crevices. The pain kept him feeling alive. He realised he had to stop soon. For the last two or so hours he had been running at a crawl. He wanted to live. He came to a stream. He drank some water. The water was still very cold, even though the sun had revealed itself fully. He contemplated filling the water flask halfway to keep it light but decided against it and filled it to the top.

He looked around the stream. He hadn't gone as far as he'd thought. Even though he had been running for five or six hours he hadn't gone that far – not with fences to climb over, maize and napier grass plants cutting into his skin and tea plantations arranged like a maze. Not with the frequent pauses to make out trees and shrubs from silhouettes of imagined soldiers and policemen with their dogs. When he was young, he and friends would sneak out of school to come and play here. What used to be an hour's drive had taken him half a night.

He walked to a mugumo tree which, contorting high into the sky, looked like many hands lifted up in prayer. It had been drilled hollow by time and now its huge trunk looked like a Maasai hut without a door. The massive tree was supported by muscular roots that ran from its round bottom like huge veins deep into the earth. They would sometimes smoke stolen cigarettes here. He sat in its hollowness, this silent witness to generations and generations. It in turn embraced his battered body. For thousands of years, his ancestors prayed and sacrificed to their God here. He remembered how he and his friends joked that back in those days, it was thieves and the poor who answered the prayers by eating the food and warm muratina beer left as sacrifice. He was hungry and regretted the food he had thrown away. He wondered if he looked around whether he would find some cured meat, a bone that he could crush to find marrow preserved over many generations.

For the last few hours, he hadn't thought about his father, girlfriend, relatives and friends and how they would take his flight, how they would cope with the harassment that would follow. He wondered if exile was a selfish act, like suicide. But no, he had to trust their judgment, they would be happy that he had escaped. He was alive and therefore there was hope. They would not, even in their imagination, sacrifice him to cosy up to the authorities. Besides, they were all doing the same work in different ways.

As he sat inside the mugumo tree, he thought about Odhiambo. They had grown up in the same town. They had gone to the same schools, and even though they had enrolled for different university degree programmes, they had been admitted and graduated at the same time. His parents were managers at Bata

Shoe Company, which made the Prefect shoes he was wearing. In addition to Luo, he also spoke Kamau's language, Gikuyu. But the thing about it all was that neither the Luo nor the Gikuyu trusted him and herein lay the stupidity of the whole thing, Kamau angrily thought. To understand other African cultures was to be diluted, to be on the fence, to be compromised. It was to be dirty. He painfully dragged himself from where he was sitting to lean against the inside wall of the tree. He wondered if, after all the sacrifices done at this tree, would the culmination of their magic save his life? Embraced by the mugumo tree, he felt safe and protected and the warmth of sleep came over him.

He dreamed that there were loud voices and army trucks and helicopters circling above the tree looking for him. He felt the heat of a bright searchlight in his eyes. He wasn't dreaming. How could they possibly have found him? He opened his eyes to find a bright mid-afternoon sun streaming into his eyes. He closed and opened them again. The sun had found a hole through the mugumo to launch its invasion.

He was relieved. But just as he felt safe, he heard loud voices, screams and then machine-gun fire that sounded like a thousand people clapping loudly at a rally. He crawled about one hundred feet towards the stream. He made it just in time to witness the last of the executions, bodies dancing violently before falling to the ground. The soldiers began to pile dead bodies on top of one another in a shallow but wide grave that resembled the first dig to lay a foundation. They stacked them like cabin logs so that each head was locked into the feet of the other until they rose into the sky. He was well hidden by rocks and the long grass by the river's bank but he felt vulnerable, like he was completely out in the open.

From where the bodies were stacked, a slow but widening flood of blood was flowing down the bank into the stream, cutting it in half – upstream, clear and frothy white water and downstream, water thick with a bright, heavy and velvety redness.

It was fratricide. The dead and the dying wore army uniforms. He lay there transfixed, a reluctant witness immobilised just like the mugumo tree. The soldiers, tired farmers leaving the field after a hard day with their guns slung on their shoulders like hoes, were making their way back into the trucks. Only one soldier, fumbling in his pockets and resembling a smoker looking for matches, remained. It was then that Kamau noticed that the place reeked of gasoline.

They were going to burn the bodies and bury the remains. He thought of the schoolchildren who would some day find the remains but realised that this area would be cordoned off. This piece of land was owned by a well-respected local politician.

For the soldiers, everything was well under control. He felt dizzy and for a moment he did not know where he was. It was then that, as the soldier fumbled through his pockets, Kamau noticed one of the bodies had come back to life and was starting to move. It was stirring. At the same moment their eyes met. The man in the pile of bodies was waking up as if from a nightmare, disoriented. As he began to grope around, his confusion lifted just long enough for him to remember what had happened and he understood why there was a pair of eyes hidden across the stream frantically telling him to be still. When the shooting started, he had felt a sharp but heavy blow on his temple and, as he fell unconscious, he believed he was falling to his death. As he was realising what was now happening, he was at the same time trying to stop his hands from moving but it was too late.

His body had obeyed his earlier command. The soldier had seen him stir. He saw the soldier drop the lit match and snuff it out with his foot. As the soldier begun to march toward him, he turned his eyes to the pair of eyes across the stream. He felt a series of unpunctuated sharp blows to his chest. He felt his head getting heavier and heavier as the back of his neck locked against the feet of another dead soldier.

It was then that Kamau realised who the dead man was. It was the soldier who had told him to run for his life the night before. He had given Kamau a list of people to be rounded up and assassinated by the Special Branch in case of an emergency. Kamau had asked him why he was giving it to him.

"Just in case we fail," the soldier replied. It was not until Kamau met Odhiambo and Wambui that he knew the coup attempt had failed. Another matchstick struck the rough surface. It lit up and then began to fade away such that the soldier had to carefully cup it with both hands as he leaned over to light the pyre which hungrily welcomed contact. As a soft but determined wind fanned the flames, they began to flutter furiously, sounding like flags in the wind. The soldiers left, save for two who were guarding the burning bodies. Tomorrow they would be back. They had ploughed the field and would be returning to plant bones and skulls into the earth. The smoke from burning flesh began to rise into the sky. He looked around and saw it was a beautiful day. Looking into the stream that had now turned from deep blood red to a mucky black colour, he selfishly thought how lucky he was to have tapped a full container of water. Then he doubled up and started vomiting. He was afraid the two soldiers would hear him but not above the flutter and crackle of the flames and burning flesh. He was a witness taking flight, taking the pictures of the dead with him.

Kamau crawled back inside the mugumo tree. As he once again leaned against the inside wall, he noticed he was bleeding heavily from his stomach. He must have crawled over something sharp. He was in a state of shock which numbed him from feeling. He wished for the pain back. Perhaps this was the culmination of generations upon generations of sacrifices. He thought of the soldier and how he had come to his house the night before, unarmed and alone. Even without his weapons he had not lost his arrogance, so that when Kamau asked him for his name, he said in an off-hand manner it was none of his business. Kamau wasn't scared of him, though a few months before, even with him unarmed he would have been – soldiers and dictators rule through the threat of violence and the uniform without the gun is the same as one with a gun. It was like colonial white skin – whether it carried a Bible or not, the most important thing was the wrath of the army it threatened to visit upon the souls that refused to be harvested and rebelled. Over time white skin became the stand-in for the army itself.

He was not afraid of the soldier. He had experienced everything but death in their hands and, short of killing him, there was nothing more they could do to him. But that was Kamau the victim and survivor. Kamau the witness wondered if this held true any more. There was a lot more to be afraid of. Like people who conduct massacres in the middle of a beautiful day as carelessly as if they were on a lunch break.

"Look," the soldier had said to Kamau, "I... we do not want to see more people dead. Especially the young people and even though we anticipate more trouble from the likes of you, you professional agitators, this is our country and you are needed. Protect yourselves and your friends. We shall deal with each other later. Like men... eye to eye. If you do not leave tonight, there is a chance you will be dead by tomorrow morning."

The soldier gave Kamau the list and left. Perhaps he had been one of Kamau's torturers, perhaps an assassin doing one act of penance or perhaps he was just being pragmatic. But no matter, the soldier had saved his life. Kamau had not doubted him. He had felt the vice tightening. After torture and release he was aware of being followed. He was sure that their house phone was tapped. Some politicians – moderates, nationalists and radicals – had disappeared into black holes. Something had to give. He understood this with that same instinct that informs soccer players in a tight match or soldiers that tables are turning in a war. He felt that the culmination of all the right and wrong moves had brought things to a point where decisions had to be made. And for him, it was victory, death or exile. Regardless of which one claimed him, he understood that things could no longer remain at the cusp of a violent implosion. Someone had to go for broke. It was not the movement that he belonged to that made the first move. It was a section of the army and the dictator had just exacted his revenge – a first instalment of a hundred or more deaths. He and those like him who were part of the Second Independence Democracy with Content Forum (SIDCF) were going to feel the full effects of whatever had just transpired.

After the soldier left, Kamau studied the list. It had been hastily written, not even typed but first written in pen or pencil then stencilled. Some names were carelessly cancelled out. He wondered if that meant they had already been contained or had won a reprieve. The ones he could make out, like his, were names of members he knew to be alive. The names were written in different handwriting. Due to promotions or demotions and being processed by different agencies, the list must change hands quite often, he thought. He became very angry. Here, on this piece of paper, stencilled and crumpled, were people's lives. How many anti-government speeches earned one an assassination? How many rallies? How about silence when asked to sing? How many silences added your name to the list? From his cellphone, he called Odhiambo, who knew to walk to a phone booth and call Kamau at a neighbour's house. Kamau gave him the names on the list and asked him to contact as many as he could. He called those he knew he could easily reach and then made his escape plans with Odhiambo. There were two meeting points, one certain and the other a contingency. He returned home and started packing.

Inside the mugumo tree, he thought about how his father had slept through the soldier's visit, his packing and flight and started to smile but the energy left him. He should have woken him up. The sun began fading. He thought it was time to move on. But it was the fire. By creating thick dark clouds of smoke, it had hastened evening. Inside the mugumo tree the smoke was swirling angrily as it looked for a place to escape. Finding the small window that earlier had streamed in the sunlight, it billowed through. His eyes misted. He realised that he was crying. The shock had begun to wear off and he was feeling the pain that comes with thawing. He shut down and, even though awake, nothing registered, not the pain, not the burning bodies outside nor the torture he had endured a few months ago, not the wound that ran across his stomach nor his father who by now would be worried. When he finally woke up from his catatonic state, the moon was out but it was dark enough to continue. Even though he did not know it at the time, and it would take him even longer to register, he swore to himself that he would live. A wounded animal, limping and stumbling, he continued with his journey towards exile. The soldier who had saved his life was dead. But he was alive, a survivor and a witness.

II

Odhiambo heard a rustling noise and, as his heart contracted into a tight squeeze, he noted just how jumpy and scared he was. With the old wooden door open and the moonlight behind the silhouette, Odhiambo's eyes did not adjust to the light long enough to make it out before it pushed the door closed. The silhouette walked in dragging its feet along the floor, which was covered with sawdust to protect it from mud during the rainy season. Odhiambo fumbled in his pockets for a match. As he struck light, he heard the silhouette gasp and shuffle towards the door. It could not be Wambui. He whispered Kamau's name and, as the light from the lantern filled the room, the silhouette turned around. On seeing Kamau, he could see that something had gone terribly wrong.

Kamau looked as if he had splashed about in a pool full of blood. His white t-shirt was soggy with it and, as he shuffled along, he left little drops of blood which mixed with the sawdust on the floor and looked like little balls of mercury, each self-contained and shimmering. He was doubled over, holding his stomach with one hand and the water bottle like a grenade in the other. His long dreadlocks were full of black jacks, leaves and little twigs and his arms, neck and face were lacerated. But it was the expression on his face. His normally jovial face, alive in debate or jokes, was gaunt. In no time it had wilted. His eyes were flashing disbelief, fear and outrage, at once vacant then full of anger, at times ashamed then exhilarated. He was experiencing a thousand human emotions rapidly; emotions that were intense, sharp and without relief.

And the light from the kerosene lantern, not quite a bright white and not quite a bright red, almost yellow in fact, the light was painting everything in the room a hue of sick colours – jaundiced colours. Lazily pulling shadows long and short as it blew through the cracked walls, the lantern made matters worse. It was a wonder that Kamau was not on the ground paralysed.

After calling out his name, Odhiambo had not said a word. He pulled a dusty wooden chair for him to sit. This woodshed in their old primary school was their contingency plan. For Odhiambo the coup attempt and for Kamau the massacre had triggered it. With the coup attempt, there were complications. There would be road-blocks and of course a list against which every ID would be checked. All their plans had changed. They could no longer bluff and bribe their way through the airport. There was too much at stake now for the corrupt immigration official. They would need a million shillings at the very least whereas before they only needed thousands. In any case here was Kamau bruised up and without his dress shirt, trousers and pants. Odhiambo did not know what to do. At that moment Wambui walked in. Kamau tried to stand up as she walked in but he was too drained. She paused for a moment before motioning to him to remain seated and walked over to him. She looked at Odhiambo as if to ask for help but he just shook his head. Kamau reached out and held on to her.

Since his ordeal had begun, even though not more than 24 hours ago, it was only when he saw Wambui that he thought he might be okay. He knew he would be safe when he saw Odhiambo but Wambui made him feel he might be okay.

Witnessing the executions had unnerved him. The last part of his journey to the school had been painful. He had never felt so much fear in his life. Not even when he was arrested for the first time. To get to the tool shed he had to walk through the open soccer field, otherwise he would have had to double back and climb the fence behind the school. He did not have the energy to change the route he had taken. But if he had known that his heart would be pounding so hard as to make him think he was going to die, or that his chest under the vice of terror would tighten till he felt like he was going to vomit his insides, or that the dull moon would feel like a spotlight on him and that he would feel so vulnerable and lonely as he waited for an assassin's bullet, and that he would be so terrified as to wish for certain death, perhaps he would have changed his route.

But Wambui was here now. He had made it. He started crying, first slowly, sobs that heaved both him and Wambui, who was standing and holding him close to her stomach, back and forth. Then the anguished wails started that were so low that both Wambui and Odhiambo felt them without hearing them.

They got louder and louder until they thought the wails would rip them into pieces. Odhiambo watched helplessly as Wambui thrust Kamau back, took one step back and then slapped him so hard that he spun on the chair which swivelled on one leg, hesitated for a moment and then came crashing down, taking Kamau with it. She thrust her arms under his armpits, lifted him up from the ground and sat him down on a plastic pail of dried-up red paint. Then she explained to them how they would get him out of the country.

Kneeling before him on the dusty floor, she took some red ochre from her bag. As if she had done this all her life, picking out the black jacks and dry leaves, she began applying it to his dreadlocks. Its richness fought the smell of kerosene out of the woodshed. She kneaded it into his dreads. At times she would treat them one lock at a time, lift them up as if they were thread and she were sewing. With the balls of her hands she worked the ochre in. She massaged it into his roots in sharp, quick movements that appeared to Odhiambo to be rough. But to Kamau it was relief as the ochre lodged deep into his scalp, a cool, gritty healing potion. When it was all worked in, she straightened up, took the lantern and held it to his face. It would need time to dry but they had to move soon. She asked him to take off his t-shirt and trousers. He did not hesitate. She pointed to the blood-soaked boxers as well. She poured some water from Kamau's flask onto a cloth and scrubbed the blood off his face, chest, genitals, thighs and legs. She took off a long green wrapper that was holding her dreadlocks in place and wrapped it around Kamau's back and stomach to stem the bleeding from the wound.

From her bag she removed a long, flowing red cloth, the red bordered by black squares. She was glad to have picked red cloth – it would camouflage any bleeding. She draped it over his left shoulder and under the armpit of the right, leaving it bare, and then let the rest of the cloth fall to his ankles. She checked through his jean pockets and found the passport, school certificates and money. It was risky to be without a form of identification but it was even riskier for Kamau to be caught with his passport on him – with him on the list, they would all be shot dead on the spot. She stuffed everything back except for the money which she first folded into a small note and then, taking the left-hand side of the cloth, she knotted the money into it. She stuffed his bloody clothes behind some empty drums in the shed. They would come back for them later when it was safer. She gave him 12 amulets made of what seemed like a million rainbow-coloured little beads to put on each wrist.

Finally, to complete the ensemble, she gave him a calabash. It was full. He opened it. It contained fermented porridge that was still warm. As he painfully lifted it to his lips, Wambui looked at him. He almost resembled a Maasai warrior now but without a sword, spear or a fighting club he would not pass. But only if a Maasai cop stopped them – and such a cop, in disguise as well, would not peer too closely. In a sense Kamau's disguise was perfect. To everybody else in the country, a Maasai wore a red cloth, had red ochre in his or her hair and stank horribly. They were not seen and when they were, they were wished away because they reminded the Africans of their having sold their culture to the European only to till his garden, work as maids, oversee his estates and manage his bank accounts. In this world called a village, the Maasai reminded the African of who had elected the Westerner the village elder and, for this, they were punished. But the Maasai trudged on wearily, land continually taken, culture under siege from other citizens and European tourists who posed for photographs with them and their gold, diamonds, lions, antelopes and elephants. They wanted the red ochre to rub off onto their skins and carry back to their capitals the smell of a true African. Now other Africans were attempting to succeed where the coloniser had failed – to conquer the Maasai.

What also made the disguise perfect was that, while Kamau might suffer some insults and gruff treatment when stopped by the police, there was no way they would expect an educated African, even a radical, to go as far as disguising himself as a Maasai. What would the Maasai think? She did not have time to ponder. Odhiambo was already suggesting that they move if they were to get to the border. "My *ilkiliyani*, let's go," she said.

Kamau managed a smile for the first time. The porridge and his new persona had given him a second life. Perhaps he wouldn't have smiled if he'd realised she had called him her 'junior warrior'. He got up and followed her outside. Odhiambo snuffed out the lantern lamp and pulled the door behind him. They walked to an old Datsun pick-up. He noticed the number plates – KVG 750. It was his father's car. It was good he was once again able to record details. They put him in the uncovered back. That was how the Maasai were transported by the middle class whose conscience whispered but was easily assuaged by such gestures.

III

In spite of Wambui's confidence in the disguise, the first checkpoint was the worst. They did not know what to expect. The police officer who walked over to them was armed with a machine-gun, a pistol, a grenade and an army knife. They were not relieved to note that handcuffs were not part of his arsenal. He was not here to place people under arrest. He screamed of what in the files of Amnesty International became extra-judicial killings. Neither did they feel relieved that he was bureaucratically polite when asking for Wambui's driver's licence and Odhiambo's ID. It meant he knew exactly what he was doing. He checked their names against the list. As the flashlight tore through it they could see it bore the same careless marks as the one from Kamau. He walked over to his car to radio in their names. They heard a voice filtering through the static to tell the police officer to be more thorough; Odhiambo and Wambui were known radicals and the car they were driving belonged to a suspect's father. He came back and politely handed back Wambui her driver's licence and Odhiambo his ID.

As he ordered them out of the car, she noticed that the one thousand shilling note she had tacked in her licence was still there. This was a senior officer and before Wambui could decide whether to continue with his bidding, he was already carefully patting them down. He flashed through the glove compartment, under the long leather seat, under the mats and even inside an unused cigarette ashtray that sat on the dashboard. The officer walked to the back of the Datsun pick-up, hand tensely hovering over his pistol. Wambui knew that Kamau would not pass his scrutiny. This officer was too meticulous, a civil servant who, while he might not enjoy his job, prided himself on doing it well. The kind whose parents, with slaps and kisses, instilled in their children the discipline that said a job worth doing is worth doing well. The officer looked under the car. He flashed the surrounding bushes. With his free hand, he looked under the spare tyre. He signed for Kamau to stand up. Both Wambui and Odhiambo knew it was all over. He tore the flashlight through Kamau. He looked under where Kamau was sitting. Looked at Kamau again and then walked back to his car. They heard him asking if he should detain the two known radicals just in case and voice over the static telling him to let them go because they were not on the list.

By this time the other police officers had begun walking towards the pick-up, interest piqued by the amount of time it had taken to process it. Before they reached it, the officer beckoned them to get moving. Their relief did not last long. When they came to the spikes he flashed for them to stop. As he walked over to the car, Odhiambo looked at Wambui to say they were going to die soon and there was nothing they could do. The spikes had not been moved from the road to make a path for them. Making a run for it only to be immobilised by flat tyres would be certain death. They could not reverse without being shot at. In any case the old Datsun couldn't outrun the new Peugeot police cars which Wambui, for lack of something else to think about, decided looked elegant painted black. The officer walked over to the driver's side, reached through the window into the dashboard and, deliberately sliding his arm across her right breast, from her driver's licence he extracted the one thousand shilling note. He ordered them to drive on. As Wambui eased the car into motion, he waved the money in the Maasai's face.

IV

Not much conversation took place between Wambui and Odhiambo. They drove in silence. They were both present but needed time to reflect, regroup, plot and allow for the months ahead. Soon they were four or five kilometres from the border post. It was not safe to get any closer. Kamau would have to get off here and find a suitable place for crossing. They knew that the border post, a stall with a thick and heavy nylon rope that cut across the road, did not consist of much but it was still not worth the risk. With the coup attempt, there were bound to be soldiers.

They got out of the pick-up and walked a few hundred metres before slowly lagging to a stop. Kamau looked at Wambui. He thought he would be seeing her soon. They would win soon and he would come back or she would leave the country to join him. And she, she looked at her junior warrior. They held each other for a long time trying to burn this last moment, before the interruption in their memories. And when they both felt that it was imprinted on their skins and on their breath and memory, they let go. He tried telling them about the massacre by the stream on a beautiful day, how he had been woken up by gunfire, how the mugumo tree had sheltered him, about sacrifices and black smoke and how the soldier who had given him the list was also killed. He spoke too fast and it came out jumbled. They could not follow his words, but it had been a strange day and they understood him intuitively – his body told the story, the cruel laceration across his stomach as if the earth had tried to cut him open as he crawled to the stream. Odhiambo remembered his eyes that alternated fear and vacancy and Wambui remembered the hysteria. He was out of breath. He stopped talking and then, as if the words had been stuck somewhere inside him, he told them in one quick flood to approach the massacre site from the side of the mugumo in case there were soldiers there. He again fell silent.

Odhiambo hugged him. As they were getting into the car, Wambui thought about their love, how he was so broken up that when she held him she could hear each heartbeat echo in a growing emptiness.

Kamau stood still for a while and watched the furious ball of dust and light roll further and further away and then he started for the border. He hadn't been walking for long when he noticed car headlights rapidly digging holes into the night, sometimes all but disappearing then reappearing as the car dunked in and out of dips in the road. He stopped to wait to see his friends again. When the ball of dust screeched to a stop, instead of the old pick-up hurtling toward him, it was a massive 4x4 full of white tourists. They wanted to take photographs of him but he signed that he wanted to be driven in their motor car to the big city across the border.

"Probably to buy a wife," one of them said.

"Well, let him hop in," another said.

They did not put him in the carrier cabin at the back as Africans would have done. They squeezed him into the back seat. "Mr Maasai, can you teach us to say hello? How – do you – say – hello?" they asked him, gesturing wildly. Odhiambo probably would have known. "Wi mwega," he said in Gikuyu. They didn't know he was speaking Gikuyu and if they did, they didn't care. They repeated after him in chorus "Wi mwega."

"Why do you people kill lions? Do you know I once dreamed of hunting a Maasai hunting a lion?"

"Man, he doesn't look too good – perhaps the hunt did not go too well."

And thus their journey continued, slowing down only once to show their white skin and their one Maasai to the soldiers at the border post. Soon they reached Kiliko town. The flashlight tore into his eyes as they took what felt like a thousand photographs of him. The townspeople, composed of natives in tribal costume, administrators with suits that had bruised collars and tourists with cameras and long hair went about their business. But even then, some of the other tourists crowded in as if on a kill to snap a few photographs of him. He had made it out of his country barely alive. But he had survived, he was still alive and for now that was enough to work with.

Mukoma wa Ngugi is a Kenyan living in the US. He is the author of *Conversing with Africa: The Politics of Change* (2003), *Hurling Words at Consciousness* (2006) and *New Kenyan Fiction* (2008). He is a political columnist for *Business Daily Africa* and the BBC *Focus on Africa* magazine. 'How Kamau wa Mwangi Escaped into Exile' was first published in *Wasafiri* 54 (Summer), London, 2008.

Zain Caine Prize African Writers'
Workshop Stories 2009

Mansa

Franka-Maria Andoh

MY GOD MANSA HAD screamed the day it happened. How could she not? Now she lay in bed, the sunlight filtering through the large windows, waking her up. The welcome aroma of tea, coffee, toast and eggs wafted in. She could hear murmurs and loud sobbing starting again from the corner. She understood. Pain. It comes when it comes, has no special time or place where you can expect it. She'd looked everywhere but at the new wound, her eyes had roved, searching for distractions. The ceiling, the plain white screen that separated her from the world.

Even the fading red varnish on her toes held her interest for a little while. She adjusted the soft white cotton cloth that offered her body refuge from curious stares. An old scar from another time and place coaxed memories out. Hot coals, scalding palm soup, ice cold water. It hadn't healed well; its texture was a rough fabric embracing the lower part of her right leg. The drugs dulled the pain, made her head feel weighty. Maybe she was thinking too much.

A few days ago, they had dragged her out of that lovely, quiet world. Even as her eyes fluttered open, she knew where she was. For a split second the possibility of pretence was explored but she was held captive by the flash of sympathy in the doctor's eyes. Mansa recognised a kindred spirit. A traveller from her homeland, Ghana.

She could see the understanding in the woman's eyes. The knowledge that Patricia Ellen Johnson, the name entered on Mansa's chart, did not exist. Patricia had never resided at No 12 Streatham Road, London SW6. It was not possible that *this* was Patricia lying in a hospital bed, her eyes wide with apprehension. Mansa had stolen the dead woman's identity and was to be punished. Mansa's thoughts had wandered to her village, Bayire. She'd thought about Papa Koo, chased out of his new dwelling by a ghost. Koo had run out of the man's house with no clothes on, shouting. "He is here o! He is here o!" The village children called him *Hiero*. He'd gone a little mad after that. The things that happened in her little village... *Bayire*. Home. She'd played with all that in her mind. The going home bit. She was prepared.

Three days ago, spurts of blood had heralded the screams that twisted her mouth into different bizarre shapes. Mansa had heard Ngozi call out her name. Or was it Jane? It didn't matter; the pain that coursed through her body had rendered her bones molten. Some fellow had swooned right by the machine that continued to hum as if to say, life goes on. The factory filled with the sound of frenzied feet, pandemonium as the workers shouted.

"Tie it up."

"Grab that cloth. Quick, quick, hand it here."

"Bloody hell."

That made sense. It made sense to her even in her whirling mind. There was blood for sure and surely only in hell could this happen. Mansa went down on her knees, howling, calling out.

Ewuradzi Nyankopon.

Nyame.

Mi Na Mansa.

Mi Nana Mansa.

Gently closing eyes took in the Ziploc bag, the ice, and its contents. Her bones softened further and, slowly abandoning their faltering grip, allowed her to plummet into a dense, quiet world.

* * *

A year ago, her first letter had arrived at Bayire. Mansa Maame Mansa sat outside the hut. "Akuba. Akuba, please where are you? Come and read your sister's letter to me again."

Akuba dragged herself out of the room, a small stool dangling on her left arm like a handbag. Mansa Maame was careful with this child of hers. This daughter who, when ruffled, used words as weapons. "I may not be pretty but I'm smarter than you are. I'd rather have a big head and no hair with something inside than a small head full of bees." With the boys who shouted "Razor Mouth" every time she raised her hand in class, she picked her battles more cautiously. Akuba's strength was not in her clenched fists. This daughter who did not have the responsibility given the first child or the indulgences gifted to the last. The vacuum was where her latent feelings existed, a cobra about to strike. Mansa Maame was grateful to have one child and a grandchild with her. Her oldest daughter had died giving birth to her grandson Koby and Mansa was gone somewhere very far. Her Mansa. She missed her little girl, the long conversations with her, right here in front of the hut. The letter smudged with charcoal and palm oil emerged from Akuba's shirt pocket.

"Read it very loud, okay, you know my ears don't work well." Akuba read slowly, a little hesitant, but her mother sat very still, listening with a smile hovering around her lips.

Dear Maame

I arrived safely in England. I hope that this letter meets you, Akuba and Koby in good health. Is he behaving himself, that naughty nephew of mine? I hope so. I will soon send him a football if he promises to do well in school. I think of him often, Koby, losing his mother, and I will do the best I can for him.

By the way, I had a good flight, really enjoyed it and met a woman who was so nice; she held my hand all through immigration. I also met a pregnant woman on the flight; she looked like Koko. She was coming to England to have her baby and the immigration man actually got off his chair and helped her through. Her husband was overjoyed to see her. James met me at the airport. You know you cannot miss him, as tall as he is. We drove to the supermarket to do some shopping. I have never seen so much food. James filled the trolley with biscuits, sweets, all kinds of things. We then got home where I met his English wife Donna and our nephew Jamie who is a very beautiful baby. I help with Jamie, sleep with him in the same room and Donna is very grateful and friendly. She sits and chats with me all evening and we watch some wonderful television shows together. What can I say, life is good!

James found me a job within a week. I am enjoying it and have already made some really good friends. I am sending money for the house and also Akuba. She tells me that she wants to continue school. I think that's a great idea, my sister was always the clever one.

I wish you well Maame and will write to you soon.

Your loving daughter

Mansa

* * *

It was a sweltering Tuesday market day at Bayire and the market women fanned themselves with newspapers, cloth – anything to cool them down. Their frayed tempers extended to uncertain customers.

"Look, if you are buying, buy. Don't waste my time."

"Is that the best price you can offer?"

"Auntie. Auntie, you won't even look at me?"

Suddenly a shrill, accusing voice cut through the din. "Thief!"

An immediate crowd gathered. Other petty criminals took the opportunity to slide furtive fingers into unsuspecting pockets and accessible handbags. In the commotion someone bumped into the tomato seller's wooden table. Her elaborate display of tomatoes rolled off and one by one landed with soft thuds into the mosquito-infested gutter that meandered through the market. She bristled at the sight of Mansa Maame. Slightly out of breath, she turned her body to face the container behind her that carried all manner of filth from the market. The smell snaked through her nostrils, landed in her throat and she spat, unable to hold the taste of envy. One tomato stayed right by Mansa Maame Mansa's foot. She picked it up and handed it back to the irate woman.

"It is the end of the story that matters o!" the onion seller declared, cutting her eyes across towards the tomato seller. "Good morning Mansa Maame Mansa. How is our daughter in *Euloop*?"

"She is well, my sister. Thank you for asking." A little smile appeared quickly. The suffering that had mapped out and aged the poor woman's face was no more. She walked past the market women; a tall, slightly bent, rather pretty, young but old woman, and her cloth whispered, as only new cloth can.

"A daughter abroad. *What* more can that woman wish for?"

* * *

Two weeks gone by, the pain was less but she still couldn't, wouldn't look. Mansa shifted her weight in the bed and winced. She let out a deep sigh; breathing out of her mouth, her nose had traffic. A loud sneeze opened it up for a brief second. "Bless you," said a weak voice from the next bed.

Memories visited her regularly. Akuba questioning their mother. "How come Mansa gets to go to Cousin James and Auntie Baby's every holiday?" "Why don't I get invited any more? Mansa Maame reminding Akuba that the last time she went there she fought with James. "Why does Auntie Baby not send me to England instead of Mansa? I am older than she is." Her mother asked Akuba if time would fade the scar she left on James' ear.

Mansa wondered if Akuba would want to be where she was now. The wet pillow clung to her cheeks and the moisture moved hesitantly towards her chin.

In the beginning, Mansa had not wanted to go to Accra to visit her mother's friend. She had preferred to spend the long holidays by her mother's side.

"You'll learn a lot of things in Accra." Mansa Maame had said. "You'll have new experiences that will help you in the future."

By the second year Mansa Maame didn't have to convince her daughter any more. Mansa looked forward with much pleasure to visiting Cousin James and Auntie Baby. She fell in love with the woman and her sprawling house in East Legon that sat amidst smooth green lawns. The pool she avoided, awed by its inviting blue that seemed to draw her into a certain death. Mansa filled Auntie Baby's house with laughter and the smell of *kontomire, aponkye nkrakra* and delicious chicken stews. Home with her mother, however, was where her childish heart really was.

* * *

Mansa remembered exactly how this part of her life started: Auntie Baby organising her trip to England; how she arrived at Heathrow that early Sunday morning. She had stepped into the airport building bewildered, amazed by the number of people. Pausing every so often, she took in new things, the clothes shops. Glamorous little kiosks that had the scent of coffee and freshly baked bread sneaking out to embrace her. She spotted Cousin James; standing out in the crowd of people like a telephone pole. He held her briefly, reached out for her small suitcase.

"You made it."

"I did."

They were enveloped by men, women, children, happy people embracing, offering light kisses on the cheeks whilst others shook hands formally. Men roved around, leaning close to passengers and whispering as if they were sharing dirty secrets.

"Taxi? You want a taxi?"

James got on the escalator first. "You okay?"

"Yes".

Her voice wavered as she stepped out quickly, gripping the sides of the escalator. When the moving stairs unexpectedly joined the ground, she stumbled, almost toppling over. In the elevator, James pressed a button and as it rapidly descended, her dinner on the plane threatened to identify itself. Swallowing hard, she caught her breath and coughed, her throat tightening, irritated. James glanced in her direction but held a silence. It seemed to her as if all she had done was sit or stand on moving things since she left home. James led her to his car.

"Do all these cars belong to people?"

"Who do you think they belong to? *Ghosts*?" He smirked. James, unchanged.

As they drove to the Sainsbury's supermarket she gazed out of the window, amazed at the speed of the vehicles. She couldn't believe that roads could be so smooth, that the new country she would be living in would smell so crisp and fresh.

"Pick only what you need." James said sharply when they entered the shop.

"I don't need anything," she said. "I want everything," she thought.

It took James a couple of months to find Mansa a job. The first morning, she walked briskly towards the Shepherds Bush station. It was still dark, as if day and night had exchanged places. Mansa felt afraid, a little sad. She looked forlorn, a hunched-up girl in an old black winter coat. Her mind revisited images of a woman that had flashed repeatedly on the television screen the previous week. "Why would you stab a person 20 times?' Mansa had asked Donna that night. Donna had shrugged.

Mansa smiled at the other women in the factory. "Hello," she said nervously. "I'm Patricia Johnson." "Hello Pat." "Hi." "Come and sit beside me," one woman said. "Come. Sit right here."

She recalled how she had always felt cold and longed for some warmth. At night, even with three sweaters and a duvet, her arm died again and again then suffered a painful resurrection, tingling with the feeling of a thousand spiders scurrying through her blood. In the morning when she clocked in and sat down to sew, her eyes felt heavy. The whirring sound of the machines in the factory did not help. It was a lullaby. How could she sleep? The baby was fretful and arguments seeped like damp through the wall. Night came with a barter of words, her name the medium of exchange. "YOU BLOODY LEECHES!" Donna had roared, just before Mansa heard the front door reverberate.

She wasn't bothered by the reference to the blood-sucking insect. How could she explain to Donna that James was borrowing money from her every week? Ten pounds here, a fiver there, out of her small pay. She had been disciplined with her budget; Donna's 20 pounds for rent always came first. She knew the month was going to be tight since Akuba had requested money for Koby's school fees. Poor Koby, she hoped Akuba was taking good care of the boy. Mansa was tired, had been rocked to sleep by the sway of the train from Leyton to White City. She'd started when the train halted, a little out of it, snapping back her flopping head. "Things really have to get better than this. Things *will* get better," she encouraged herself, staggering towards the front door of James and Donna's flat.

There were sounds of people laughing loudly inside. The sound of breaking glass. More laughter. When she opened the front door, the noise from the living room was deafening. It was worse than the Mozama Disco Kristo church in the middle of Bayire. She'd managed to creep into bed and slip under her duvet when a man stumbled into the room. Mansa jumped out of bed. She pushed him out onto the narrow corridor and heard him grunt as he fell just outside their door. Jamie was fast asleep, oblivious to the wild, crazy party his mother was having.

The next day, a heady cocktail of vomit, beer and urine wandered around the tiny flat. The toilet seat had been flung into a corner and remnants of the curtains hung off the rod. As Mansa crept past, the man she had shoved out of their room remained slouched against the wall by their door. She wondered where James was. She hadn't seen him since the night he had taken his keys and banged the front door so hard that Jamie had woken up screaming. Mansa had it all sorted in her mind. She really had made a decision.

Two weeks later, he finally talked to her.

"I've moved out, James. I thought you should know."

"I'm busy, Mansa. That's entirely your business."

There hadn't been much to take with her. One suitcase and a few 'Ghana must go' bags. The taxi had waited. When she dropped her things into her newly rented room, she laughed out loud. She didn't care that it was a small room with bad wallpaper, closed in even more by her few belongings. She knew that from now on when her body met the bed, her eyes would not open until the dark dawn came.

It took Mansa a little while to settle. New environment, new rules.

Just outside the block of flats where she lived, she waited for a young man to finish his call. He seemed agitated and she stood looking away from him as he swore continually and finally banged the phone. She rummaged through her bag, eventually finding the international phone card she'd bought at the corner shop. Mansa leant against the side of the booth and with the phone tucked between her shoulder and chin she scratched the card with a coin. It took a while to punch in all the numbers. She had to try a few times before she heard a funny click that preceded several long ring tones.

"Auntie Baby?" she asked hesitantly.

"Mansa. Is that you?"

Mansa had been avoiding this conversation. The only thing that had driven her to the phone booth was concern for her mother. The niggling feeling that somehow, something wasn't right at home. She wanted Auntie Baby to make that trip to the village, to see her mother. She needed reassurance.

"Oh my daughter," the surprise and delight in her mother's voice came through clearly. She sensed her mother's wonder at being able to talk to her daughter so far away.

"I am so glad you are doing well. Akuba reads all your letters to me. She tells me you are now a secretary and live in a big house."

"Akuba is never home when I want to talk to you on the mobile phone, Maame."

"Mansa, I can't hear you. Can you shout? "

It was a comforting thought to know her mother was alive and well. But a secretary? Big houses? Who told her mother these things?

"Mansa, I will thank Auntie Baby for using her phone to call you. She came to the village yesterday. I cannot hear you, but I know you are there. That makes me happy."

"Goodbye Maame. Stay well."

It was the weekend that a new love had taken her landlady Glynis off in a flurry of sexy lingerie and red boots. Mansa looked forward to having the flat to herself, fixing some tasty *jollof* rice and getting into the world of Nigerian movies. She planned to stop at the African store in Balham where Ghanaians bought exotic foods and cussed each other out.

There's always something going on with us, she thought to herself. She'd walked past two women deep in conversation, their bulging carrier bags leaning against their legs. Plantains peeked out of one bag. She heard the word, 'deportation.'

"Can you imagine," one woman said. "Her own brother reported her to immigration and she got deported just last week. They didn't even let her take dross. Not even dross back home."

Mansa missed the other woman's response. Walking home from the station, she thought about Glynis, the new glow that seemed to have appeared on her face in the last few weeks. A spasm of envy was exactly that, a spasm. Mansa hadn't met anybody, apart from the Jamaican boy who had threatened to "bust her cherry".

She shivered when she pushed the door open with her shoulder. "Someone's dancing on your grave," her mother would say when you shivered like that. The hurriedly written note propped against the toaster explained everything. The heater was gone. She didn't take her coat off and walked around the house rubbing her hands together. Hot cups of tea dropped a little warmth into her body. Her mind played back her latest conversation with her mother. She had sounded a little slow over the phone. Maybe it was the distance, a bad connection.

The weekend dragged on endlessly and she welcomed the warmth in the factory, Monday morning.

"Hi Ngozi." She greeted the Nigerian woman.

"Hello Pat, enjoyed your weekend?"

"It was alright."

Was it really alright? It was freezing in the flat. She had been anxious all weekend, her mind going back to the long conversation with Auntie Baby on Sunday. Mansa shook her head, to clear it of the worries and doubts that clouded it. Mansa was late to work, needed to catch up, concentrate. She straightened up in the chair, placed her right fingers on the cloth and then came the pain.

* * *

The smell of medicine was stronger than usual. She woke up to find the man and woman from immigration already there. They sat comfortably, legs crossed

84

as if they had all day. The man was nervous, kept tapping his fingers on his knee. He was kinder, Mansa felt instinctively. She managed a smile. Thoughts of her sister travelled through her mind. How would Akuba handle this? Akuba who when pushed to the wall, scratched, bit and hurled verbal missiles at the end of the playground.

"How long have you been in the United Kingdom illegally?"

"Where were you living in this period?"

"How did this accident happen?"

The questions seemed never-ending. Mansa was tired, almost relieved when she saw them again. She knew that it was time to go home.

* * *

It took three weeks to summon the strength to go to her mother's home. Mansa approached the hut. Nothing much had changed. There was the rubbish heap; the one that people came protected by darkness to 'go to private'. The whole place looked worse than she had imagined. Oh, look at the roof! What happened to the money for the new roof? Her mother lived like this? God, she had been suffering for nothing. Her mind went back to the many evenings she and her mother sat outside this hut. They stirred leftover palm soup, stirred until it turned thick and delicious to eat with boiled cassava. Koby was always tucked into her arms, his thumb right behind his front teeth, sucking away. Akuba stayed inside, reading an old book borrowed from the mobile library that came round every month. Mother and daughter would talk about anything that popped in their heads. Koby always fell asleep and Mansa would take him to his room, place him gently on his mat.

Mansa saw Koby running towards her. His long legs were so thin. She wondered what he was doing at home at this time of the day, a school day. She wrapped one arm around his neck, drawing him tight. His bristly, uncombed hair brushed her chin. A tall boy, she wasn't sure if he would sit on her lap now. Then she saw her mother's stool: it lay on its side, dusty, neglected, unused. She began to wail. Wailed so loud the market women looked at each other, puzzled.

"You said everything was fine," Mansa shrieked. "Carried her to a herbalist when I sent money for the doctor."

Akuba stood silent, legs slightly apart as if she needed the ground to support her. "You kept saying to send money home. You lied to me. Wouldn't let me speak to her when I called! I never lied to Maame; I always told her what life was like in England. I hoped she would tell me I could come back."

The market women could hear Mansa shouting. They again exchanged uncertain glances. "Why does she scream like one whose mother died this morning? Did we not bury Mansa Maame four months ago?"

A group of young children clustered outside the hut to watch. A free show. Two cloth patterns pursuing a savage dance on the red ground. The coal pot nursing a young fire turned over, spilling hot coals, porridge and ash onto the floor. Mansa had pictures flashing in her mind like a slide show. The hospital. The flight home. She whimpered when Akuba tore her dress. Her left hand struggled to cover her breasts.

"I have to leave this place, I cannot stay here," she whispered to herself. "I have to go."

Koby stood in the room, silent, his frightened eyes darting towards the door. He pointed towards Akuba's bed. What was he trying to say? Why was he so scared? She paused a while and then, grabbing her bag, walked out. Akuba stood still like a statue surrounded by the excited children. Mansa could hear her sister's rage; the jealousy.

"*You* got all the nice things, *You* went to London. *You* were prettier, but *I* was smarter. It was all about you. Mansa this. Mansa that. It was always about you. I'm happy you suffered. You made *me* suffer."

Mansa shook her head, didn't look back. Her mouth was set in a terrible upside-down smile. She walked, head high, a beautiful girl, oblivious to curious stares. Only when she arrived at the bus station did her face crumple again as she remembered her mother's words. "You will learn many things." She adjusted her third-piece cloth that covered the ripped top, wiped her damp face with the back of her hand. Koby leant his head against her shoulder. Still a child. "Accra! Accra! Accra!" The bus driver's mate had spit flying from his mouth as the vehicle filled up rapidly.

EPILOGUE

It has been 380 days since the final parting with Bayire and Akuba. Not that she's counting for any reason. Just that it's taken this time to arrive at a calm place, where thoughts of Akuba can be tolerated once in a while. Her clever sister, reading the letters Mansa sent home to suit *her* needs. Koby had told her everything.

The canopy came on the hottest day. She is very pleased; it will protect customers from the blazing sun. Kofi, the canopy guy, has done it just the way she'd asked him to. She chose a jade green colour and he has MANSA MANSA SPECIALS emblazoned in a bright red on the front. He even made the SPECIALS stand out by writing it out in a curly, stylish way that she adores. She feels good and stands there admiring it for a few minutes.

Even when the customers start coming, she steps out from behind the counter when there is a lull to check it out. It's a busy day and there are ten customers already working through the different meals that she has become famous for. *Red red, kontonmire*, it's all written out on the little black board propped against the wall. She paid the canopy man immediately after he set it up. Pulled the money out of the heavy, brown envelope she had removed from under Akuba's bed. She feels better every time she takes money out of that envelope. Actually, she feels better than she has in a very long time. More customers arrive and she spies that man who has been coming every day for two weeks. On the first day, he smiled at her; looked away from her hand. He's a gallant man, she thinks. Maybe one day she'll explain to him why she refused the prosthesis. Felt it would make her clumsy, an oddity. Not that she didn't feel odd anyway. She can tell he has questions. He orders lunch for the day.

"How much meat?" she asks.

He isn't listening. Mind is elsewhere. She asks again.

"Oh sorry. Three cedis, please, my sister. Three cedis."

She smiles and flicks stew onto the rice, the meat placed daintily on the side: presentation matters to her. It's amazing how adept she's become with her left hand. The man asks her a question that has nothing to do with the food. She laughs softly, assured somehow by the uncertainty in his eyes.

Some customers look up, briefly caught up by the magic of a new beginning.

Franka-Maria Andoh lives in Ghana with her daughter. A Communications graduate of Croydon Business School, she owns a coffee shop and PR company in Accra. Franka was a part of the Crossing Border's writing programme. Three of her children's stories set in Ghana will be published this year.

Ekow

Ayesha Harruna Attah

MY BODY IS GLUED to the seat of this impeccable taxi. My eyes are fixed on the gate. Was it always this colour? A light green splash of mottled paint. It couldn't have been. I would have protested.

The vomit-green gate is flanked by already high white walls that have been elevated with a double layer of concrete blocks. My eyes wander, but they come back to rest on the gate, and I wonder what goes on behind it. My stomach juices churn. Behind that bile-coloured portal, how are they managing?

"Sister," the taxi driver says for the third time. "Isn't this your house?"

"Hmmm," I say. "I can't go in."

"Ei, sister." He's turned around and is looking at me, his neck craned above his blue and brown-checkered shirt. He seems like a decent man – his skin a richer chocolate than mine, his hair shaved close to his skull, and his eyes shockingly white. Maybe he's never had malaria, I think. Ekow never caught malaria. When we were children, I was always the sick one. The driver flicks the Christmas tree-shaped air freshener hanging from his rearview mirror, rattling the brown prayer beads hung behind it. "So what should I do?"

"Hmmm," I say again. "What's your name?"

"Moustapha." His voice is soft, and his gaze moves in the direction of the gate.

"Moustapha, please take me somewhere else. Anywhere."

"Eh?" He is now staring me dead in the eye. I'd have laughed, at any time, at the expression on Moustapha's face. On it is a combination of bemusement and amusement. His brow is furrowed and the corners of his lips are unsure whether to shoot up or down. I would have laughed, because I'd be as confused as he is. If Ekow were here we'd both be in stitches. Why wouldn't you want to go into your own house? But I haven't laughed and I am not laughing, and Moustapha is reversing, and the gate is growing smaller and smaller, and yet I can't take my eyes off it, until the dust on the road rises so high, I can't make it out any more. It's gone. I look forward now, at Moustapha's green air freshener. It's still swaying.

"OK," I relent. "Please take me to Kanda, near the Accra Zoo." I have a feeling Ewuresi's not there. She's probably behind the green gate like everybody else.

Mourning.

"You have stayed long outside," Moustapha is telling me. I look at his milky eyes through the rearview mirror. His eyes are like his voice. Soft. A little watery, though. Like he'd cry at the slightest provocation. I haven't laughed and I haven't cried.

"Not really," I say. "About six years. Why?"

"Ah, sister. It's only you people who've lived with *obronis* who become strange. How can you fly all the way from London here and now tell me you don't want to go home?"

"Hmmm," I say. I want to tell him I've arrived from New York, not London, but what difference does it make? I want to tell Moustapha that it's not that I don't want to go home, but that I really can't. I stared at that gate, at its bevels and dents, but couldn't bring myself to cross its threshold, because somebody isn't there. Instead, I clutch the peach zipper bag on my lap.

He's driving along with the Accra Sunday morning traffic. We are whizzing by on roads I can't remember being here. Once, to my left, crawled the Odaw River, barely coursing along with orange peels, pure water bags, Malt and Milk wrappers and faeces, but now I can't see it, and instead we're flying over tarmac, overlooking a crisscross of concrete. I see Accra rising and falling with orange, yellow and dust-strewn walls of houses topped with rusted roofing sheets.

"Accra has become very nice," Moustapha says. Is he reading my mind? I really like his voice. His velvety words are comforting.

"Yes," I say and watch as he passes by a copper-brown building – what was once Caprice Hotel. It was converted into the Boomerang Nightclub before I left but I can't get Caprice out of my head. He's cutting corners and turning and turning and now I'm lost. And yet, not a single heartbeat is skipping out of place. I am numbly calm.

* * *

We're in front of Ewuresi's house. The royal palms she planted before my departure are now towering above everything on the street. Her saffron walls seem to have been recently repainted. Ewuresi – the kind of woman whose walls look freshly painted even at the end of the rainy season.

"Sister, we're here," Moustapha says. "Should I remove your suitcase?"

"Please wait. I don't think my sister's home. I'll be right back."

"Today is Christmas Day for me," he says and chuckles. He doesn't mean it. His eyes assure me he's not going to milk me dry.

I sling my zipper bag over my shoulder, get down and walk to Ewuresi's burgundy gate. That should be the colour of Mommie and Poppie's. But it's not like they'd even consider my opinion, small girl like me. They never listened to Ekow either.

I press on a black plastic bell that pushes in under the pressure of my finger. The gate is being opened and a man about the same age as Moustapha ambles out.

"Yes?" he asks, his left hand clamping his hip, his eyes rolling about in their sockets. I wonder when he started working here. I find him presumptuous and rude. Ewuresi is the type of woman who wants her staff on their best behaviour at all times. These thoughts aren't original. Ekow's the one who'd say something like this.

"Is Mrs. Ahwi there?" I ask. He nods and opens the gate. I recall when Ewuresi first moved here. I was still in secondary school, and she was my age then. Twenty-two with a husband and a four-bedroom house. I can barely afford the one bedroom Holly and I have converted into two rooms. Thank God she was able to find someone to sublet for January.

I pass the side of the house, along full-blooming cat whiskers in beds filled with well-shorn grass. Apart from pruning the flowerbeds in Achimota Secondary School, I have never planted a thing in my life. The brown mosquito-proofed door is just like I remember – not sitting well in its frame. I swing it open, and it sings a long slow dirge.

Ewuresi's at home. She's standing in the kitchen, a plastic bowl cupped in her left hand, her right hand stirring whatever is in the bowl. Her black T-shirt is snug around her frame. Her middle is pudgy. It was never pudgy. She's looking at me, but recognition hasn't sunk in yet. She places the bowl on a marble surface. The spoon bounces off the bowl and lands next to three fat plastic cups.

"Oh, Araba!" she cries. "We knew you'd arrived, but weren't sure what had happened to you. Mommie and Poppie have been worried out of their minds! What are you doing here?" Her arms are outstretched, their undersides wobbling ever so much.

I walk toward her and let her engulf me. I feel her soft stomach on my chest. It's not easy being the dwarf of the family. "Why aren't you there?" I ask.

"Jason caught chickenpox yesterday. I want them all to get it once and for all. Let's call Mommie now."

I am shaking my head, trying to widen my eyes as much as I can, to transmit to her how I really cannot deal with Mommie and Poppie without Ekow. I can't go home.

"Are you all right? You must be hungry. You've lost so much weight. Why? You don't eat in New York? Why? That glamorous New York magazine doesn't pay you?" She's not far from the truth. Except for the glamorous part.

"I ate on the plane." Rice, beans, rotisserie chicken, *maduros* and shreds of algae-green lettuce, on 11th Street. The last real meal I ate. A week ago. I threw up after Mommie called, and have since been getting by on Twix bars and cans of coke. Even they have no taste.

"Please help me," Ewuresi says, handing me the bowl of creamy Cerelac she'd been whisking. She opens the fridge and extracts a bottle of milk, a jug of berry-red liquid, and is picking up the three cups from her marble top. Superwoman. I can't even handle grown-up Holly – washing up after her, cleaning the bathroom she clogs with her wispy strands of hair and wiping the sludge she leaves on the carpet. The carpet we can't afford to get dirty before our lease ends.

We're climbing up the steps and I remember. Easter of 1999. I had come in from Achimota, and Ekow had made the trip from Mfantsipim. When Ewuresi got her own house, it was much more fun for us to come here. She was almost like the cool parent, what with Mommie and Poppie being so old and conservative. So here we were racing up these very wooden stairs, with their forever-glossed look, trying to see who would get the bigger of Ewuresi's guestrooms. The one with the bathroom.

We're walking into that room now. The walls are salmon, and the curtains a bright orange. It's the girls' room, I presume. Jessie and Janet's. But everyone is in here. The twins – Jason and Jessie, and Janet and John. Their faces are covered with a pinkish white layer. The girls on one bed. The boys on the other.

That day, Ekow had won. He'd squeezed his wiry frame by me and dumped his dirty red satchel in front of the door. "Victory's mine, my little cow! All mine!" he'd shrieked and smiled, revealing his large PK teeth. He always conveniently forgot that I had two years on him.

"Mummy, who's this?" Janet is asking.

"Auntie!" Jessie volunteers, wrapping her arm around Janet's shoulders and pulling her in toward her. But I'm sure she can't remember me. I left when she was four. And now she's ten?

"Auntie who?" Ewuresi asks Jessie and hands her a cup.

"Auntie Ekow!" John shouts and giggles. He's missing two front teeth. Ewuresi's looking at me, shaking her head.

"Yes," Jessie says. "You look like Uncle Ekow!"

"Shhh!" Ewuresi says. They are right. People thought we were twins until he went off to Mfantsipim and went through that insane growth spurt, but our facial features are identical. Same eyes. Same nose. Are. Were. What tense does one use when one part of two isn't there any more? I walk out of the room.

"We have to call Mommie," Ewuresi says behind me and draws the door close.

"She's worried sick. She already has one person..." She hiccups and purses her mouth. Her deep dimples stretch out on either cheek. If I looked like Ewuresi at twenty-two, I'd be modelling in New York City, making shitloads of money, but now lines radiate from the corners of her eyes, which are welling. She used to have the smoothest face from here to Kumasi.

"Ewuresi," I start. "I didn't say goodbye. The last time we spoke, he made me so angry, I hung up on him..."

"Mummy!" Sounds like Janet. "Stop it, STOPIT! Stop it, John, ah! Mummy, John is eating my Cerelac!"

"Why didn't he just ask for Cerelac?" Ewuresi mutters under her breath, wiping her eye. "He said he wanted milk." She's heading back into the girls' room.

As I descend the stairs, I see the golden-framed blown up photograph of Ewuresi in kente cloth, a blue sash draped across her chest. Her sash reads, "1st Runner-up, Miss Ghana 1994". My eyes drift left. Here's a picture of Ewuresi clad in a shiny lace dress, sitting atop a black stool, Jason, Jessie, Janet and John dotted in a circle on the ground around her. I see more pictures of Ewuresi and the children. And only one of Mr Ahwi. I wonder where he is today. My eyes are fixed on his photo and his overgrown jet-black hair. Ekow and I call him the Bushy Lizard. BL for short. Back then every time BL came home, he'd sniff the air, his head bobbing, waiting for his dearest Ewuresi to tell him what she'd cooked him for dinner. All it'd take was one glance at Ekow and I'd burst out laughing. Ekow always wore the stupidest looks. But I was the one who ended up looking like the fool. That cow!

I don't know why I am still here staring at the Bushy Lizard. This rollercoaster in memory-land is no better than if I'd gone through the puke-green gates.

My feet lead me back into the kitchen, through the whiny ill-fitting net door, along the cat whisker flowerbed and out the burgundy gate. I am opening the back door to Moustapha's taxi and find myself staring at the Christmas tree air freshener. "Royal Pine," it reads.

"Moustapha." I'm looking at his rearview mirror. "I beg you. Take me somewhere else."

The pupils of Moustapha's eyes move up to touch his eyelids, circle and come back to rest in the middle. He fixes his gaze on the clock below the Christmas tree air freshener. I can't make out the figures from here.

"Sister, I think you're hungry," he says, and we're driving off again.

* * *

We're turning left, right, right, then left, leftrightright. And I am lost. But I don't feel anything. I don't know where we're going and I don't care.

Moustapha noses the car into a space between a blue car without tyres and a red-yellow Tico taxi. I get whiffs of ginger, bean cakes and firewood and I'm reminded of my grandmother's house in Kumasi.

"This is my house," Moustapha says, pointing at a blue wall, with patches of grey concrete spotted on it. Two benches lie against the wall, and men sit on them, hip-to-hip, licking *koko* off the plastic bowls before them. Beyond the benches, a queue snakes along the spotted blue wall. One man holds the tip of the bowl against his lower lip, and I hear slurp-slurp-slurp.

We get down. As Moustapha and I walk to a small blue gate, out comes a girl with a metal tray balancing five bowls. She smiles at Moustapha and curtseys. "Sala, *kwallafiya*," he says.

"*Lafiya lau*," Sala says back. "Welcome, sister."

I thank her, but wonder if my suitcase is safe. We're inside the compound now and somebody catches my eye – this large woman on a small stool. Her buttocks spread across the stool's sloped top. Her lime-green *boubou* creases and straightens as she stirs the colossal aluminium pot in front of her. Moustapha starts towards her, but she turns round before he gets to her and she beams. From the corner of her mouth, a gold tooth shimmers. Her eyes. They're bright white and I see where Moustapha's come from.

"Hajia, *kwallafiya*," Moustapha says, kowtowing.

"You're back so soon," Hajia says. She's looking straight into my eyes and the corner of her mouth shoots up. She raises her right palm, her fingers curl over and she's drawing the hand to her bosom. Come, she's gesturing. And I am going, transfixed to her shiny white eyes and smile. "Ei, Moustapha! She is nice papa! *Laa ilaa illa llah!*"

Moustapha's bemused look has returned, and his eyes are twitching, trying to send a nonverbal message to Hajia, but she hasn't seen him, because she's looking at me, and I'm looking at him. And her.

"What's your name?" Hajia is asking me in Twi.

"Araba."

"SALAAA!" Hajia is screaming, "SALAAA!" and a string of Hausa words. And now, Sala has brought me a stool. "Why do you make me shout, eh, Sala?"

Hajia's right hand is wielding a giant metal ladle. She dips it into the pot and collects a steaming thick grey gruel she's pouring into a silver bowl. "My dear," she says, "you look like bones! Have this!" She thrusts the silver bowl in my face, and sticks a spoon in my hand. Even though the thought of food going down my throat makes me gag, I dutifully place the spoon in the porridge.

"I'm coming," Moustapha says, plods toward a door covered with a purple cloth with pink feathers and disappears behind it.

Hajia's eyes linger on me. "This is the best *koko* in all of Accra," she says. "That line you saw outside. Ho! That's nothing! It's Sunday, so the businessmen are at church. Come see this place tomorrow morning! Shieee!" She slaps her thigh. "The Benzes and BMWs. Hmmm!"

My stomach is heaving and I still haven't put the spoon to my lips.

"EAT!" Hajia bellows. Her command stills my churning insides. I twirl my spoon around in the grey muck. I lift a mouthful and lead it to my lips. The spoon is on my tongue, and I get a kick of ginger, pepper, cloves and spices that I haven't tasted in years. Hajia's right hand is now whipping an orange paste, and yet she manages to keep her eyes on me. "It's nice, eh?"

"Very good," I say. I am leading a second, a third, a fifth spoonful of *koko* to my lips. The first time all week anything has taken on flavour on my tongue.

"So, Araba," Hajia says, shifting about coal on a Dutch oven, "how did you charm Moustapha's heart?" I choke. Did the *koko* just spurt out of my nose? "It must be serious," she's going on, "because since that little prostitute Naa trapped him into getting her pregnant, he hasn't brought anyone to greet me."

"Oh, Hajia." I am smiling. The first time all week I've smiled. "We're still getting to know each other."

"He's too good," Hajia says. "That's how that witch trapped him. If not for her, he would have been just like my businessmen – driving a Benz!" She sucks her teeth.

I am scraping the bottom of the silver bowl. Moustapha is walking out of the room he'd entered. He trudges toward us, his checkered shirt tucked into his khaki trousers.

"Sister," he says, "are you ready?"

"Oh, OK," I say, hoisting myself off the stool. I turn to Hajia. "This *is* the best *koko* in the whole city."

"Thank you, my dear. Come back, eh. This is your home now."

"Thank you, Hajia."

* * *

It's Moustapha and I again. Moustapha-Araba. Araba-Moustapha and the Royal Pine Christmas-tree air freshener.

"Thank you," I say to him, looking in the rearview mirror. His brows shoot up. They are thick and are angled along with his soft, liquid eyes, not a single hair out of place. Maybe he tweezes them.

"For what?"

"Taking me to your mother and showing me your home."

"But that's Ghanaian hospitality," he says.

"I'm still grateful. What's your child's name?"

"That woman just opens her mouth," he groans. There's something in his eyes I haven't seen before. They're set on the road ahead. They've become hard and distant. "Listen, sister," he says. His velvety voice is roughening around the edges. "Some of us have real problems. Not you. You don't want to go home." He kisses his teeth. "Please, don't waste any more of my time. Your house or the airport?"

I must have really hit a sore spot, but we all have problems. "We all have problems," I am repeating aloud. "Moustapha, I have plenty of real problems."

"Yes, I know. You don't want to go home. What a problem! Tell me. Tell me your plenty problems."

"I'm sure in one day you make more money than me."

"Now you think I'm a fool?" He chortles.

"No, I'm serious. I've been going to school for so long. I've finished university but work like an apprentice. Do you know what I do?" Moustapha's quiet. "I photocopy. I buy coffee for my bosses. And when they pay me, I use all the money for rent."

His eyes meet mine in the rearview mirror and he lowers his.

"At least you're in London. Life is easier there than here." His voice is thawing.

"Next year if I don't get a real job, I'll have to come back home. With absolutely nothing."

"Ah ah! Then why is everyone trying to go to Babylon?"

"I don't know, Moustapha. It's so lonely there. And when something happens to your family and friends here, you don't know." We're both quiet. The sun is now high up in the sky, casting a mirage above Moustapha's hood.

"My son's name is Razak," he says.

"That's beautiful."

"My mother used to say I'd be great." He pauses. "She stopped saying it when Razak was born." I want to ask him why, but I don't need to. He continues, "I wanted to start a fine taxi company. Plenty cars people can hire. If you want to go to the Western Region, Volta Region, you come and hire my car and driver."

"I know how you feel," I say. "But at least this taxi is yours."

"Yes."

"I own nothing."

"You have your mother and father."

"Moustapha, they can't support me forever."

"Why don't you want to go home?" Moustapha's gaze is piercing through me. His eyes say, "You can't escape this time. I've shared. It's your turn now."

"My brother died." I look out the window. We're back on the new highway that hides the Odaw River. This is the first time those words have come out. They are chased by a swelling in my chest, a round nebulous thing lodged in my throat. I haven't said those words because saying them makes them come true. I try to swallow but can't. My eyes sting. My lips are pursing, shaking. My brother died. A tear falls onto my peach zipper bag. Stains it a dark salmon. Ekow really has left me.

"I'm sorry," Moustapha says, cutting in front of a black Volvo. "Were you close?"

"Like twins." I wipe the corners of my eyes. "But I haven't seen him in six years."

"Allah," Moustapha whispers. "What happened to him? If you don't mind..."

"He was in an accident. Kumasi road. He was coming down from the university."

"Ay, Allah!" A filmy sheen covers Moustapha's white eyes. Mine are blurry.

We're back on the dirt road. Through a haze I see Miss Andoh's house, the Bindies', and now we're in front of the mustard gate. Moustapha pulls up to the gate and grinds the engine to a halt. He says nothing. We are sitting outside. Moustapha-Araba. Araba-Moustapha. Time is ticktocking away.

"How much do I owe you?"

"Nothing, my sister."

"No, Moustapha," I say, opening my zipper bag. "I can pay for this."

"We're now friends. Next time." He's opened his door and is walking out. He's popping the trunk open and I descend from the taxi.

"Thank you for everything, Moustapha," I say, and approach the green gate.

Ayesha Harruna Attah has worked as a freelance writer for publications in Ghana and the United States. Born in Accra, Ghana, Ayesha studied biochemistry at Mount Holyoke College and holds a Masters in journalism from Columbia University. She wrote her first novel, *Harmattan Rain*, at the Per Sesh Writers' Workshop in Senegal.

Simple Economics

Brian James

I HAVE NEVER FELT my heart beat the way it is beating. Rather than its usual steady beat, it flutters erratically. I know that nothing is wrong with me – not physically anyway. I settle further into my velvet seat trying to shrink out of sight. My eyes stray to the elegant napkin on the table in front of me. It is white with gold trimming. Like the parquet floor, the crystal glasses, the chandeliers and, most of all, like the customers engaged in their hushed conversations, the napkin exudes opulence. Before tonight I had never known that such magazine-page restaurants existed in Sierra Leone. I toy with the idea of using the napkin to hide my face. But there really is no need. I might as well be invisible to all the Italians, Arabians and Americans around me who are buried in their own business.

As though accessing my thoughts, the waiter materialises beside my table, reminding me that I am not quite so invisible. His starched shirt is so white; it is almost painful to look at. Raking me over with the most disdainful look he can muster, he pulls himself to full height and raises his nose in the air.

"I have been asked to inform you that your... companion is on the way."

His attempt at a snooty upper-class British accent is terrible. It is clear that he has never set a toe out of Sierra Leone. Any other time I would have laughed aloud. But this is not any other time. The sound of my fluttering heart fills my ears. I watch the restaurant's plexiglass entrance. I am unable to see outside to know who is approaching. All I can see is a reflection of myself sitting alone at the table. I try to straighten out the collar of my best t-shirt so that it looks less frayed. The table cloth isn't quite long enough to cover my shoes. No amount of boot polish can hide the fact they are beyond redemption. Anyhow, it is far too late to change any of that. The show is about to begin.

The plexiglass doors open. My heart slams painfully against my chest. A rotund, reddish-faced man enters, with an anorexic local girl hanging onto his arm. His eyes are tiny and cotton wool-white hair shoots out of either side of his head. Her face is broad, her eyes heavily lidded and her black and gold lips appear to be stuck in a vacuous smile. The light skin on her bare shoulders is covered with dark blotches. As they choose a table, the fluttering in my ribcage resumes.

So does my surveillance of the plexiglass doors. Over in a corner, the waiter glares at me again. I ignore him.

A sudden vibration on my left thigh startles me. I fish in my jeans pocket for my phone. Even before I look at the screen, I know who it is. I contemplate not answering. As the phone continues to vibrate, I realise that not answering would only make room for questions that I would rather do without. I raise the phone to my ear.

"Hello?"

"Why aren't you home yet? Where are you?"

"I'll be home soon," I respond, "I just have a little business to take care of."

"Is it about the bike?" Melissa asks.

"Yes."

"Where are you?"

"I'm meeting with someone who might lend me the money to pay Mr. Kuyateh back for it."

"When will you be home?"

"I don't know. The person is not here yet."

"Well, when you get home please try not to wake me. I'm very tired."

"Don't worry."

I turn the phone off completely. Once again I try to play out in my mind how this evening could go. I imagine how I am going to negotiate this transaction; what strategies I am going to use. Thinking is difficult though. Between my peculiar heart rate and the constant opening and closing of the plexiglass doors, I am rendered incapable of structural thought. I will have to rely on the strategy plans I laid out earlier if I am to get through this evening... if I am to come out looking good.

Just a few days ago, like many other Sierra Leonean youths, I was out on the streets trying to face the struggle for survival like a man. In college, it hadn't crossed my mind that I would be unable to get a job. Years after the end of our ten-year civil war, the economic and political climate had calmed somewhat and commercial institutions had begun springing up all over the capital. In the past three years, 13 of them had been opened or were about to be opened. They needed workers and they were rapaciously absorbing college students. Don't get me wrong, I wasn't naïve enough to think that managing directors would be waiting out on the front steps of their institutions for me to pass so that they could beg me to work for them. I mean, economics students weren't exactly a rarity in Freetown. There were at least a hundred in my class alone. Like me, they realised that there were prospects in this field of study. So I never lost sight of the competition around me but I was confident of the fact that amidst all the fortune seekers, I got some of the best grades. Just like I defeated my colleagues in class, I would overcome them in the world of work.

I was so confident of powering my way to the top that when Melissa informed me that she was pregnant, I gallantly offered to marry her immediately after graduation. I never went through the emotional lashing that many jobless young men go through when they ask a couple for their little girl's hand in marriage. Melissa's parents loved me right from the start. In an ultimate show of their approval of our relationship, they paid for the whole thing. It was a simple little ceremony but filled with love and laughter.

"We know that you will take good care of our daughter," her mother whispered in my ear as we danced. At that moment I could almost feel the warmth from my parents' smiles as they gazed down at me from the Great Beyond.

Like all honeymoons, ours eventually came to an end. It was time to take on the system. Melissa suffered frequent bouts of sickness that made it difficult for her to go job hunting. So it was all up to me. Clutching my first-class degree and my admittedly scanty curriculum vitae in hand, I took to the streets of Freetown.

As I searched for possibilities perched on commercial *Okada* bikes, I imagined profiles that would be written about me in five to ten years. *This economics wizard,* they would write, *started his phenomenal career by going from bank to bank atop the "poor man's transport".* It was childish but it helped me focus on what I wanted out of life.

The months flew by and it became increasingly difficult to hold back my frustration. Melissa was great. She went about our meagre accommodations quietly performing her wifely role as best she could. Not once did she complain. Her growing belly, however, was always a constant reminder of the added responsibility to come. A man should feel pride at the sight of life growing inside the woman he loves. I could not help seeing it as a ticking clock; telling me that I was running out of time.

Out on the streets I noticed that many of my contemporaries were proving to be luckier than I. Often, I would walk into plush, ultra-modern financial institutions and recognise former colleagues sheathed in executive suits, walking up and down the marble floors.

An old school friend of mine, who was now in charge of personnel at the Central Bank, asked me to accompany him to lunch. Over a beer, I asked him to share the secret.

"No secret," he replied, snapping his fingers at a waitress for the bill. "It's not about how good you are. It's about who you know. Look at me. My mother's friend is having a thing with the Public Relations person. He helped me get this gig. It's all about *sababu*."

"So why don't you hook me up with someone," I asked.

"I'll see what I can do," he said.

I called him four times after that. The first three times, his reply was that he was still working on it. The fourth time, he had changed his phone number.

It came to a point where I had been to every institution that was even remotely linked to my educational discipline. With no money left to take an *Okada* home, I leaned back heavily against the perimeter wall of a girls' school out of sheer exhaustion. The best part of the day had gone when I finally persuaded myself to begin the trek home. As I dragged my feet along the wall, I noticed that it was covered in posters advertising Christian crusades and conventions. COME AND RECEIVE YOUR FINANCIAL BREAKTHROUGH, they screamed. THIS IS YOUR YEAR OF DIVINE PROSPERITY. Unlike Melissa, I had never been much of a church person, but the words "Financial Breakthrough" and "Divine Prosperity" began to sound very good.

Much to Melissa's delight, I took her to one of the crusades. After that I began following her to church. As the Sundays came and went, I saw no change in my situation. My year of divine prosperity was running out and I hadn't so much as landed a job.

"You can't expect it to happen right away," Melissa chided me. "It takes time and faith."

It took all of my restraint to keep from telling her what she could do with her time and faith. It wouldn't do to take my frustrations out on her.

The thought of resorting to African magic darted provocatively in and out of my mind. I was smart enough to know not to mess with the stuff but it remained a constant presence in my subconscious. One day I mentioned it to Melissa... and she exploded.

"What kind of nonsense are you talking about?" Do you know what that thing can do to a person? Especially a pregnant one? Do you want me to give birth to a duck?"

It took plenty of sweet talking and a foot massage to assure her that I had no desire to father a duck. I had merely succumbed to a moment of weakness, I told her.

Melissa's medical bills mounted. I hated the idea of having to borrow money from friends and family but I had little choice. We'd been married only a few months and in that time, three birthing mothers in the Kalaba town community where we lived had died during childbirth. Two more had lost their babies soon after birth. The papers gave significantly higher body counts from around the country. According to them, ours was the highest infant and maternal mortality rate in the world. Whenever I saw Melissa wince in pain as she got up from the bed, my heart screamed. I had to make sure she had all the required medical attention. I also had to figure out a way to pay up if I didn't want to spend the rest of my life in debt.

I was in the powdered milk section of a shop grieving at the prices when I heard a man talking with attention-seeking loudness. "First of all, you identify a market. Then you search yourself and see what you have to offer that market. It's simple economics." I peered over the topmost cans into the next aisle to have a look at the would-be economist. A tall man with oily slicked-back hair, a gold earring and reflector sunglasses was talking on a mobile phone. His light skin had the unmistakable quality of one that has not been repeatedly exposed to the ruthless African sun.

"It's simple economics," he said again. "My brother, when you look hard enough, you'll find that there is always a market. There is not a man in existence with nothing to offer. Everyone has a market, therefore everyone is a potential millionaire. That is what most people don't know."

I had never heard economics explained like that before. As he left the supermarket, I ran after him, forgetting my original mission to purchase milk.

"Excuse me," I said as he slid behind the wheel of his black monster of a four-wheel drive.

"Yeah, 'sup?" he said.

"I couldn't help overhearing your conversation in there, just now."

Suddenly he grinned at me. "Ah! You want to unlock the millionaire within?"

"Well... yes."

"It's easy, my brother. When you look at yourself, what do you see?"

"I see a broke guy drowning in financial trouble."

"That right there is your problem," he told me. "It is that kind of thinking that keeps you from your potential. Ask me what I see when I look at you."

"What? What do you see?"

He came down from his car and moved so close to me that I could smell his breath. It had a hint of minty freshness.

"Guys like you are the reason I came back home. When I look at you I see an African powerhouse. My man, a guy like you, you're a walking cash extravaganza."

My mouth was suddenly dry. "How... how do you think I can get my hands on some of that cash?"

He considered me for a moment. "I'm going to tell you something that any other African guy would keep from you simply because he doesn't want you to get ahead. I'm going to do it because you're a brother in need and I'm a humanitarian who only wants to help."

And he leaned to my ear and told me. When he had finished sharing the secret of his success, I looked at him in disbelief.

"That's it?" I asked. "You can't be serious."

"Find the market, baby," he said with a toothy grin.

As he entered his vehicle, he had the self-satisfied look of one that has just done a big favour. Shaking my head, I went back into the shop wondering why some people were wired the way they were.

I decided to forget about my pursuit of the banks and begin to hustle. I now spent my days (and some nights) scouring the streets for information on anything that would make me a little money. When you're a hustler, your eyes and ears must be on full alert at all times. Sometimes the call of opportunity comes as a mere whisper. Sitting in a taxi on my way to see a man about some DVD players, my ears latched on to the conversation of two young men sitting behind me in the back seat.

"What kind of bike is it?" the first one asked.

"I haven't seen it yet," answered the second, "but I heard it's a Yamaha."

"That's better for picking up passengers, isn't it?"

"I prefer my old Honda Civic any day but it's a job so I'm not complaining."

"What's the new employer like?"

"He's a fellow named Kuyateh over on Dundas Street. I haven't met him yet but they say he doesn't have a problem. As long as you keep his bike clean and you give him his percentage on time, you can do whatever you want with it. He doesn't interfere. When we meet this afternoon, he gives me the key and then I start work."

Right there and then I got down from the taxi and made tracks for Dundas Street to look for the man named Kuyateh. After some asking around, I caught him on his way out of a two-storey house with red bricks.

"Good morning, sir," I said.

He gave me an empty look. "Good morning."

"I'm here about the *Okada*."

"You're Karimu Jalloh?"

"Yes sir."

"Are you sure? You don't look like a *fullah*."

"My... er... mother was from the south."

"I see. Didn't I say we should meet this afternoon?"

"That is what you said sir, but I just remembered that I have a doctor's appointment this afternoon. I don't know how long it will take."

Mr. Kuyateh looked at his watch.

"Hmm. I suppose we could talk for a few minutes. Let's go inside."

I followed him in and once I had dazzled him with my non-existent history of commercial motor biking, the job was mine. Just like that. I did eventually go on to see the guy about the DVD players but was told that the deal had been given to someone else.

So I plunged into the *Okada* business. The money was lousy but I was able to scrape some kind of living together. True to what I had heard in the taxi, Kuyateh never interfered with how I conducted business so long as I gave him his handsome percentage every evening.

About a month later, Melissa was due for a trip to the antenatal clinic. Fortunately, she wasn't averse to riding behind me on the bike in her condition. But that was where the good fortune stopped. In the doctor's surgery I listened with a rising sense of doom as the doctor gleefully ticked off all the payments I had to make to see Melissa through to delivery. Feeling rather dazed, we walked out of the clinic only to find that the bike was gone. There was nothing under the mango tree where I had parked it but a few dead leaves. I slapped my pockets. The keys weren't there.

Melissa reached out to support me as the world began to spin. If telling my boss that I had lost his bike was hard, sleep that night was impossible. A combined debt of about 15 million leones hung over my head like the hammer of a vengeful god. With less than 100,000 leones in savings, I had finally reached a wall that no amount of street hustling could overcome.

The plexiglass doors open again. A woman walks in. She is tall and heavy-set, with stringy blonde hair that fans her pale white shoulders. Her eyes scan the restaurant. The fluttering in my heart stops dead. Slowly, I raise my hand. She notices and with a smile, begins walking towards me. As she draws closer I notice lines around her eyes and mouth.

"Hello, I'm Andrea," she says extending a hand. "You must be Daramy." Her accent sounds German but it could be Dutch.

"I am Daramy," I reply, shaking her hand. I gesture to the chair opposite me and she sits. The words of the oily stranger come back to me. *You are young, virile, good looking and charming if you work at it,* he had whispered into my ear. *Your market is plentiful.*

Sitting across from me, the 'market' smiles again. One of her lower front teeth has a brownish tinge. I make a fair attempt to return the smile, noticing that the roots of her blonde hair are dark.

"So," she says, leaning towards me. Her pale blue eyes have a watery quality to them. "You're a pretty one, aren't you? You African men never disappoint."

My tongue is frozen. I try to recall my negotiation strategies but end up wondering whether I had any to begin with. My eyes flit to the balding man and his emaciated companion. Her vacant smile is still in place as she feeds him a piece of fish.

"Come on, darling," Andrea continues, forcing me to look at her. "You're not shy, are you?"

My tongue is dead. All I can manage is an imbecilic shake of the head. Her thin lips curve into an almost motherly smile.

"First time?"

I am not sure whether she is inquiring after my sexual status or whether she wants to know if this is my first time in a situation such as this.

"No," I reply just to be safe. She gives an amused laugh. Before I can say anything else, the waiter swoops down on us with a menu.

"Enjoy," he smiles looking squarely at Andrea and handing her the menu.

"Think you could bring one for my friend?" she asks. He hesitates, his smile wavering dangerously, and then with a low bow he replies:

"But of course, madam."

Without so much as a glance in my direction, he turns sharply and walks away.

Brian James was born in Lagos, Nigeria to Sierra Leonean parents. He lives in Sierra Leone, where he works as a consultant editor, screenwriter and documentary filmmaker. He has won various short story and poetry competitions at national level. Prior publications include 'On the Road to Godiva' in the *Book of Voices* anthology and 'Devils at the Door' in the *Dreams, Miracles and Jazz* anthology.

The Sky Above Nagala

Blessing Musariri

THE BODY FLEW INTO the air right in front of their eyes and disappeared into the dark verges of the road. The offending car sped on, tail-lights soon disappearing over a rise. Antonio automatically came to a stop, leaving the engine idling. In the passenger seat next to him Carlos was silent. The brothers sat for a moment, peering into the path of their headlights trying to process what it was they had just witnessed.

"Jesus!" Carlos exclaimed. "Did you just see that? A motherfucking hit and run."

Antonio was too stunned to respond with his usual internal grimace at his younger brother's colourful language. It had been a long and trying day and he was beginning to wish he hadn't forced Carlos to accompany him on this trip, but it had been his father's dying wish and Antonio was going to make sure that Carlos did at least this one thing. It had cost him the price of a second-hand, slightly beat-up car but, to be honest, as annoying as he could be, it was better to have Carlos along than nobody at all. Maybe Carlos would even thank him later for the closure. Antonio senior and Carlos had not seen eye to eye since Carlos' 15th birthday when he had come home with a tattoo on his upper arm and an earring in his ear. They hadn't always been enemies but once the opening salvo had been fired, neither would back down.

Reaching into the glove compartment, Antonio drew out a torch.

"Hey! Antonio," Carlos called out as his brother opened the door and stepped out of the rented four-by-four.

"Antonio, man, what the fuck are you doing? Let's get outta here. This ain't our business. Why do you always have to be a do-gooder?"

As he cautiously approached the spot where he thought he'd seen the body land, Antonio sighed wearily. He felt weighed down – by Carlos, by the recent death of his mother, soon followed by that of his father, by his return to Nagala, a country that had flung its people far and wide at the onset of the war and never reclaimed them. Twelve years later, here he was in the country of his birth, the place where his memories began and held him captive and it had been as alien as if he were seeing it for the first time. It was as if the war had tossed everything up into the air and let it settle back down at will. Nothing was as he had remembered it except this one thing; a curious sense that things were about to happen over which he had no control.

"We should leave, man." Carlos had come up behind him and they both stood looking at the battered spectacle in the beam of torchlight. The man had landed at the foot of a large tree a couple of metres from the narrow strip of tar on which they'd carelessly left their car. The faint tick-ticking of the hazard lights blended into the subtle orchestra of night rustlings in the underbrush.

"Shit." For once Antonio echoed his brother's sentiments but he still wasn't up to speaking to Carlos after their most recent altercation in Nyampuli. It had been brewing since they'd boarded the plane from Chicago – Carlos mutinous and unbending and Antonio resisting the systematic draining of his patience with all his strength but slowly losing the battle. They'd been looking for the village where Antonio senior had been born and where he'd wanted his remains to be laid to rest.

"What does it matter where his ashes are scattered really? The old man won't know any better now that he's gone to join those ancestors of his that he was forever talking about."

"Carlos, have some respect. Whether you believe it or not, the man loved you. I just don't know why everything has to be a fight with you all the time."

Carlos snorted, "I don't think he truly believed I was his son. Did you ever see the way he looked at me, like I was some kind of small dirty animal that was littering his yard? He never had anything good to say about me."

"Because you went out of your way to do nothing good! Carlos, what happened to you? What made you so angry and so disagreeable? I just... look, let's just find this place, okay? The sooner we do this, the sooner we can leave and we can both be free to go about our business."

* * *

"Sir, can you hear me?" Antonio asked, in what he hoped was passable *Cheche*. He had begun to lose his native tongue along with his memories, even as his parents had struggled to keep them alive, but 12 years were too many to lose all at once; strong traces remained. The man was unresponsive. Moving the beam of light from head to toe, Antonio examined the body lying at awkward angles at his feet – a wiry middle-aged man in a dirty and now bloody white T-shirt and dark trousers. There was a large gash on his forehead but, other than that, Antonio was not able to immediately ascertain his other injuries.

"Sir?" Antonio tried again.

"What are you calling him for, Antonio? We didn't hit this guy, he's not our responsibility." Carlos was looking nervously around him. "If someone else comes along and finds us here, they'll think we did this and I can tell you these niggaz don't play when it comes to shit like this."

Absurdly, Antonio found himself wondering if his brother would ever speak another proper sentence in his life, but regardless of how he put it he had a point. Over the years, their father had received copies of *The Nagala Herald* through friends and Antonio had often read stories about drivers being lynched for hitting pedestrians but still, it would be wrong to walk away. The man was still alive, they couldn't just leave him to die alone. Antonio was sure that, if they did, in some way, at some stage in his life, he would be punished for it. Call it karma or simple guilt, he didn't want to carry this wrong-doing with him when he left Nagala. After this trip, he had a feeling that he would not be back again, even if his father's ashes now lay scattered on Nymapuli Plain. If he had ever had a connection with his ancestors, it had now been severed by time and distance and the simple fact that Nagala after ten years of war was not the country of his childhood. He had not even been able to find his way back to the village.

"Help me." Antonio had gently taken hold of the man's head and shoulders and now gestured for Carlos to lift the man's legs.

"Heeeelllllll no!" Carlos burst out. "You wanna take this trouble with us? Antonio man, just think for a minute. I ain't going to jail for this."

If this was the last thing that he would ever force Carlos to do, so be it, he was going to do this – Antonio had made his mind up.

"Carlos," he ground out his brother's name in a tone that Carlos knew boded ill, "what you did out on the plain today, I'm letting go." Antonio had always tried to be a good brother to Carlos and he had been a good son. He knew that this had made him appear to be their father's favourite, their mother's darling, but there was no need for any rivalry between them. Carlos' response, however, seemed to be to behave as badly as he could. Often, Antonio had sensed that almost as soon as he'd done or said something, Carlos regretted it but after the first few times of not taking it back, it seemed to have become simpler to keep going on his trajectory of rebellion. Antonio wished Carlos could have shared in the easy camaraderie that had existed between him and their father, wished he could have joined in when they spoke of their life in Nagala, people and things they had known, but he was too young to remember. He wished his mother could have looked at her younger son with something other than concern and fear for his future. Antonio wondered what Carlos wished for himself, wondered what went on in that head of his.

"Do you understand what I'm saying? Take his legs."

Grumbling, Carlos did as he was told. Carlos had been grumbling all the way from O'Hare, through customs at Nagala-Luni, about the inconvenience of their father's expectations: "Mama was happy to be buried in America even though she also has ancestors in Nagala, this old man of ours always has to ask for things that are inconvenient."

The customs procedures: "What, do they think I got drugs or something, what's the deal with this place anyway?"

The heat: "Goddamn! It's hot enough to roast a weiner on a stone. Dang!"

The hotel: "Geez! You mean that dirty water I let out of the tub was what we had to use for bathing and shit?"

It was nothing that Antonio had expected either, so much worse than he remembered, even though he knew that modernisation had been lagging far behind during their years in the US. Somehow Nagala seemed stripped of all dignity, joyless, a place with no knowledge of itself. The streets were filthy and littered with homeless people, cars, stalls and buildings in varying stages of decline. Ten years of war would take a lifetime to erase. Antonio wondered at the survivors who had never left, wondered if they too felt as stripped and bereft as their towns and villages, wondered if they felt the heaviness of a loss he felt more keenly now than he had at the time of their leaving. He'd felt lost from the moment he took the first step into a country he no longer knew and he'd envied Carlos his ease of disconnection.

A new resentment was building up in him towards his irreverent younger brother. It was so easy for Carlos. He felt nothing but annoyance at the disruptions his family caused in his life. He'd anticipated nothing from Nagala except more inconvenience and thus managed his expectations well. On the other hand, Antonio was sliding down the gentle but unsympathetic slope of disillusionment. What use was a bunch of memories with no place to return?

"Antonio man, I'm telling you we shouldn't be doing this. This is exactly the kinda shit that gets niggaz into trouble. We ain't got no call acting like Good Samaritans – why the hell do you think the guys who did this didn't stop? Ah man! if it wasn't so damn dark I'd get out and hitch-hike. Dang!" Continuing to mutter under his breath, Carlos slammed the car door. Antonio glanced back at the injured man lying still on the back seat, the only indication that he was still alive being the wheezing sound of his breath.

"What's the next town from here? Check your notes." Antonio had made Carlos write down the route they had taken so that it would be easier to map the way back in case they got lost.

"Ummmm! Well, I didn't exactly write down the last few towns 'cause I was kinda tired and..."

"Carlos, I asked you to do one simple thing..."

"...'Coz you always yelling at me and shit, makes me crazy man. I can't think straight."

They were simply going round in circles. Antonio switched tactics.

"Okay, just try and think, we're about an hour and a half out of Egoni. Can you remember if there is another town coming up and how soon, or do you think we should go back?" Maybe a little bit of responsibility would spur him into being useful.

After a brief discussion, they decided to continue forward, both agreeing it made better sense and neither said much else after that. Antonio glanced at the digital numbers of the clock on the dash: it was going on ten o'clock. They had at least another four hours to go to reach Nagala-Luni, not counting the time it would take to stop and deliver the injured man to a hospital. It was a closer drive from Chicago to Indianapolis but what a difference there was. Even though he was used to the efficiency of his life away from Nagala, it seemed almost natural to him that things in Nagala should be disordered and difficult. Life had never been convenient here, even at the best of times. There were no guarantees that one's life would go as planned from one minute to the next and that kept you on your toes. Sometimes it was something small and sometimes something that could turn your world up on its end but there was always a way to win.

"Hey Antonio, what are you slowing down for?"

"What? I'm not." But, sure enough, the car had begun to lose speed. Antonio stepped on the accelerator, it went all the way down and nothing happened. He edged towards the shoulder where the car rolled to a complete stop and the engine cut off. Antonio turned the key in the ignition but there was no response from the engine. He tried again.

"Great! Just what we need right now."

In the back seat the man was still wheezing as he breathed. Carlos turned back to check on him.

"Geez, this guy's freaking me out, man."

Antonio popped the bonnet and stepped out of the car, telling Carlos to bring the torch which he was shining onto the back seat. He followed Antonio and together they stood and peered into the silent engine.

"What do you think it is?"

Antonio shook his head. He walked back to the interior of the car and returned with a wheel spanner which he used to tap the battery terminals after checking to see if the connections were secure.

"Try and start the car," he instructed. Carlos ambled round to the driver's side and turned the key in the ignition. Nothing happened.

"Shit." Antonio muttered. Lighting his way with the torch in one hand he reached in with the other and worked through all the possibilities but at each turn of the key, nothing happened. Neither brother had more than a basic knowledge of motor mechanics and working by torchlight added a degree of difficulty. Carlos stomped off in disgust, cursing and kicking at whatever it was he could see in the dark. Antonio didn't worry about him, he wouldn't go far. In Nyampuli he had done the same thing. They had returned for the third time to the same spot when Carlos had jumped out of the car in disgust declaring that he was sick and tired of going around in circles, man!

In the tall sea of golden grass he'd stood with his arms dramatically flung out and shouted that this was as good a place as any in Nyampuli.

"Where the fuck is this goddamned village?"

"It doesn't exist, man, I'm telling you. He was going a little bit crazy and it was all in his head. If it's here why can't we find it, huh? I'm not stupid, I can read a map."

Evidently not, Antonio had thought to himself. Leaning against the front bumper, he had watched his brother's antics, but apparently neither could he read a map, because for the life of them they couldn't seem to find the right village no matter how hard they tried. People kept giving them conflicting directions so they'd given up on that, thinking they would eventually figure it out themselves. Antonio had walked towards a large flat rock in an area left clear by the tall stalks of grass. When he looked beyond the scars left by bombs, guns and people, Nyampuli was beautiful again. The blue sky above it had remained untouched and nature was reclaiming places that had been left broken and abandoned. It would be okay again, maybe not soon but one day. He hadn't realised how long he had been lost in thought until Carlos emerged from a copse of trees dusting off his hands, the silver tin that had held the ashes clutched just under his armpit.

"It's done," he'd announced triumphantly, "so can we go now?"

He'd promised Carlos he'd let it go but he had done so more out of self-preservation and the knowledge that if he didn't, he might never speak to his brother again. He'd wanted to find that village, needed the release that would have come from having finally returned but here he was again, stuck in between places. Cursing under his breath, he kicked at the iron grill fixed to the bumper.

"Damn!"

A car sped past, not even slowing down to see what might be the problem. This was Nagala, people here didn't stop to borrow trouble. He turned back to tinker with the engine – he might get lucky and hit upon the solution. He was fiddling with the battery again when Carlos came barrelling out the darkness.

"Ey-yo 'ntonio! There's lights over there," his arm pointed in the direction from which he'd come, "I think we're close to a town."

Antonio turned to his brother, wiping his fingers on some tissue he'd found in his pocket. He felt the first relief of the tension that had his head in a vice-grip.

"Okay, good. What do you suggest we do?" Sticking to his earlier tactic, he waited for Carlos to come up with a suggestion while he mulled over the options in his own mind.

"Umm! Let's see if we can jog over there and get some help."

"What about this guy?" Antonio gestured to the back.

"He ain't going nowhere."

It was the best option but Antonio did not feel comfortable leaving the injured man for anyone to find, in a car rented in his name.

"One of us should probably stay behind while the other goes for help." Even as he said this, Antonio also knew it was not wise to be a sitting duck for anyone to take a shot at. The war was over but the recovery was just beginning, there was still too much uncertainty in the air, the residual traces of danger lurking.

"Say what?" Carlos' eyes bugged out. "You're playing. I ain't staying here and I ain't going nowhere by myself."

It came as no surprise to Antonio: Carlos, for all his fronting, was brave only in concrete spaces, places he knew, built up and defined. Out here, any further than out of sight, on his own, he was completely cowed. There was only one thing to do.

They wiped down the seat as best they could with a dirty rag and some water, packed their few belongings into Antonio's backpack and secured the car. A truck had trundled by, heading in the opposite direction, but hadn't stopped. The road remained deserted and Antonio couldn't decide whether he was relieved or not. On the one hand, he didn't fancy the prospect of dragging the injured man for kilometres on end, in the hopes of making it to a town, and on the other, involving anyone else in their dilemma at this stage could mean the difference between being forcibly detained in Nagala and choosing to leave – again. Already he'd involved Carlos and that was all he could deal with for now.

"This shit is straight played out, Antonio. This is worth at least a set of rims." They were lugging the man in a crude sling they'd constructed out of an old blanket they'd found in the boot of the car and a broken tree limb that was proving to be more supple than they required. There weren't many large trees in the area that was mostly grass and shrubs so they had to be thankful they had at least this much, even if it was threatening to break at any moment. They'd been walking in silence for the last twenty minutes, heading towards the lights in the distance.

Antonio scoffed at Carlos' assertion. "On that old thing you're fixing to buy? Might as well put a diamond on a monkey and call it a day." To Antonio's astonishment, Carlos doubled up and hooted with laughter, bringing their progress to a sudden halt. The sling had reached the ground abruptly but there was no sound from its occupant. Antonio let his end drop as Carlos continued to laugh uncontrollably. He'd fallen to the ground and was bent over, arm around his sides. Antonio felt laughter well up inside him in response but he knew what lay under the surface and he quelled it. Carlos was wiping tears from his eyes.

"God, Antonio!" he gasped. "Can you imagine that?" He flung himself down on his back. Antonio took this as a sign for a break and sank onto the ground. He was exhausted. It was hot out and, once they had become accustomed to it, not so dark. The sky was an explosion of stars. Antonio's head fell back as he breathed in and out on a deep sigh. He didn't quite know what he was doing any more. It didn't seem real somehow, that he should be walking in the bush in the middle of the night with Carlos and an unconscious stranger, swinging in a blanket between them. If he didn't want to continue, could he just stop right where he was and let the world take its course around him? Things might never be all right again but he would take this moment and own it. He would lie here beside the stranger, who might die, or might recover eventually then get up and walk away. Carlos would eventually stop laughing, curse a bit then get bored and get up and also walk away, and he would continue to sit here and watch the sky above Nagala.

Blessing Musariri is a published and award-winning children's author who writes many other things besides. Her publications to date are *Rufaro's Day* (Longman Zimbabwe 2000) and *Going Home; A Tree's Story* (Weaver Press Zimbabwe 2005) and *The Mystery of Rokodzi Mountain* (Hodder Education UK). She is also published in various international anthologies. Blessing mistakenly believed she would be a lawyer but came to her senses after sitting and passing the English Bar Finals in 1997. She also holds a Masters in Diplomatic Studies from the University of Westminster.

Ravalushan

Mohammed Naseehu Ali

WE AWOKE EARLY ONE morning to the blaring sounds of martial music on our short-wave transistor radios. The music was all too familiar to us Zongo Street folks. It was the music the soldiers played whenever they made a coup. Out on the street and in the city proper, people gathered wherever they found a radio, and waited for a speech by our new leader at ten o'clock. With very few people owning a radio set, long before the appointed time, folks began to gather at the two places a radio was almost guaranteed to be on: Aliko's barbershop and Mallam Sile's teashop.

By nine-thirty, Gado's barbershop was filled to capacity. All the *booklong* people like Mr. Rafique and Uncle Azeez – daily regulars at Gado's, where the men do nothing but argue – were present. Gado imposed a hair-cutting moratorium until after the speech. "These are serious times," he said, and waved his scissors in the air. He twisted his moustache and sat with keen eyes listening to the martial music on the radio. An out-of-towner, obviously clueless about Gado's infamous temper, walked in and asked for a trim. Gado chased him out with scissors dangling in his left hand, threatening to cut the customer's ears.

At Sile's teashop the mood was not as tense. The children, on automatic holiday from the catholic school and the madrassah, gathered in front of the shop. They seemed excited in the way kids are when things, good or bad, happen to somebody or anybody. The adults looked frightened and alert, a change from the torpid manner in which we normally carried ourselves about the street.

As we waited for our new leader's speech, Mr. Rafique told his pompous, semi-educated crowd at Gado's barbershop that what was taking place was not an ordinary coup, but an actual *ravalushan*, and that the Soviet people themselves were the ones who had helped the new leader to make the coup. There were counter-rumours that the white people of England, and not the Russians, were the ones in charge; and that they had come to take over the reins of government and to take us back to colonialism all over again. In truth it was a confusing time for us. You see, we Zongolese never dabbled in any other philosophy or psychology or religion apart from ours, Islam. In short, we never strived to know more about the complexities of the modern world. We lived our lives one day at a time, from hand to mouth, as they say, and worried ourselves about nothing. We stuck to our mantra of existence: Insha Allah. And with people such as Suraju the Swindler, Hamda One the Night Soil Man, and Mansa BBC, our most authoritative rumourmonger, Ee Hey and Mr. Brenya, our two resident lunatics, and lastly Mr. Rafique – with his big English, creating one scandal and laughing matter after the other – we consoled ourselves with the ironic humour of our existence, and in so doing dodged the pain of our poverty.

But that 16 February day wasn't one for humour or jolliness. By the harshness of the early morning heat, by the white man's martial music on the radio, we knew and felt that something we had never experienced before was afoot, and that the tranquil state of our lives was about to be altered. Forever.

* * *

At exactly ten o'clock the martial music stopped. Everything and everybody – including the lizards that roam the street's crevices, bobbing their heads up and down – froze in their tracks.

From the radio we could hear several voices arguing in the background. Then the new leader's voice came on the radio momentarily. It was a deep, husky and frightened voice.

"Good morning, fellow comrades, countrymen and women," he started. "I am speaking on behalf of the New Ghana Revolutionary Council, NGRC."

The voice of our new leader sounded foreign to our ears. We began to wonder if what Mr. Rafique said was indeed true.

After his introduction, our new head of state, whose name was Sergeant Leader, didn't waste any time. He moved on quickly to explain to us the reason for the coup. Some on Zongo Street said Sergeant Leader had taken power so as to give power back to the people. Others insisted that his main goal was to help poor communities like ours, and to stamp out all the corruption that had infested the moral fibre of the country's ruling class.

During the speech, an intermittent bang was heard on the radio, causing breaks in the transmission. We later learned it was the sound of Sergeant Leader banging on the desk in front of him, an act that became the symbol of his ravalushanary style. The speech by our new leader took all but five minutes, and he ended it with the announcement that a six to six curfew had been imposed on the country, in order to stabilize the situation. We were told that some soldiers were still trying to make a counter-coup. And when Sergeant Leader finished speaking and the music was turned back on, a deep and uncomfortable silence engulfed our street.

Then, suddenly, a roar was heard across the length and breadth of the city. The next thing we saw was a massive crowd, numbering in the thousands, marching toward our street. A mad euphoria suddenly gripped the whole Kumasi. Taxi and trotro drivers bleated their horns; women waved their scarves – some even their veils – in the air; young men and women cried, "Power to the people! Power to the people!"; the university students sang, "Aluta Continua". We joined them and sang the songs over and over again, though the real meaning of those words was lost on many of us.

We, like other communities, joined the throng when they reached our street. We marched with them like a herd of cattle to Justice Park, where it looked like a huge rally was about to begin. And it was much later that we realised that the march arose from the spontaneous giddiness that followed Sergeant Leader's speech, and that it was not commanded by anybody in particular. We milled around the dusty and treeless park, and waited for the speech of nobody in particular.

As the jubilation continued we forgot the passage of time. In our heightened, intoxicated state, we lost track of the rhythm of our biological clocks. The racy beat of the new songs of struggle and ravalushan confused the cautious drumbeat of old that had always guided our actions. By the time we realised it, it was less than ten minutes before six o'clock – curfew time. Someone from our street shouted "curfew *yakai*", alerting everyone familiar with our Hausa tongue that it was time to vamoose. The moment we started running, others in the crowd quickly sensed their folly too, and joined us in flight. In a desperate attempt to flee, an instant stampede ensued. People ran in all directions, stepping over each other and screaming in their various languages and dialects, in a scene that resembled the fall of Babel tower.

Luckily for us Zongo Street folks, our neighbourhood was just five minutes from Justice Park. But the story was not the same for the people of Ash Town, AEB and Bantama, where the majority of the marchers came from. As the curfew siren went off at six, hundreds of gun-carrying soldiers emerged from nowhere, as if they had lain in wait the whole time so they could attack the crowd at the strike of six. We cracked open our windows and watched people being beaten to the ground. Some were even shot dead right on the spot. People ran helter-skelter into houses in which they knew nobody, to seek refuge. We hid many of the marchers in our houses and gave them mats to sleep in our courtyards.

There were sporadic gunshots throughout the city that night. We heard the following morning that more than 50 people had been killed by the soldiers. But we had no means of knowing the truth about the figures, as none of the daily newspapers made mention of the impromptu march and the consequent attack. So, the rally that never was ended up being like a bad dream in our minds. People were afraid to talk not only about the march, but also about anything to do with the new ravalushan, even if they supported it.

* * *

Zongo Street had only one truly rich person. His name was Baba Ila, a stockfish and dried goods importer. Baba Ila was an honest, god-fearing man who never engaged in *kalabule* deals. Comfortable that our richest man was not in any harm's way with the ravalushan, we tacitly supported the assault on the country's wealthy folks, on whose head the soldiers blamed the country's economic problems. We sat idly and watched big-money individuals in the city being stripped naked and flogged in the market square for all to see. We never thought that the ravalushan would one day be brought to our doorstep.

By the second week of the coup we had got used to the curfew. We and our sheep, goats, chickens and ducks locked ourselves in our houses before the siren went off. The children enjoyed the new schedule very much; they got the attention of their grandparents, who spun one tale of *gizo* after another throughout the evening.

New laws, plenty of them, were made every day. It became a ritual for us every morning to gather on our verandahs and shopfronts to listen to fresh guidelines and edicts on how to conduct our lives, so as to stay clear of the rising tide of the ravalushan. Like religious converts, we listened with heightened and feverish interest to the new edicts from our leader and his lieutenants, who constantly reminded us that those laws were meant to protect us, the People, and to right all the wrongs that had been done to us by past leaders.

One of the new decrees was the formation of the People's Vigilante Committees, the grassroots wing of the ravalushan, meant to infiltrate the country's cities, suburbs, and communities to root out anti-ravalushanaries. The creation of the Zongo Street branch of the PVC ushered in an era never before witnessed by our folks. The booklong Mr. Rafique stated that it was the end of the old ways, and that our people should wake up and accept the spirit of the *zamaan*. Respect for the elders, part of our age-old Hausa-Islamic tradition, was pushed aside in the name of ravalushan, which worshipped the youth.

* * *

Days elapsed into weeks, and weeks into a full month of the ravalushan. By this time, the effects of the coup were becoming visible in our famished looks. We got hungrier and hungrier, as food prices had risen beyond our means. We began to grow so lean that our collarbones were bereft of any flesh. A secret name, Sergeant's Chain, was given to this, but we dared not mention it in public.

Our old ways had begun to change quite rapidly. So busy were we with trying to survive that we didn't even realise that the two madmen who lived on Zongo Street had disappeared. The first lunatic was Ee Hey – a giant, thong-wearing lunatic, who got his nickname from the shouts of warning people made when he approached. His favourite pastime was to stand near a blaring radio and laugh hysterically at the sounds coming from the speakers. The other resident crazy man was Mr. Brenya, who had been reading the same newspaper article for the past 27 years. Like Ee Hey, Mr. Brenya hardly said a word to anybody, except when he challenged passers-by to a word definition contest, the only passion that consumed his life. Those two madmen did not only entertain us, but protected our street from vandals and petty thieves at night, as they walked on at the sight of the lunatics. But we didn't think that madmen, too, were citizens of the country and therefore bound to the same new laws of the ravalushan that bound us all. We merely thought: why would soldiers waste their precious ravalushanary time dealing with crazies on the street? At any rate, we never saw Ee Hey again. Mr. Brenya eventually returned to the street, but he wasn't the same grammar man we knew: his face, too, bore the same macabre expression imprinted on our faces.

The day we realised our madmen had disappeared was the day we stopped laughing on Zongo Street. Everyone's eyes bore the same sad expression, our lips pouched as if we were about to burst out crying at any moment. We walked about with mournful faces, only nodding our heads, not saying a word to each other. For weeks, not a single laugh was heard on Zongo Street, not even from the little kids who were usually immune to the harsh realities of life. Even Hamda One, the constantly laughing latrine man who, despite his horrendous vocation and social status, found mysterious ways to be the most cheerful person on the street, lost his humour. He avoided eye contact with people and sped on with his latrine bucket perfectly balanced on his head.

* * *

Two months into the government of our Sergeant Leader, the ravalushan was yet to happen on our street. With the exception of our missing lunatic, no house on the street had been bombed and no-one had been abducted or tortured.

But all that changed when, at exactly six-thirty on the morning of 11 June, four *abongo* lorry-loads of soldiers wielding machine guns, rifles and grenades that hung loosely on their waistbands, descended upon our street. There must have been over 200 of them – Mansa BBC claimed they numbered 500, even though she didn't step out of her room during the entire operation. The soldiers stood at intervals throughout the length and breadth of Zongo Street. About 50 of them trotted into the house of Baba Ila, whom we never thought would become a victim of the ravalushan, given his honest and generous ways.

We heard banging and the cracking of doors from within Baba Ila's house, a modern three-storey concrete building, with a penthouse atop its magnificent structure that Baba Ila's children used as a study. We stopped all our activites that morning to pay attention to what went on in his compound. Gado barber didn't even attempt to open his shop. Mallam Sile's teashop was empty; he was left with all the fresh bread he had ordered that morning for his early customers.

We gathered in alleyways and on our rooftops, and watched as the Alhaji was led out of his house. He was a tall, robust and muscular man in his mid-fifties. He was clad in only white cotton underwear, and wore nothing at the top to cover his wide, hairy chest. With hands raised above his head, six soldiers, each holding a machine gun, escorted Baba Ila outside.

The abongo boys then carted loads of imported stockfish and hundreds of boxes of sardines, corned beef and other dried goods out of the house and stacked them in a pile on the street. They then broke into the front stores of Baba Ila's house and moved all the merchandise onto the street, next to the goods from the main house. There was a provision store, a textile retail store, and a rice wholesale store. And even though Baba Ila didn't own any of the businesses in those three stores, which he had rented out, the soldiers still held him responsible for the "hoarded" goods they claimed to have discovered in his house.

Before our disbelieving eyes, the soldiers started beating Baba Ila, kicking him with their combat boots and knocking his head with the butt of their guns. Blood started streaming down from his head onto his face. His eyes swelled quickly, though that did not stop the abongo soldier boys from beating him. One soldier slapped his face, another one kicked his groin, and yet a third soldier came from behind and hit the Alhaji on the head with the barrel of his gun. Unable to withstand all the beating any longer, Baba Ila fell to the ground like a tipped cow. They shouted, "Get up, if you don't want to die!" Baba Ila made an attempt to stand, but fell back down on his face. The soldiers continued to kick him, and as they did so continued screaming: "Get up, you *kalabule* man. We go kill you today!"

Women cried hysterically from the insides of their houses. The men just stood and watched in frightful silence. We wished we could approach the soldiers, and to vouch for Baba Ila's honesty and integrity, to tell them that the poor man never hoarded goods of any kind, and that many of the street's poor and destitute depended on him for their evening meal. Instead, we watched as our true saviour was being bludgeoned to death.

Suddenly, the worst thing we had dreaded all along seemed to be happening. A stout soldier hit a beer bottle from which he had just finished drinking against the wall, and using a large piece of the broken bottle, he began to scrape the hair off Baba Ila's head from where he sat on the muddied ground. Blood was everywhere on the old man's body. Next, the soldiers opened a bunch of sardine and corned beef tins and ordered Baba Ila to eat them. They then forced him to chew on the raw and uncooked dried fish. Baba Ila ate until he began to choke. He finally vomited all that he had taken in, and that too, created another opportunity for a fresh round of beatings. The soldiers whacked him from all sides like a pack of lions taking turns at tearing into the flesh of a prey.

"*Aboa, Alhaji banza*. Now you dey vomit?" screamed one soldier. "We go make you eat all your kalabule t'ings till you die," shouted another as he dealt Baba Ila the final blow that rendered him unconscious, falling from his sitting position to the ground, his head hitting a rock.

They loaded Baba Ila's almost lifeless body and the tons of merchandise they had seized onto the trucks. One by one, in a show of dexterity mixed with showmanship, the soldiers jumped onto the lorries, started the engines, fired lots of shots into the air, and sped off, leaving a cloud of dust behind them.

The ravalushan had finally taken place on our own street. We began to whisper our disgust with Sergeant Leader and the whole ravalushan. We couldn't speak so loudly, though, still mindful of the PVCs among us. That night, in the secret of our inner chambers, we kept vigil on our prayermats, and for the first time since the coup, asked Allah for the destruction of the ravalushan.

* * *

One bright morning 13 weeks after the ravalushan had started, we heard Hamda One laughing hoarsely. It was the first time we had heard anybody laughing in a few weeks, and so we were a bit shocked by it. Some immediately suggested that Hamda One had gone mad. The crowd at Gado barber's suggested that the carrion stew Hamda One had been eating at Mallam Bawa's pito bar had finally damaged his senses.

Until we stopped laughing a few weeks into the ravalushan, Hamda One was sometimes called the laughing jackal; he laughed at the slightest trivia, brandishing his shiny teeth. But something about the manner in which Hamda One went about himself alarmed us a bit that morning. The cacophonic sound of his laughter clearly told us it wasn't only Hamda One who was laughing under that skin of his. Mansa BBC claimed that some spirits may have entered and

121

occupied Hamda One's soul the night before. He laughed so hard that tears began streaming down his face.

Hamda One's real name was Atandana Pwalugu, though only a handful of us knew of this name. The commonest story as to how Hamda One got his new name went like this. Once, during our annual eid-el-kabir festival, when we slaughter hundreds of goats, sheep, and cows for sacrifice, Hamda One had gone round to the houses on the street that patronized his latrine collection services, to get the alms of fresh meat people gave to their neighbours and families. And each time a cut of fresh meat was tossed into his wide raffia hat, Hamda One, for no apparent reason other than his exuberance at getting so much fresh meat, began saying Hamda One, Hamda One. He was calling the name of a young boy he saw, though the actual pronunciation of the boy's name was Hamdawaihi. But the more meat Hamda One got, the more creative he became. "Hamda Two, Hamda Three," he kept on to six, from where he skipped two numbers and jumped all the way to nine when the stingy Baba Musa gave him a tiny cut of the goat he had mustered to sacrifice for his family. Ever since that day, Atandana Pwalugu had been known to us as Hamda One.

As friendly to people and as jovial as Hamda One was, the streetfolks avoided him even when he wasn't carrying a latrine bucket. Hamda One never seemed embarrassed by what he did for a living, but due to his polite nature he walked quickly through the street, returning a greeting or a wave only when someone cared enough to acknowledge him. However, on this fateful day, Hamda One walked the length of the street as slowly as he could, with the latrine bucket perfectly balanced on his head. He came to a complete stop right at the navel of the street. Then he burst out in roaring laughter for no reason whatsoever. We were quite taken aback and everybody looked reproachfully at him, as if by his laughter he had committed a big sin.

Hamda One then began to sway sideways, causing the excrement in the bucket to spill onto the ground. Many different voices yelled, "Useless man, carry your shit to some other place." Hamda One didn't seem to hear anything anybody was saying. He continued to laugh and scream maniacally, swaying to the left and then to the right. And as he did so, "more shit begin to hit the ground," as Mansa BBC stated. People, standing at a reasonable distance away from him, afraid of being doused with excrement, continued to urge Hamda One to "stop spreading shit on the street". Then Hamda One started dancing and singing in his Frafra tongue. Since we understood not a single word of Hamda One's language, the syllables we heard sounded very ominous to our ears. His words sounded like a litany of dark phrases. It was a pitiful sight to all of us; that day, even the booklong folks at Gado's barbershop sympathized with the latrine man.

Hamda One continued to laugh and scream: "hehehe, hehehe, hahahoooooo, haaaaaa, he, he!" Some of the spilled latrine found its way into his mouth, which seemed to increase the intensity of his laughter and incoherent speech. The hysterical laughter soon gave way to violent, ricocheting coughs. By now, half the excrement in the bucket had spilled onto the ground. We watched as Hamda One, who had used laughter to mitigate the harsh realities of his life, applied the same tool in confronting his death. He laughed and coughed until his knees buckled and gave in to the weight of the bucket. He fell to the ground in one heap. The bucket fell with him as well, reaching the ground seconds after him, spilling its remaining contents all over the place. Hamda One died instantly: his smeared visage, mouth agape and in mid-laughter, was the last thing we saw of the latrine man.

Some folks on the street suggested that in Hamda One's laughter that morning the latrine man had informed us of the birth of new religions that have black figures as gods. Others swore that they had heard Hamda One re-spin the tale of the chicken, who after being consistently absent at the seasonal grand conference of the animal kingdom, was unanimously voted to be the sacrificial animal the kingdom offered humanity in a deal that was supposed to bar them from indiscriminate hunting or killing of other animals. Mr. Rafique claimed that the shit carrier had, in his final lament, tried to re-ignite the stagnant spirit in us, to free us from our collective cowardice, and that in his violent, last coughs, Hamda One was asking us to raise our voices, if not our fists, in protest at the indignities that were being heaped on us.

It was as if the same spirits that had stifled our laughter for weeks had suddenly realised our immense suffering; as if Hamda One's death symbolized that of a saviour, who came to Zongo Street purposely to suffer and to die in order to atone for our shortcomings and prejudice. Instead of crying and heading for the mosque to pray for Hamda One, the street erupted in laughter. We couldn't make eye contact with one another without bursting into uncontrollable laughter.

To atone for our sin of prejudice against Hamda One, our Imam instructed every adult on Zongo Street to fast for a day. This was unheard of in the history of our community, and this was because we treated the non-Muslims among us as infidels, folks we weren't even allowed to pray for. By his death, Hamda One taught us that all humanity was woven from the same fabric, and that the suffering of one human affects us all.

* * *

The owl is an animal of darkness. And yet it is also an animal of vision – for its gifted ability to see its back. The very sighting of the Shy One – as we Hausas call an owl – was at once ominous and sinful by the same token. The owl lived its life far from human gaze, so as to protect us from the potential ill-luck that could visit us just from seeing it; when we did see it, we gave alms to the poor and prayed for Allah's protection.

On the day following Hamda One's death, we knew the worse had yet to come. The white owl, the most ominous of them all, showed up on our street and sat comfortably for more than five minutes on a limb of the goji tree near the mosque. Some said the white owl had flown all the way from the bush to make a special appearance on Zongo Street, to reveal a secret to us. The animal didn't blink or turn its head away to look back in the usual manner of owls. Instead, it stared right back at many on the street whose eyes accidentally caught his.

Mallam Ibrahima, one of Zongo Street's many self-inducted spiritualists, who had previously given one false prediction after another of the date of Sergeant Leader's demise, swore by the grave of the Prophet himself that the owl's sighting had just revealed the destiny of the whole nation to him.

"This is it for him," said the spiritualist, referring to Sergeant Leader. "This time he is leaving us. By Allah we shall not wake up with him next week." But we had heard many such predictions by our mallams before, and had already begun not to take them too seriously.

With the mystery of the owl still looming over our heads, with the fear of hunger and the brutality of the soldiers threatening our very existence, with the uncertainty of Baba Ila's fate, with the remnants of the clouds of smoke from house bombings that still hung in the air, with the ominous death of Hamda One still unexplained, and with the stench of the pool of excrement that was still fresh in our noses, we became more scared than ever and resorted to our blind arguments and constant prayers, forgetting that we had done the same thing during previous coups.

Mohammed Naseehu Ali, a native of Ghana, is a writer and musician. A graduate of the Interlochen Arts Academy and Bennington College, Ali has published fiction and essays in *The New Yorker*, *New York Times*, *Mississippi Review*, *Bomb*, *Gathering of the Tribes*, and *Essence*. He was shortlisted for the 2008 Caine Prize. He lives in Brooklyn, New York, where he has worked since 1996 as a Senior Publishing Operations Analyst for LexisNexis Publishing.

The Sound of Water

Thabisani Ndlovu

A CAR HONKS OUTSIDE. Halleluiah! It's *Mdala* Walter to the rescue. On a good day he can stand you a whole crate of beers. He is leaning out of the window of a massive metallic-blue SUV and wearing big dark glasses like a 1970s pop star. Mdala Walter is living positively. He has just returned from America where his body gets "fixed" periodically. He looks like an overfed cat. His wife died more than ten years ago and the fingers of both hands are not enough to count the number of schoolgirls people say died after he infected them with HIV. You need your toes too and possibly somebody else's fingers and toes.

"Professor," he says with a mock bow before I even get to him, and his pitch-black hair sparkles suspiciously in the copper rays of the evening sun, "I'm back and I thought we could have one-one with the boys and celebrate life. What do you think? Fanuel is around. I left him with Shingi a while ago." He smiles his meaty smile. When Old Walter left a few months ago, his lips were a raw pink and he didn't like that. They are a healthy brown now. I'm not a professor but the "uselessness" of my education never fails to tickle him. I can't blame him really. The creaky ladder of education has been kicked from under the feet of some of us educated lot and we have fallen hard on our degreed asses. It hurts so much to rough it up with all kinds of riff-raff, like the guy who controls the bread queue and says, "Hey, you there. Yes, you with a head like a brick. Stand in line with the others, you're messing my queue." Look at the money changers. Filthy rich idiots, most of whom could never tell the difference between a chicken run and classroom. God help us. Here's one such monkey in silk.

Old Walter shakes my hand and, as usual, holds it for too long. Also as usual, his hand creeps up my upper arm, like a rude customer fondling and pressing fruit like pawpaw, feeling for the perfect firmness, leaving dents and bruises behind. My skin crawls. But I suppose one can stomach this sort of thing, considering I need to ask him, for the first time, a favour, and of course he will make beer flow until we vomit. One thing for sure, he will make a nice corpse one of these days, the kind that makes people go, "Aah, shame mahn. He died fresh. *So so* fresh. Shame."

He is still smiling like a toothpaste advert. A few months ago these small teeth were tobacco-stained. They are so small and sharp, like hacksaw blades. I say, "Great Bra Walter. That's the greatest news I've heard in days. Why don't you wait a bit while I change?" He nods and continues to flash the new whiteness of his teeth, satisfied with the world.

Maybe I should tell Smangele that I'm going for a drink with the boys. Well, the boys and this imbecile of a recycled teenager. Mdala Walter makes plans. "Make a plan *mfana,*" he is always saying. Everybody is talking about making a plan. Smangele wants me to make a plan. One of Old Walter's plans is hoarding just about everything in short supply, including, of all things, burial space, which he sells at drop-jaw prices. He says all the space left at Athlone Cemetery is his. When people want to bury their dead there, they are told there is no space but they can talk to him. Now, that's *pathetic.* At least I'm relieved that when Old Walter tried to run for Mayor of this town he failed. A law had just been passed – a mayoral candidate needed to hold a full Ordinary Level Certificate including Maths and English. He doesn't have even a Grade Seven certificate. But he would have won, I can assure you. He is still smarting from the missed opportunity and insists he knows no less than ten parliamentarians who bought their certificates and some whose only piece of paper is their birth certificate.

But what use will it be to tell Smangele I'm going out when she'll say the most correct thing in the voice of a seasoned newsreader and look at me with the corners of her eyes. She drives me nuts sometimes. If she carries on this way... One of these days... Just one of these days... And this bathroom rubbish... I can't remember when she started it but it's really getting to me. Why doesn't she just stop me or flatly refuse? She just lies there. Occasionally an eyelid, hand or leg twitches but other than that she might as well as be dead. When I get off her, she quickly goes into the bathroom. Initially there's the angry sputter of water rushing into the tub, then the purring of shallow water before the full hum of what I suspect to be a half full bath. I wish to go in there to see her washing away my mess; to see it float briefly in the water before floating gently to the bottom; to see it spinning headily before being sucked into the drain hole; to ask her: "What are you doing?" But I always wait for the last two noises in this madness of hers – the obscene sucking that quickly runs into the satisfied burping of the drain hole. Then she comes back to bed smelling sweetly of scented lotion and roll-on deodorant, lies down facing away from me and soon she is snoring gently. Are we becoming the perfect pop song of good love gone bad? This is silly. All because she wants me to cross into South Africa and find work.

"Why don't you make a plan like other men?" she has been saying. What does she mean, *like other men*? Luckily, she has stopped yammering, "Go to South

Africa like other men or we will die of hunger." She has always been a little on the over-imaginative side. Too many women's magazines with their fix-it-now airiness haven't helped either. True, we no longer have three meals a day and we certainly eat less. But die of hunger? She'll come right. She has these moments of occasional madness. Men leave their families behind just to become bum cleaners in the UK and gardeners in South Africa. She is too keen to see me gone. Is that something an educated woman should wish to see happen to her man? And what do the wives left behind do? Ha! She'll come right. Always takes her a bit of time to see what's what. We can't all flock to Johannesburg.

Cars are parked in knots, laager fashion, opposite Barclays Bank along Herbert Chitepo Street. There has been no power for three days but what the hell? We are coaxing happiness with canned South African beer sold by vendors on Bulawayo streets. Shafts of light from car headlights dance like drunken ghosts as the moving vehicles swerve to avoid potholes on the dark Herbert Chitepo Street. Some cars fall into potholes. Momentarily, the lights fall eerily on the four of us – Mdala Walter, Shingi, Fanuel and I, sitting in the back of Fanuel's one-ton truck, on the edge, our feet inside. The truck still smells of newness. Fanuel bought it yesterday, he says, in Botswana where he now works. He'll be paying for it through his ass for the next three years, but it's worth it, he says. Can we wet it a bit? Sure. And we each spill a good amount of beer on the rubberized floor of the truck and the foam hisses. "Yah," Fanuel says, "this car really burnt a bloody big hole in my pocket. I don't have a frigging cent to my name. I'm embarrassed that it coincided with my niece being sent home for non-payment of school fees. You know, when I told my sister that I couldn't help her pay my niece's fees, she congratulated me again on buying this car." There goes my back-up plan of borrowing from Fanuel. Why can't people live within their means? He gets a good chance and decides to show off. Stupid.

"Don't worry *mfana*," Old Walter says to Fanuel, "Haven't I always bought you beer, heh? You have this Botswana job but you're still a teacher aren't you? You're still earning a pittance. Look at me, The-iron-that-never-bends. I make so much money I don't even know what to do with it. You think those who call me 'Walie of too much money' are joking, heh?" He laughs. No-one can sing his own praises like this old idiot. As the fizz of beer goes up my nostrils, I desperately wait for happiness to start. Cheers to the darkness. Cheers to us. Cheers to life. Cheers to fools who don't know what to do with their money. Cheers to fools who get a chance to make money and immediately jump into a cesspit of debt.

Light falls on men urinating at the beginning of an alley between Barclays Bank and Mushemushe Stores. No-one dares to go into the alley in the dark, in case they step on shit. "You know what?" Shingi says, "I'm thinking of John

Saunders. You remember that white guy I used to hang around with. He said his father used to say that now that blacks have their independence, they'll start shitting on the streets."

"And what is wrong with that?" Old Walter asks. "Is there anything wrong with that, Prof? Independence means you can pee on your country, and if peeing is not enough, you can crap on it too." He laughs like a hyena. He thinks it's funny.

A big four-by-four pulls up to join the cars about ten metres from us and, before its doors are opened, a rumbling bass threatens to crack the car's windows. Two men open the doors and the bass shakes something in my chest while the tweeters shrill into my ears. It is the hit song these days:

Ndourayiwa kani ndourayiwa
  Ndourayiwa munyika yamatsotsi
  Ndourayiwa
  Ndourayiwa munyika yembavha
  Ndourayiwa

They are killing me
  Oh they are killing me
  They are killing me in the land of thugs,
  They are killing me
  They are killing me in the land of thieves
  They are killing me

Bloody repetitive. And just how can a song with those kind of sad lyrics, just one chorus really, have such a fast beat? But Mdala Walter jumps off the truck and starts gyrating and then making big pelvic thrusts, whistling like a thrilled herd boy. He looks up at the starry sky as if a heavenly message will appear. Fanuel helps with the whistling, and claps the farce on. Then Old Walter tries to dance the 'razor wire'. He doesn't have the required feet of lightning and his sagging beer belly says no. In less than a minute, he is out of breath. Most people would have known that old lungs can't hold enough air for the 'razor wire'. But this is Old Walter. See? He is coughing and laughing now, trying to catch his breath, "Yah ei, I can still move, *bafana*." Cough cough. The volume from the moving disco is turned down. People with such loud radios grew up without radios in their homes and so make a vow to buy the loudest radio possible. Those decibels are enough to rupture an eardrum. "Professor, cheer up man," cough cough. "Hey you, I want beer."

"It's 60 rand for a six pack," the vendor says when he gets to us.

"Do you think I care how much it costs? How many six packs do you have?"

"Five left," the man says.

Going back to his pelvic thrusts, gently this time, singing under his breath, Old Walter pulls out a wodge of notes, extracts a few and hands them to the vendor. The lights of one car fleetingly catch three or four girls in miniskirts leaning against the low wall adjoining Barclays Bank. "Where there's a man, there's a woman, eh, Professor?" Old Walter says.

"Sure Bra Walter," I say.

"Shingi," Old Walter says, slapping Shingi on the shoulder and then doing the pawpaw massage on him, "don't you want to be happy tonight, my boy?"

"Happy? How, Bra Walter?"

"Keep your eyes on the wall there. The writing will appear," Old Walter says, pointing into the gloom and cackling like an old woman. "They want a hundred million for short time. But that's less than 10 rand, you know. Less than one US dollar. Ever heard of a fuck that cheap?" He throws his head back, laughs like a braying donkey, as if he is the inventor of laughter. I bare my teeth. "You can have two at once, Shingi, if you like. Ever tried a threesome? Here, take this," and he hands Shingi what I think, from the brief flash of a car beam, is a 50-rand note. Time was when we used to drink from bars and all of us could buy a round. As it is, it's only Mdala Walter buying. Less than a dozen beers equal my rent.

Should I ask Mdala Walter now? It's not much to him, surely? The best thing would be to take him aside. Maybe I should wait for his closing-eye stage of drunkenness when he is slurring, and laughing the laughter of the mad. All these years of drinking with him, I've never asked Old Walter a single favour. He can't have a problem granting me one. If anything, he'll be happy to help so he can secretly laugh at me.

Yes, maybe poor Shingi needs to be happy tonight. His wife cleaned him clean clean. Poor Shingi. He wanted to make a plan but I told him right from the start that he was doing it all wrong. His wife persuaded him to sell his house and car so she, a nurse, could go to England. And what did this fool do? Bought the idea. He probably cried at the airport too. Of course, no tickets were sent to him and the children. And, sure enough, news filtered back that she was staying with another man in England and those in the know, like Fanuel here, said she was screwing the guy when both of them were still back in Zimbabwe. And Shingi still thinks his life will take first prize for the best hard-luck story in world. Some things never change. At least he is beginning to come out to play. His well of tears is drying up. So Shingi swaggers to the wall. Enjoy brother, I make a silent toast and take two huge gulps of beer.

"Fanuel, you want fun too?" Walter asks.

"No no no, Bra Walter. Not tonight. Thanks anyway."

"Professor, you want?"

"You know Bra Walter I don't do this stuff."

"Yes, yes, I forgot," Old Walter says slapping his forehead with an open palm. I should ask him now before he becomes a babbling moron. I should ask him now when he is wildly generous. "I need to talk to you briefly, Bra Walter. Do you think we can whisper a bit?"

"Of course, whispering is a good thing Professor. Fanuel, we'll be back now now."

We pick our way through the parked cars. We stop outside the laager of cars.

I clear my throat and say, "Bra Walter, I'm in a bit of trouble."

"Aren't we all, now and again, Professor?" I can smell his warm breath as he pushes his face close to mine. "Shoot," he says and a fine spray of saliva dots my face. Some of it falls on my lips and I wonder whether I should wipe it off and if, in this near darkness, he will notice and hold it against me.

"My rent is in arrears. The landlord wants the money in rands. He doesn't want Zimbabwean dollars any more."

"How much?"

"Two hundred."

"And you don't have that kind of money, Prof?" I imagine a smug smile in the dark.

"Yes."

He laughs, holds my right elbow and starts his paw-paw massage.

"We can talk about it, Prof."

I free my arm. "I'll pay you back as soon as I can."

"*Really?*" he asks and brings his face close to mine again. His beer breath is warm against my forehead, "and where will you get the money from?"

Bastard! It's only a few drinks to him. Why is he making an issue of this?

"You know very well, Prof, that your salary isn't even a tenth of what you're asking for and you have no way of getting forex. Why must I lend you my money? I don't like bad debts…"

"I'll make a plan, Bra Walter…."

"What plan?" and he titters. Asshole. "I was wondering just when you people would wake up to realise it doesn't make sense to have a job." He puts his arms around my waist.

"No, no, Bra Walter," I make to break away, "I'm not made like that."

"I can clear all your debts, Prof, and you can have one of my *murambatsvina* houses for the whole year, for free. How's that? In any case, do you think it's about what way you are made?" Murambatsvina – those poky two-roomed things Old Man Mugabe built after destroying a lot of houses that were even better? The whole thing was called Operation Murambatsvina – say no to filth. Must say the Old Man has always maintained his ironic sense of humour. Destroys shacks together with good houses and puts people in these idiotic matchbox structures with no running water or electricity. People shit in the nearby bush that is fast dwindling. These things are meant for the poor, the jobless, but Old Walter has 20 of them and collects rent from the tenants every month, in forex too. You have to be Old Walter to collect rent for these things in various stages of incompleteness – no windowpanes, no cement floors and, in some, no doors.

Am I hallucinating or is Old Walter's penis really stiff against my body? Why I don't punch the bloody old goat, I really don't know.

"It'll only be a few minutes, Prof," he says, breathing heavily, pressing harder against me. He is now squeezing my buttocks. Fuck! I snort and say, "Old Walter, you can't be serious," and lean back. I remember Faith, the first girl I kissed in the semi-darkness of a street corner, squirming away from me. I shove Old Walter away. I hear him scrambling for balance in the dark. As I walk away I hear him say, "Offer valid for tonight only. If you change your mind, you know where to find me."

I swing my hands and take long strides. Soon I feel very hot. I don't know if it's anger or the brisk walk. Or the thought that tomorrow the landlord is coming to throw us out. No matter how many houses or how much money Magayisa has, he'll always remain thin. The sort of evil spirit that saw him bring two monsters to fling our ever-shrinking possessions out of the house three months ago will stop him from enjoying anything he has. Smangele ran across the road to borrow the money from her friend and we still haven't repaid her.

"What are we going to do?" Smangele asked me this morning. I shrugged. She sighed in that way that says, "Didn't think you'd have a solution, dickhead." I can see Magiya's monsters hurling out the little that's left of our property tomorrow. It will be easy work. There is nothing much left. Shit. Maybe this time Smangele won't have anyone to borrow from. I don't know if I can stand the way she looks at me through the corners of her eyes any more.

A few minutes... but... no no. I cross Lobhengula Street, heading for the minibus terminus, put my right hand in my pocket. No money. Not even to catch a minibus back home. I freeze at the entrance of the terminus. Smangele might be right. Maybe I should buy us a bit of time, and then I'll just go to South Africa. And Smangele? And our son Thando?

Old Walter drops me off in the early hours of the morning. I jump out of the car and watch the tail-lights disappear in the distance. Just a few months in this house and then we will have to move. Smangele, living in a murambatsvina house? Smangele, citified as she is, squatting in tall grass or in the open for a toilet? Smangele carrying a 25-litre container of water on her head, like a woman going to the well or borehole in a village? It's so silly I almost laugh. But Smangele is a good woman really, in spite of everything. I remember her saying "Thank you," in the voice of someone who has run a long way. I remember the stickiness of sweat on our bodies as our hearts stopped galloping bit by bit. I remember that she had a huge store of kind words and a heart I could feel thumping against my chest. All is not lost. Not yet. What I desperately need is a good bath and to hear Smangele's soft "Thank you".

Water trickles out of the hot water tap and stops immediately. The cold one hisses, then gurgles. Nothing. Shit. Maybe there is a bucket of water in the kitchen. The two buckets that Smangele uses when a water cut is looming are empty. If she wasn't so crazy about bathing there could still be some water in the geyser. There must be water in this house. I look and look. Nothing. Damn! Let there be water in this house. It's her fault. I yank the bedroom door open, switch on the light and shout, "Smangele! How come there isn't even a drop of water?"

She opens one eye and says, "Shh… you'll wake up Thando. He's got a temperature. Come," she says patting the spot next to her on the bed. "Come," she says again. I haven't heard this softness in her voice, nor seen the softness in her eyes for months.

"Okay. Just give me a second," I almost whisper, and drag my feet back to the bathroom. Slowly, I turn both taps until the heads stop turning. Not even a hiccup. I look at the thread of water on the basin of the tub and wonder just how much water it takes to wash away a couple of bad memories.

Thabisani Ndlovu has an MA in English from the University of Zimbabwe and is currently studying for a PhD at Witwatersrand University, South Africa. He has won several Zimbabwean prizes for writing, the most recent being first prize in the Intwasa Arts Festival Short Story Competition.

Work in Progress

Henrietta Rose-Innes

IF YOU BEGIN A story with a high building, it's supposed to end with a fall. But that's not where this story is going. In fact, when I remember that apartment up on the 22nd floor, that summer before I turned 19 – and sometimes it does still come into my dreams – the dread is not of a fall; the fear is of staying up there forever, of never coming back down to ground.

It was one of those fancy blocks of flats that they were building everywhere in central Cape Town – "New York loft-style apartments", they called them. I was too poor for a car then, so I took a taxi to town and walked from the station – not easy in my new shoes, black leather with a heel. I was conscious of the dust on their soles as I stepped into the building's cool lobby. The entrance was imposing but seemed hardly used; the people who lived here, no doubt, entered only through the underground parking, feet never touching ground from highway to home.

Certainly the porter at the front desk seemed brand new, his face less creased than his pale-blue shirt, which still held its folds from the packaging. Did I look as green as he did, in my clothes bought specially? No doubt our tensely held expressions were much the same. We might have burst out laughing, if either one had let slip the first smile. But as it was, I was keeping my charm for someone else.

"I've come to see Mr. Muller," I said. "Mr. Bernard Muller?"

I waited for some response, but he gave no sign of recognition; just swivelled the fat ledger around and pushed it across the counter at me. I hesitated, then carefully wrote in my name, avoiding his eye. He got up from his seat and passed an access card over a sensor next to the lifts.

The doors snapped open briskly. Like the rest of the building, this elevator was sparkling, new-made; as if it had never unsealed its brushed-steel doors before. I stepped inside, held my breath, pressed 22. The machinery was quiet, barely a hum, and there was no sensation of movement; but still I sensed the dizzy speed of my ascent. Discreet amber numbers spooled higher – seventh floor, eighth. My heart winding tighter with every floor.

Alone in the lift, I examined myself. My reflection in the machine's steel sides was clouded, a girl unformed. I bared my teeth, turned left and right. My body was pleasingly elongated. I'd pulled my dark hair back into a ballerina bun, and my head looked small, but long-necked and elegant, like a deer's. I'd worn fitted dark clothes, those heeled shoes. Not my usual gear of jeans and sloppy t-shirts. I'd told myself they were working clothes: professional. But the shirt pulled tight on my breasts, the dark tailored trousers skimmed my thighs, and underneath there was new black lace underwear, a little scratchy and tight. I put my hand on my hips, slung one hip higher than the other, feeling the point of my hipbone in my palm.

I'd been a plump child and teenager, and I was still getting used to these new bones. I couldn't stop looking at myself in mirrors, discovering new angles. I felt raw to things, dangerously light.

Twenty? You seem much more mature, if you don't mind me saying. And you write?

He'd touched my shoulder as he'd said it, looking up from the table where he was signing copies of his latest novel. Behind me, a long queue waited. His hair was greying but his eyes were alive with suggestion, causing the blood to rise up my neck to my cheeks. I was not surprised; this was what I'd known would happen. What I had been imagining all through both his readings, which I'd been so lucky to get into; and for a long time before that, staring at that moody black and white photo they used on the back cover of all his books. The deepset eyes, the lean, intelligent face, the hair swept back from his brow. Everyone knew the stories.

Of course I'd read all about him: the awards, the ex-wives and girlfriends, the public outbursts and rivalries. He had a temper, they said. I wondered what it would take to make him raise that deep, smooth voice. To make it break, or sigh.

I have a book, a manuscript. It's not finished, but I thought, I hoped…

And I'd held out the fat envelope, trembling slightly. At that moment, I saw clearly what it was – a clumsy thing, adolescent, smudged – and nearly snatched it back in shame. But Bernard Muller was taking it from me, was weighing it in his hands, was looking into my eyes.

How wonderful. Come and see me this weekend – Sunday? Drop in, we can discuss your work in a more comfortable environment. My flat has great views.

I'd run that voice back and forth through my mind, fingering it like a bolt of fine cloth, all the time I was shopping for clothes. It had guided me to sheerer fabrics, tighter fits. To the low-slung tailored trousers, the slimline shirt. New bra and panties. The shoes.

But now, looking into the grain of the lift door – 13th floor, 14th – I wavered. The clothes were too much, too after-dark, too obvious. A blush pushed to my cheeks and I laid my cheek to the steel. I have thin skin; the blood shines through, so treacherous. I buttoned up my top button. And then the doors sucked open and I stepped into the brightness of the lobby beyond, and there was no retreating now.

Perfect carpeted hush, the light steady and diffuse. I picked up a low hum of some electrical system, and the sound tightened my heart another turn. The door was at the end of the corridor, beyond a stairwell. I knocked and waited, not sure how to arrange my legs, how to fold my arms. I unbuttoned the shirt again, slouched a leg. Sucked in my cheeks just a little, tried to soften the clench of my jaw. Slouched the other leg. I was about to knock again when the security peephole went dark. Then came a series of clicks and scrabbles on the other side, as if of many complex locks and latches; whole minutes passed. At last the slide of a bolt.

The woman who opened the door was very tall. Her silk dressing gown, which she held tight around her body, emphasized a fine bust, hips, a long waist; thick gold hair fell unkempt to her shoulders. She smelled both tawdry and expensive, of crumpled sheets and perfume. The long fingers that held the gown closed were tipped with perfect oval nails, shell pink. I was not good at putting ages to people, but I knew she was what I was not: a grown woman, full-size, full formed. She leant her head back to look at me over broad cheekbones, a fine strong nose. The face of an eagle.

"Christ," she said. "Now this."

Before I could speak she turned around and walked away into the dim room behind, letting the silk fall open and billow from broad shoulders. She had a very straight carriage, but as she walked away I saw she favoured one side. In fact she was limping.

"Take your shoes off at the door," she said over her shoulder. A flutter of pale silk as she turned into a room halfway down the passage.

Uncertainly, I entered. Against the walls was a neat row of men's shoes: polished brogues, sandals, tennis shoes. To save the floors, I supposed; they were gleaming wood. There was also one pair of knee-high leather boots – crocodile skin, needle toes, spike heels – which had been carelessly tossed aside. I took off my own black shoes and saw how cheap and dull they looked; and so much smaller.

I stood listening, although I could hear very little over the panic of my heart, the shock of entry. I sensed a large, high room, but dark. Tall orange curtains fell across the picture windows that lined the room to the left. The morning sunlight lit them with glowering colour, but did not penetrate. In the dimness I sensed disorder: a sharp disturbance in the air, a suspended energy, as if a very loud noise had just stopped.

"I need a cigarette," she called.

135

She was in the bedroom. Slumped back on the cushions of a double bed, her gown hanging open. I looked away from the heavy globe of one exposed breast. Smooth, strong legs were crossed at the ankles. She had an extraordinary body, the body of a large voluptuous doll, long and full; but there was something strained in her pose.

"Cigarette," she said.

"I don't smoke."

"Here." She nodded at the bedside table, and I went close to pick up the pack of smokes and the lighter and pass them to her. She fumbled, and at last gave up with a cry, letting the unlit cigarette fall into her lap and curling her hand into her chest. There was something wrong with it, with both her hands. She tried to push herself up on the pillows but whimpered again, and fell back clumsily.

"Oh dear," I said. "Are you okay?"

"So you're here for Bernard, I take it?" she said, talking over me. "You're his new one?"

She looked at me sideways, almost sly. Hair fell across her mouth and she blew it away.

"Maybe I should go."

"Well Bernard was here," she said. "Look – see." She held up her hands to me, laughed. "Look at the size of it. This one's broken, I think."

I saw now that one wrist was badly swollen; the knuckles of the other hand were red and scuffed and she held them stiffly. Several of her fingernails, I saw now, were snapped off.

"Do you want – should I call a doctor?"

She snorted, dismissing the thought. She looked at my bare feet, then moved her cold gaze up my body to my face. I stood quite still. The only movement I could not control was that of the blood into my cheeks, again.

"I just came to pick up my manuscript," I said.

"Did you, darling," she said. "Now please would you light my fucking cigarette. I can't do it myself, you see."

I placed a cigarette between her lips and lit it. A broad mouth, beautiful full lips, clearly defined. Lines were beginning to cut down on either side of her nose, but they only added emphasis to her features. I watched her smoke, the cigarette propped between cramped fingers. At length she finished, let the butt fall on the floor. I watched it singe a black mark on the wood.

"So. I need a hand here," she said. I stood, reaching out to take her arm. She yelped and pulled away.

"Not *that* arm, Jesus!" I went around and supported her under the other arm as she rolled off the bed and struggled erect. Her armpits smelled strongly, a mix

136

of sweat and scent.

"Over there." She nodded towards the dressing-table and I led her there. After staring bleakly into the mirror for a while, she tried to hold her hairbrush but I could see that her hand was weak. She shoved the brush at her hair, and then let it drop with an irritated click of the mouth.

"Please," she said.

I picked up the brush. Her hair was tangled, and not like mine: the texture and wave so different that I didn't know how to shape it. I had to lay my left palm flat on her head to hold it still while I brushed. Up close, I could see that the honey colour was dye, the silver roots showing; but the texture was still lush. The hair, catching on my fingers, felt dead and warm and damp. I controlled the urge to rip my hands away, pull out the clinging strands, and run.

In the mirror, my body was eclipsed behind hers. Heat came through the silk of her gown, from her strong fleshy shoulders, her sculpted neck. I could not ignore the red marks that sat there like a collar, or her suddenly wet eyes. But when I tried to meet her gaze in the mirror she evaded me so fiercely, and with such rigid shoulders, that I knew I should not speak. Slowly her back straightened and her shoulders pulled back, and she was queenly again.

"It's done," I said, the hair combed out at least, the strands persuaded flat.

She nodded. I pulled back the chair and she hobbled to the centre of the room, shrugged her silk nightdress to the ground, and stood tall.

She was no longer a very young woman. Her skin was slightly creased and scuffed with the marks of age; but she was long and strong, her skin bronze in the low light, almost golden in the reflection. Shaved everywhere. Her breasts and buttocks were rounded, her shoulders straight, the muscles in her back long and clearly defined. She did not look like a woman who has been beaten up. She looked like a woman who had been in a fight, like a wounded warrior.

"Fetch me my clothes," she said, not looking at me. Her tone was distant. Her eyes were fixed on her own body in the mirror, staring as she touched the marks on her arms and her neck. I turned and found the underwear lying on the floor. Leopard print, a matching set. Tacky, sexy, expensive. She put her feet through the holes in the panties and I drew them up, face flaming and turned away. I had never been so close to another woman's body, except perhaps my mother's. I looped the bra straps over her arms and fastened the hooks behind her back; she managed to ease her breasts into the cups by herself, hooking her thumbs under the wiring and bending slightly, wincing.

Her dark-brown wrap dress was easier. A heavy slithery material, cut to hold her curves. She led me barefoot to the front room. I stood the leather boots upright for her to step into, and zipped them up one by one, kneeling at each of her feet in turn.

"Bag," she snapped. "My makeup's in there."

I had not thought I would ever do this for another person, but I did. I barely knew how to put makeup on myself, then; but under her terse instruction I twisted out the lipstick and carefully filled in her lips with deep blood colour. Her lips were so well defined it was easy, like colouring in. The silvery green eyeshadow was trickier, and she impatiently twitched her face away from my attempt with the mascara. But she let me dust her cheekbones, rusty red. Under my hands, I saw her face taking shape, animating, hardening. We were painting a face of fury, until nothing else remained.

At last I put the makeup kit back in the leather bag and hung it off her shoulder. Then I opened the front door for her, and walked a step behind her as she headed for the lift doors. I pressed the button.

Just before the lift arrived, she turned to look down at me. Magnificent, restored, as if her body had grown younger and stronger with each cosmetic layer.

"Stay, if you like," she said, "He'll be back soon. I'm sure he's eager to see you." Her eyes were clear and her voice strong, each word precisely cut.

The lift was swift in arriving. She stepped inside, facing away. Pressed the button for the ground floor with her thumb, without a flinch. I watched her face in reflection. Her image was golden in it, gleaming, sharp. Hers was the form for which this machine had been made, for which its sides had been polished to a shine. And then the doors pulled closed across this vision, and she was gone.

The lobby was silent again. I went back into the flat and pulled back the long curtains, wanting to find my bearings, a sense of where I was. On the other side of the picture windows, there opened out a blue, enormous view: the side of Signal Hill; the tiny bright houses and mosques, the harbour, the sea. So high.

None of it mattered, I thought, as long as I stayed up here on the 22nd floor. All this belonged to the sky world, to dreams. Only when my feet touched ground again would time resume, would it all be real.

In the sunlight spilling into the room, I saw now what I hadn't wanted to see before: the broken glasses, the overturned furniture. On the wall, a framed print of the familiar author photograph. Blown up large, but revealing nothing new, no detail that I'd overlooked. It remained a stranger's face. Those two handsome profiles, his and hers, must have clashed ferociously: kisses like bites, teeth bared. How much I'd wanted, only this morning, his lips against my neck.

Under the photo was a telephone table, and I saw that something had slipped behind it and lay against the wall. It was my manuscript, still in its large envelope, untouched. I bent to pull it out, brushed off the dust. A lot of work had gone into those pages, I thought. And I still wasn't sure how it ended.

138

I put on my shoes and went out into the lobby. The numbers above the lift door were changing: someone was coming up. I pushed open the fire door into the stairwell. Twenty-two floors was a long way to walk in heels, in shoes that still needed wearing in; there would be blisters. But I liked those shoes I'd chosen, I decided; they suited me. I tucked my book beneath my arm and started down.

Henrietta Rose-Innes was born in 1971 in Cape Town. In 2008 she won the Caine Prize, for which she was shortlisted in 2007, and in 2007 she received the Southern African PEN Literary Award. She has written two novels, *Shark's Egg* (2000) and *The Rock Alphabet* (2004), and her short pieces have appeared in various international anthologies.

Half-man and the Curse of the Ancient Buttocks

Mohamed Gibril Sesay

I LEAVE BED EARLY, sleep hanging onto me like some resilient beggar. The toll on my eyes is heavy. Ramatulai has seen the toll but what can she do? Sleep is not something you help someone to do.

Okay, let me say it straight: since I married Ramatulai I haven't been able to sleep well at night. It is not for those usual reasons: the nagging wife, the spouse who asks for too much of what people expect newly weds to do when the imams, in-laws and friends are gone, or the wife whose body language with other men makes the husband think the bodies might be exploring themselves much more beyond language. No, Ramatulai is no harbinger of those cliché causes of relationship insomnia. I cannot sleep because her sleeping form is so supernal that it gives me magical happiness to watch her sleep. I love the way she does her sleep. Face facing me, her eyes refocusing their lights towards her soul. I tell you, brother, you can see her dreams meandering within her being, dancing to the tip-tap of her heart.

I would stand up, to get a better view of her sleeping form. The way she raises her arm as she turns in her sleep, her fingers like she is holding some staff, index pointing to whichever direction the moon is… I hope I am not lying. But even if I am lying, one thing is certain, I love Ramatulai with all the manhood in me.

Brother, and you too, sister, looking at my head as if you are some psychiatrist sent to tether it to reality, Ramatulai's sleeping form makes me the happiest man in all Africa. No, sister, it is not because she is most passive when she is asleep. Love for submissive women is not in my genes. And you, brother, why are you looking at me like that, am I breaking the taboos of any male cult by saying what I am saying? Are you one of those who say a man who talks too much about his love for a woman is a foolish man? That a man's love is a thing of the heart and not of the lips?

Okay, okay, let me move my story in another direction. Because I could not sleep at night, I started sleeping in the office. My office mate said he could tell the depth of my sleep by how my open mouth moved from oval to round. It was roundest when I was deepest in sleep. He had several names for me, that office mate of mine. The latest one was Sleepo. He printed out some instructions to the other workers: mouth open slightly, you may wake him up; mouth open very wide, do not disturb. We called my office mate Orlangba, which in Temne means the fucker.

At first my sleeping was tolerated because of the belief that newly weds spend so much time in bed without sleeping that they need to make up for it during the day. Maybe you know the saying: do not make an early-morning appointment with a newly married man.

But I always leave bed early though I am newly married, so an early-morning appointment with me could have been alright. But you would not catch me at home for that appointment because I have to rush away from Ramatulai before she starts chewing breakfast.

I do not like the way Ramatulai chews breakfast. It is so ugly: her right jowl sulks as her left jaw bulges, lips rickety like those vans that face sideways whilst moving forward. I now see ugliness in human chewing. If you want to spoil my day, force me to watch human beings chewing. It is worse with Ramatulai because the contrast between her sublime sleeping form and her ugly chewing is so great that it turns my wits into fits. To save my wits, I have to flee before she commences the rituals of uglification.

I did not see ugliness in chewing before I married Ramatulai. Perhaps it is the morning tiredness that now makes me see funny. The optician had another story: "Your left eye shows evidence of a great slap, so now it sees far less than the right eye, distorting the angles of what you see."

"I get you, optician," I replied. "My visions now come to me hunching like hags in rags toting memories heavy with beatings from dead husbands."

"No," said the optician, "I think they come to you zigzagging like a man whose scrotal hernia weighs more heavily on his left foot."

I searched my memory for evidence of the great slap of the optician's diagnosis. There were many, but the champion slap was delivered by a cinema attendant. We were little, with no money to watch the third film on the matinée show. The cinema attendant asked for our jaws as fees. I gave my left jaw, slanting it the way some people do when they want others to think they are asking a clever question. The sound of the slap was like the shot that kicks off a hundred metres race. The other urchins ran home faster than the speed of wailing. I was the only one amongst them that submitted to the ritual of the great slap of the attendant testing the strength of his manhood on the jaws of my childhood. My trophy was the third matinée film and the tired vision of my left eye. That is me, brother, caught between the consequences of the great slap and the repercussions of the little sleep. Brother, I don't know how to handle this. I am a man, yes, but I don't know how to handle this.

Brother, the first time I saw Ramatulai she was winnowing fire with an abused plate, separating soot from the useful lumps put within the stony trinity of our cooking places. When women play with fire you get food. When men play with fire you get hit by stray incidents. Mangy thoughts bite you. You get rabies. You loll your speech like I did on my first day with Ramatulai.

Man met woman for the very first time. Man fell in love. Woman saw man funny. Woman laughed. Man felt successful. Man caught fire. Woman winnowed man, to separate lust from love. Man proposed marriage. Woman accepted. Parents did not. Woman and man went ahead anyway. Parents placed a curse: man, you will have sleepless nights; woman the mouth with which you accepted the proposal shall be a source of discomfort.

Some people say Ramatulai and I are living without consent. Their problem is that we did our wedding at the government registry office. There were no imams, no elders, no relatives. There was no funny talk from my relatives telling Ramatulai's relatives that we see a flower in your garden that we want to pluck. Don't they know that plucked flowers die too soon? There were no grandfathers posing as the original husbands of Ramatulai whose wedding expenses must be reimbursed before we start our own wedding. There were no false brides that we must bribe to go bring the real bride. There were no bitter kola to remind Ramatulai that her marriage could sometimes be bitter. There was no white cloth inside a calabash that should receive blood from the torn hymen of Ramatulai and then be hoisted as a flag of pride on the rooftops of her family name. So some people grumble, what type of wedding is that without relatives? Did the couple just fall from the sky as adults, without mothers, cousins, fathers, brothers, sisters?

Even my own mother takes us for some fornicating couple. She once asked Ramatulai: "What are you turning my son into, did you give him the last drop of your first defecation after menstruation to turn his eyes upside down?" She is old now, my mother, heroine of my birthing. Tomorrow is my birthday, I'll visit her with presents to commemorate her achieving my birthing. People said I nearly killed her with my big head. Many murderers in this country are infants. But my mother would have none of that, she would be no victim of matricide.

"You should have been tried for attempted murder," Ramatulai once told me after drinking too much of the alcoholic narratives of my birthing.

"Why?" I asked.

143

"As an example to other would-be killers of mothers." She said this with that smile of hers, lips opening slightly, revealing the lower parts of upper incisors, colour like the insides of a young coconut.

Ramatulai has a way of saying serious things lightly, like we sometimes talk about our war: armed men who amputated limbs called cutting off wrists 'long sleeves' and cutting off elbows 'short sleeves'. They met this woman and asked: "What do you want, short sleeves or long sleeves?" The woman replied: "Well, you are the designers, you should know the sleeves that fit me well."

Or like the man rebels met hiding in a cemetery. "What are you doing there?" the renegades asked. "Don't you remember me?" the man replied. "I was amongst the people you killed last year." A rebel called Kill-man-no-blood, with eyes the colour of hurriedly spat-out kola chaff, looked at the man and said: "Well, you better hurry off from this place because our colleagues who kill people again and again are on their way."

Or like the mother and daughter the armed men met and asked: "Who is the older amongst you, for she is the one we will kill." The daughter replied: "This is my mother, she is older than I." The mother replied: "Yes, I am her mother, but she is very old too, I gave birth to her a very long time ago."

Ramatulai has barrel-loads of these stories, and one sometimes wonders whether they are all true. Like this other one about a bus full of travellers stripped naked by the armed men, who burned the clothes, ordered the travellers back into the bus and instructed the driver to speed away. A busload of nude people moving through the countryside. They stopped at the first village, descended *en masse* to solicit clothes. The villagers took to their heels at the sight of 70 naked beings. They moved to the next village, same story. So they moved on, fulfilling the ancient prophecy: naked you come, naked you go.

Our people say the good storyteller heals, relieves the stresses of eking out survival from soil and sea. Maybe that's why Ramatulai loves to tell stories in the evenings, between sunset and eyes-set, between waking and sleeping, preferably when the moon is at its fullest, tweaking the brain waves of the storyteller, making the storyteller a little madder, for only a person with the daring of a lunatic could knowingly talk like she is telling a lie.

Ramatulai is fun to be with when she is not chewing. She tells me dreams in the evenings, says she could not tell me them in the mornings because I leave bed early and rush out. So she captures them in a notebook for narration to me in the evenings. She once had this dream about my mother urging her on in a race. She was the only woman in a race of a thousand men. My mother was the only woman spectator in a stadium of a hundred thousand men. And all these men were against Ramatulai, shouting at her, raining invectives on her, testing the abusive metaphors of their manhood on the waki waki of her speeding buttocks. But my mother was praising her, urging her on. And my mother's voice was louder than the combined voices of the hundred thousand men: "Go on, daughter, use the skills honed in the kitchens and farmlands of Africa, use the lungs that raise up the fires of the cooking places, use the muscles that pound the rice, use the spines that tote the babies, use the resilience that they underestimate, win the race for me, your mother-in-law."

Ramatulai says dreaming is storytelling by self to self in the privacy of sleep. She says a lot more: that her name means 'Grace of God,' that it was the name of her father's first love who died long before he met and married her mother. When her mother found that out, she demanded a change of name. But her father would have none of it. This Grace-of-God was a source of many a palaver in their home. Ramatulai often sided with her father because she believed the name made her the first love of her father. She could not understand how her mother could be so jealous of a dead woman. One day her mother sat her down and said: "Baby pig once asked mother pig why her mouth was so long. Mother pig replied, 'as you grow up you will know'."

The week before last I saw Orlangba around these parts. He was going into one of those houses that leak during the rains. The inhabitants had covered the rotten zinc on the roof with polythene bags scavenged from many places. The bags were in all shapes and colours. Roofs of many colours, that's what we have in the slums of our living. People put big stones on the bags to stop them from flying in the rain. They say a president of ours was once with a visiting head of state in a helicopter flying over our town. The visiting head of state asked our president: "Why are there so many stones on the roofs of the houses of your people?" Our president replied: "Custom, ancient custom, each stone represents a dead relative."

It was one of those houses of many dead relatives that I saw Orlangba going into. That fucker knew how to put women under pressure to get them to acquiesce to his loins. He would pay some guys to find out discreetly where the woman stayed. If the woman was residing in those houses of many stones on the roof, he would ask his men to count the number of stones. He studied economics, that room-mate of mine. He said the extent of hunger in a house is directly proportional to the number of stones on the roof. So. A house with a hundred stones on the roof is a house with very hungry people. So. He would go there, if that was where the woman was staying, with a bag of rice in the first week. So. Second week, he would come with a bag of sugar. So. Third week he would come with a carton of tinned tomatoes. All this while he would not even say a word to the woman of his heart. But the women in the house would know anyway, and they would put the woman of Orlangba's heart under immense pressure to become the woman of Orlangba's loins.

Ramatulai once told me that women easily spot out men on heat. I asked her, "Has it got to do with their noses, is their sense of smell better than men's?"

"Of course,' she answered, "women home in their sense of smell whilst cooking."

"Or has it got something to do with their sense of sight?"

"Of course," Ramatulai answered, "women home in their sense of sight by looking for bulges, in their own chest; on men's trousers and on their own tummies. They are particularly watchful for bulging in trousers, for you know the saying, bulging penises have no conscience."

"Mine has a conscience," I protested.

"Of course," said Ramatulai, "else I would have cut it off."

I instantly clutched my penis as I heard this, like a woman would her groin should a strange man open the door to where she is bathing. You know how a woman does it, bending one knee towards the other, her shins move horizontally apart, creating an opening between her two insteps large enough for the biggest football to pass through. I had to do like that, brother, I had to hang on to my penis, for it was all over the news, about how Orlangba's wife cut off his penis with the sharpest knife in her kitchen.

Women these days do not make empty threats. They say the woman had warned Orlangba, "stop messing around, else I'll destroy your manhood." But he thought the woman was like the guinea fowl whose flurrying of feathers could not even take it to the lowest branches of the shortest trees. Brother, let me tell you, surprise knoweth no shocker like a woman underestimated. Just like that, when the woman caught Orlangba with a girl in a house of many stones, she sliced off his penis. We now call Orlangba Half-man – his banana was cut midway, with a single slash of his wife's kitchen knife.

"Of course," said Ramatulai, "women are experts with knives, they home in their skills in the kitchen slicing onions, potato leaves and turgid bananas."

Orlangba's wife was arrested for what the police called aggravated bodily harm. Ramatulai organised women to get her out. Forty-one women went to the police station slashing bananas with kitchen knives.

The police at first put up some resistance. But an old woman in the group, hunching like a passenger telling her destination to the driver of a little taxi cab, bared her buttocks to the commanding officer. He turned his face away to avoid the curse of the ancient backside and ordered the immediate release of Orlangba's wife.

When my mother heard about Ramatulai's march to the police station, she said, "My son, God will protect you from what God has given your generation; if

God gives you big teeth, He will give you big lips to cover them."

Yesterday, I read in the notebook of Ramatulai's dream that she, Ramatulai, saw my mother handing me over to her as a gift for having led the women to the police station. It was also written in the notebook of dreams that I was clutching my manhood as I was being handed over to this woman of my heart, Ramatulai, Grace-of-God.

Ramatulai says she thinks my mother loves her, despite her anger at us for having our wedding at the registry office. Brother, I am a little frightened. For you have heard it said: "When the main woman of your past and the main woman of your present are united, know that your manhood is in for some great shocks." That, my brother, is something I don't know how to handle. Sister, I am still having sleepless nights. I am a man, yes, but I don't know how to handle this.

I leave bed early, these thoughts hanging onto my manhood like hernia. The toll on my manhood is heavy. Half-man has seen the toll, but what can he do? Manhood is not something you help someone to carry.

Mohamed Gibril Sesay grew up in Freetown, Sierra Leone. He was educated at Fourah Bay College, University of Sierra Leone, where he currently teaches Sociology.

No Windscreen Wipers

Alba K Sumprim

"ESI, CAN YOU BORROW me ten Ghana to buy petrol for my *trotro*?"

Agya Yaw's wife, Esi, who is as fragile as reinforced concrete, stops tying her headscarf and snaps her fingers, *pka, pka, pka*. "And what about the money for Paa Kwesi's funeral contribution that you have been promising me since? You know I can't show my face in the village until I have that money. But it is rather you who is asking me for money!"

Agya Yaw reminds her that she didn't like Paa Kwesi in life, in fact, she'd called him a shameless goat the last time they met, so why the fuss now that he has thankfully died? Momentarily stunned, Esi grips the side of the table, "Eh, so that is how you now talk about my relatives? Shameless goats!"

From the tight shape her lips have formed, Agya Yaw knows there is no point in reminding her again that she is the only one who insults her family members. Not him o; he wouldn't dare.

"Hmm, they told me not to marry you, but would I listen? Now, you see the way God is punishing me? Anyway, it's my fault o, I don't blame you!" She takes her purse from her basket and makes a drama of showing that he's getting the last of her money, "Take," she spits, and thrusts the ten-cedi note at him.

Agya Yaw rolls his eyes and sighs deeply as Esi launches into the next scene of their seemingly never-ending marital script. Raising her hands dramatically to the heavens, she sighs, "Ei God," and slaps her chest hard, "so my husband has turned me into the man of this house?"

Though it wasn't like this when they got married, shouting and causing a palaver had somehow become Esi's forte, useful skills when haranguing customers, other rivals at the smoked-fish section of the market and, of course, her husband. The petty insults had become as normal as drinking pure water, and Agya Yaw had swallowed it quietly all these years.

Like a wound-up toy, Esi could shout and shout and shout, but eventually, by God's grace, she would shut up.

This time, though, Esi has been cruel. How could a woman talk so harshly to her husband? But then, what could he do? Because that crispy green ten-cedi note, held tightly between his fingers, they both know, has stripped him of his manhood, therefore, all Agya Yaw is able to morally muster is, "Esi, as for this one dee, I think you have gone too far."

"You think? I haven't even started o. Agya Yaw, Agya Yaw my husband, don't come back to this house if you don't find my money. You will not disgrace me in front of my family, *w'ate!*" She yanks her earlobe. "Have you heard?!"

Avoiding Esi's blazing eyes, he folds the money slowly into his shirt breast pocket, "Esi, I have heard you."

"Look at you," she runs her finger through the air taking him in from head to toe and back up again, *"berma ti se wo!"* She jabs her finger at him, "And you call yourself a man!"

At the same time as Agya Yaw is being blasted, the daily hustle and bustle of the busy trotro station has started with a vengeance. It is hot, hot, hot, and threatening to heat up further, the cacophony of noise doing its best to keep up, as if it were some sort of competition.

Trotros in varying battered states leave the station; many belching out obnoxious exhaust fumes, while their mates shout above the racket. The race is well on its way.

Esi's skin-stinging early morning tongue lashing leads to Agya Yaw's late arrival at the trotro station. It leads to him missing his place in the queue, and then finding out that Sammy, his trotro mate, hasn't turned up for work. Still, Agya Yaw is light-spirited, even though working on his own today is going to be a great challenge.

The trotro station has been a place of refuge where no-one harasses him. On several occasions, including today, he fantasises about getting a student mattress and moving into the Union's office, an Esi-free zone where he would have complete peace and quiet. But then what would people think, especially his colleagues, who treat him well and to a certain extent respect him because of his age and his many years as a driver. Saying that, people like kokonsa too much and are always ready to gossip, sneer and mock anyone whose life seems more wretched than their own miserable lives. Apart from the very fact that Esi would surely make him return home, therefore, the thought of walking off into the sunset with his student mattress remains a dream that serves to lighten up the drudgery of his daily life.

After sitting in the queue and sweating in his hot trotro for what seems like ages, it's Agya Yaw's turn to load. The passengers board, he collects the fares and is thankful that many of them have coins; at least God is favouring him, small.

His first few runs go without any hitches. He gets full loads and makes back Esi's loan, two crisp five-cedi notes which he tucks into his shirt breast pocket for safe keeping, a portion of the daily sales he renders to Mr. Blege, the trotro owner, and a little something towards the contribution for that useless Paa Kwesi's funeral, who he's sure died specifically at this time just to spite people. He wonders how people can just selfishly get up and die without taking into consideration that others might not have money for all the funeral shenanigans.

By late morning, passengers have thinned out and the station resembles a morgue; even the sellers have relocated to the streets. Those who are lucky enough to have jobs are struggling to earn their daily crust. The children are in school, unless they have been sacked for non-payment of fees, and the market women, including Esi, are in the market dishing out the 'Makola Special' to those who look at goods longer than they ought to, and especially to those who ask prices but don't buy.

After enjoying Auntie Mercy's delicious kenkey, pepper and fish, washed down with two sachets of pure waters, Agya Yaw washes his hands and pays his food credit for the week, which eats into Esi's money, but at least it stops Auntie Mercy making unnecessary noise in front of people who are always waiting for a scandal.

He has always waited patiently in the queue to load at the station and leave with a full trotro, but today the passengers are not coming and he can't wait any longer. Today, he has to get his trousers back from Esi, or, at least, have some peace and quiet at home. In order to do that, he has to battle with those daredevil trotro drivers, who weave in a death-defying manner, horns beeping, making all kinds of illegal manoeuvres, scattering street sellers and overtaking with such speed it's a miracle there aren't even more accidents.

From the moment he reaches the overhead bridge bus stop, where two mates are struggling over a passenger, he regrets his decision and contemplates returning to the station to wait for passengers. Without his mate, Sammy, how did he expect to compete with the aggression of mates who have been known to push passengers into their trotros by force? Some resort to insults and blows and Agya Yaw has too much respect for himself to get involved with that. Not to mention that they could easily beat him if they wanted. The youth have no respect for their elders nowadays.

Shaking his head, his eyes scan the hullabaloo and land on an elderly booklong-looking gentleman, sporting a batik shirt, a colo haircut, and a rolled-up newspaper in his hand, backing cautiously away from the crowd, which includes mothers with tiny babies strapped to their backs, fighting to get onto trotros. A loud scream rends the air.

"God help us," Agya Yaw mutters as a woman with a baby and a heavy Ghana-must-go bag crashes to the ground.

Moments later, Agya Yaw makes eye contact with the elderly man, standing apart from the crowd, and calls out, "Abeka, Circle, Accra," while pointing his index finger in the direction of Accra. The old man gets into the front passenger seat, "I don't know what this country is coming to. Look at them, fighting like animals!"

Agya Yaw smiles, "Hmmm," and pulls away from the bus stop. He has made it a policy not to get involved in any discussion or argument that takes place on his trotro, and goes through a noncommittal repertoire of, "Ei!" "Hmmm!" "Eeehhhh!" and "It's not easy o!"

Further down the street, a lady in her late twenties and dressed for the office, stands on the roadside making a circular motion with her hand, the signal for Circle. Agya Yaw pulls over, jumps out of his seat and runs around to open the door. She gets in, cutting her eyes at the elderly man whose eyes have locked onto the opening of her shirt. She pulls out a romantic novel from her bag and buries her nose in it. The elderly man turns away under Agya Yaw's reproachful gaze, and opens his newspaper, rustling it loudly.

Agya Yaw's trotro arrives at Tesano bus stop first. He barely makes it out of his seat before other trotros arrive and aggressively snatch up all the passengers. He gets one passenger, a young mechanic in dirty overalls who had to push away a competing mate who had blocked entry into Agya Yaw's trotro. At this rate, Agya Yaw is in serious danger of not making any more money and the thought of going back empty-handed to Esi, who would spit fire, is more than he can tolerate. Other trotros whiz by, triumphant cheeky grins on the mates' faces, mocking him, boys young enough to be his sons and yet he is scared to challenge them. What does a man who only wants peace and quiet do in a world that starts with harsh words and ends with mocking grins?

"Driver, are we going to sit here all day?" The mechanic's voice cuts into his thoughts.

Heading towards Abeka Junction, packed with potential passengers, Agya Yaw, frustrated by the bullying and belittling smirks on the faces of his competitors, feels his foot pressing hard on the accelerator, something he has never done before. The elderly gentleman grips onto his seat in alarm.

"Driver, be careful o," the office lady exclaims.

Deaf to the alarmed gasps of his few passengers, he swerves around street sellers who dive for cover and throw insults. With a determined glint in his eyes, he speeds past, eyeballing his competitors racing each other towards the bus stop; the feeling of exhilaration is fantastic.

Agya Yaw calculates that if he could get at least ten passengers, and if by God's grace, they were all going to Accra, he would be sorted out for the day. After that, he would go back to the station and spend the rest of the day playing *oware* with his colleagues until it was time to go home. He has a plan. "Young man, what is your name?" he asks the mechanic excitedly.

"I be Adjetey!"

"I am Agya Yaw, my mate didn't come today, so, if you can help me collect the fares, I will give you something when we get to Accra."

Adjetey agrees and Agya Yaw cruises confidently towards the stop. The passengers rush noisily and try to board even before it stops, violently shoving each other and demanding in desperate loud voices where the trotro is going.

"Kaprice, Circle, Accra!" Adjetey shouts, enjoying his new role.

The passengers who manage to board include a large woman, who uses her considerable bulk to her advantage, an old woman, three students, a young hiplife wannabe whose jeans hang precariously around his knees, a sexily dressed young girl wearing revealing apushkeleke clothing and a man who gets in last, enjoying the view. The old woman, offended by the waist beads hanging out from the sexy girl's mini-skirt, stretches out and tries to yank her top down, which only reveals more of her bust hanging out of her low neckline.

The girl spins around in anger, "Adɛn? What is your problem?" The old lady shrinks back and turns to look out of the window.

The man wades in mischievously: "Don't mind her; she's doing 'I'm aware'."

The students titter with delight as the sexy girl kisses her teeth loudly. "Is it on a trotro that I'll do 'I'm aware?' In front of useless men who can't buy their own cars?"

The man fires back, "What do you mean useless?"

"You should know," she hurls back cheekily.

From that point, the insults fly, with passengers tossing in their ten pesewas' worth.

Agya Yaw keeps a determined eye on the road and half an ear on the elderly man's complaints about the decay of the nation, complaints that started the moment he entered the trotro. If it's not the youth, it's the rubbish and stinking gutters, or thieving politicians. He refers Agya Yaw to the front-page news, another sleazy corruption scandal. "Just to think, he was using money meant for improving hospitals to buy cocaine benzs for those small small campus girls."

Agya Yaw smiles, "Ei!" and leans to turn on the radio – maybe that would stop the elderly man trying to force him into an unwanted conversation.

The office lady comments loudly to the air: "Imagine, the pot that nearly cooked my breasts with his hot stares calling a kettle black."

The elderly man swings around to reply but the mocking, dagger-like 'I dare you' glare that is returned freezes his vocal cords. The women laugh heartily.

On the radio news, a Minister is interviewed about the Government's policy of zero tolerance on corruption. Agya Yaw hands Adjetey some cedi notes and a few coins in a plastic bag and tells him to collect the fares.

Adjetey snaps his fingers, "Yes!"

The large woman pulls a handkerchief from inside her brassiere, "Accra, ɛyɛ ahe?"

"Forty pesewas."

"Are you sure it's not 35?"

Adjetey raises his voice, "Maame, Accra, 40 pesewas."

She passes him a five-cedi note, "Two!" Then mutters, "Every day, you are increasing the prices. Where are we supposed to find the money, eh?"

The hiplife wannabe puts on LAFA, the locally acquired foreign accent. "For real, maaan, you know war am sayin'."

The old lady asks, "What did he say?" Everyone ignores her because they don't know.

The elderly man snorts as the Minister gives examples of how corruption should be tackled.

"Ho, don't mind that man. I know him well, he's always at the casino and clubs," the sexy girl laughs.

"Ehh, so those are the men you like to do 'I'm aware' for?" The man teases.

The sexy girl throws him a vicious look, hands her money to the large woman to pass on and turns to stare out of the window.

The large woman laments, "And their children go to schools abroad, but our children have to go to the *nyama nyama* government schools here. You go to the market and the money passes through your hands like water."

Adjetey joins in, "It's true, everything is too expensive." He snaps his fingers, "Front seat, bring your money." The elderly man doesn't hear him, "Old man, I said bring your money!"

"Young boy, take it easy. Am I going to run away? I will pay."

"How many times do I have to ask you?"

The elderly man hands over a ten-cedi note, "It's okay, it's okay."

The large woman sticks her hand out: "Mate, my change!"

Adjetey waves his money in the air for her to see, "Exercise patience, can't you see the coins are not plenty."

"Oh, I should exercise patience, so you can chop my money."

"Maame, abeg, watch your words, I'm not a thief!"

Adjetey collects the rest of the money as the radio voices discuss issues that make it difficult to tackle corruption at the grassroots level.

"Which grassroots? The tail follows the head," the office lady sneers. A chorus of voices agree with her, touting exaggerated rumours they've heard about thieving politicians as the gospel truth.

Eternal road works are going on and again the traffic lights are not working, the police to sort out the chaos are nowhere to be seen – fists wave and insults fly with abandon. Traffic inches very slowly forward as the sun beats everything with intense heat. Like locusts, the street sellers swarm in, jostling each other and shouting out their wares: you name it, the street mobile shops will provide it, even *mogya eduro*, which cures all diseases known and unknown to humankind. Suddenly traffic frees up onto an open road. Agya Yaw steps on the gas pedal – soon he will be in Accra and his money woes for the day will be over.

As if someone had juju-ed him, an elderly policeman springs out from nowhere onto the roadside. Agya Yaw groans.

The elderly man sneers, "Look at his shinny coconut head, *okom de no!*"

The passengers' laughter converts to mutters of agreement when the large women states, "Hmm, Daddy, we are all hungry o!"

As Agya Yaw pulls up to the roadside, the grinning mate of a competing trotro whizzing by, hangs out of the window and jeers at him.

"Stupid boy," Agya Yaw mutters as he pulls out what is left of Esi's money. He bends down and tucks a five-cedi note into his shoe. Exchanging a 'what can I do' look with the elderly man, he folds the rest of the money inside a bit of paper and jumps out of the trotro, slamming the door. The policeman looks at the money with disdain and thrusts it back to Agya Yaw, who refuses to take it. The passengers hang out of the windows, their ears flapping unashamedly. Agya Yaw pulls out his empty pockets and holds out his hands pitifully. The policeman looks him up and down with disdain, snatches the money and turns his back on him.

As the trotro pulls away the passengers jeer at the policeman, "Thief! Look at your face."

"How much did he collect?" Adjetey asks.

"One cedi," Agya Yaw sighs, Esi's angry "And you call yourself a man!" words slapping him around the face.

"Why did you give him?" the large women demands angrily.

Agya Yaw ignores her.

The sexy girl laughs, "Ho! One cedi pɛ? Our policemen have become cheap pa pa! No shame at all."

"For real, maan, you know war am sayin'," adds the hiplife wannabe.

Once the first insult lands, there is no stopping them, disdain and sarcasm dripping from their mouths.

"One cedi! What can anyone do with one cedi?" the man sneers.

"My son, ask me?" the old woman responds. "It wasn't like this in our days."

"Beh, he's buying pure water," Adjetey jokes. The passengers have a good laugh.

The large woman wades in, "Listen-o, one cedi, 30 times a day! Sometimes they collect more. It's not a small matter."

"True talk. The corruption is too much in this country," the man shouts, "and you, Mr Man, you are among. It's people like you who are spoiling this country."

"Eh, why did you give him?" the elderly woman demands.

Agya Yaw holds his tongue and absorbs the heckling. He doesn't want to break his rule but the passengers are pushing him too far and that large woman is sounding more and more like Esi.

"You should have stood up to him like a man," the large woman lectures.

That does it.

Agya Yaw swerves and screeches to a halt. "You people, stop talking or get out of my trotro." A loud collective surprised 'ei' rings around the trotro but no one moves. "Because your bellies are full, you are talking plenty."

The elderly man taps him on the shoulder, "Agya Yaw, it's okay, eh, let's go."

The trotro moves off in silence, the only sound coming from the radio; a discussion show about which woman a man would prefer, one with no teeth or one who wets the bed. The DJ laughs likes a demented hyena.

"Bus stop," the office lady calls out. Agya Yaw stops for her to get down, but just as he's about to move off, the sexy girl asks to get down. The sounds of "Apus!" follow her off the trotro. She makes a rude hand signal to the man: "Foolish man!"

All stays quiet on the trotro until a scrawny young policeman, as if by juju again, appears on the side of the road.

Agya Yaw exclaims, "A a, what again?" But this time, Agya Yaw doesn't budge from his seat. If it's not Esi, he's not giving any money to anyone.

The policeman strides up to the trotro and Agya Yaw immediately hands over his licence and trotro documents. The policeman ignores them and tries to intimidate Agya Yaw with his intense stare. It doesn't work. The policeman walks around the trotro checking for something.

"A a, driver," the man states, "dash im someting, make we go!"

Agya Yaw's angry glare stops anyone else from commenting.

"Eheeeeeh!" Something catches the policeman's attention. He jabs at the windscreen, "Where are your windscreen wipers?"

Casually leaning out of the window, Agya Yaw looks up at the sunny sky and drawls, "Ah, but is it raining?"

"My friend," the policeman rants, "I am the one asking the questions here. In fact I am arresting you for not having windscreen wipers." He jumps into the trotro, which becomes as quiet as a cemetery.

Agya Yaw turns to the policeman, stares at him very well, and raises his eyebrows.

"Cantonment police station," he barks in reply.

Agya Yaw nods his head and drives completely off the Accra route.

The passengers grumble as the trotro heads towards Kokomlemle, but quickly shut up when the policeman straightens up his shoulders and shouts: "Hey you, shut up there. No-one is getting off."

The only sound in the trotro now is the radio playing the hiplife song, ' ... *I dey mad o, I dey go crazy!*' A few passengers laugh nervously.

The policeman slowly becomes unsettled by Agya Yaw watching him closely through the rearview mirror. Agya Yaw smiles: "Officer Kwame Boadi, Cantonment police station? I like it – my brother-in-law is the chief over there." The policeman begins to look sick. Agya Yaw notices the change, "Boadi, today we will see who is who."

Officer Boadi fidgets and finally gathers the courage. "Eh, bus stop!"

There is a sharp collective intake of breath, plus giggles from the students.

Agya Yaw jabs at his temple. "Are you correct?"

Officer Boadi develops a stutter. "Em, I'll, hmm, I said I will get down here."

In a matter of seconds, Officer Boadi loses his authority and the passengers laugh freely, commenting loudly on how unserious policemen are. Some go as far as to call him a two by four policeman. "You be *azar paaa!*"

"But you have arrested me," Agya Yaw reminds him.

"Oh, my brother, hmm," he scratches his head, "this time, I'm considering you. So, I think I'll get down here."

"No, we are going to the station," Agya Yaw insists.

"Aden?" The large woman shouts, "He says he wants to get down, let him get off so that we too can go."

The man wades in. "Eh, she's right. Can't you see we are in a hurry?"

"Agya, don't mind him," the elderly man consoles, "you know what these policemen are like. Let him down."

Agya Yaw snaps, "Were you people not here when he arrested me? Why are you behaving like goats?"

"Bushman, who are you calling a goat? Nonsense. Stop this trotro," the man screeches.

Agya Yaw is furious. "My friend, save your saliva. As for the station deɛ, we will go!"

The man jumps up in his seat. "Mr Man, stop this trotro or I'll give you a dirty slap."

Officer Boadi gathers courage: "Eh, stop this trotro, you have kidnapped us."

Agya Yaw laughs. "You're the one who hijacked my trotro, I will show you where power lies today. Boadi, you are a very foolish man."

The old lady taps Agya Yaw gently on the shoulder, "Driver please, exercise patience, wae".

Agya Yaw pulls his earlobe. "Were you people not listening to the news? It is people like you who are allowing people like him to spoil this country."

A few passengers moan, "Oh driver, you are talking too much."

Officer Boadi pleads, "Agya, *abeg*, stop this trotro." He begins to struggle with Adjetey to open the door but the trotro speeds up.

"Adjetey, keep the door locked."

The trotro becomes a riot of noise as passengers climb over each other trying to get to the door, while the large woman swings her bag viciously at Adjetey.

"Driver, my children are still small o," the man wails.

The passengers' yelps and pleas become incoherent frantic screams, but the more they scream, the faster Agya Yaw drives, causing those on the streets to dive for cover. Insults fly at him from inside and outside the trotro but he is oblivious to them.

Officer Boadi grabs a wad of money from his pocket and peels off some notes, "How much do you want to let us go? Twenty, fifty, a hundred?"

The elderly man implores, "Please, take the money and let us go. Don't kill us today."

Agya Yaw snorts and waves him off, stepping on the gas and pushing the trotro which begins to rattle. He guns for the traffic light which is just turning yellow. Passengers start to pray, "Jesus, Jesus, Jesus." Others speak in tongues.

A terrified Officer Boadi waves multicoloured notes in Agya Yaw's face, shouting, "Let them go, take me! We can sort this out. You and me!"

Agya Yaw brushes his hand away and inhales sharply as he lurches towards the car in front of him. He slams his foot hard on the brakes and swerves, throwing the screaming passengers around the trotro and leaving a trail of black skid marks and the stench of rubber. The traffic lights are red and the street in an uproar of fearful wails, insults and some scraped hands and knees. Grabbing the opportunity, Officer Boadi throws the money at Agya Yaw, elbows Adjetey, yanks open the door and sprints off before anyone can recover. The other passengers step out of the trotro in a daze as sellers and onlookers surround them demanding to know what's going on.

Before walking off, the elderly man jabs his newspaper at Agya Yaw, "Don't mind this man, he is too known." The onlookers stare at Agya Yaw and make comments.

The large woman grabs Adjetey from behind. "Mate, my change."

Adjetey pulls away roughly. "Is the trotro for me?"

She turns to Agya Yaw. "Driver, my change."

Agya picks up a green ten-cedi note from the money scattered all over him and hands it to her. She snatches it with force, "*Wo yɛ kwasea pa-pa! Fooooolish* man."

The hiplife wannabe strolls off last. "For real maaan, you da man. Yo know war am sayin'?"

Agya Yaw shakes his head and smiles, counting his money, happily ignoring the insults and car horns beeping as the traffic lights turn green.

Alba K Sumprim is the author of *The Imported Ghanaian*, a collection of humorous homecoming experiences. A graduate of the Cuban film school, she freelances for the BBC World Service Trust as a writer of radio and television dramas.

Double Wahala

Uche Peter Umez

Okuko na-aboputa mma na-egbu ya. The fowl digs out the blade that kills it – **Igbo Proverb**

CHUX FLINGS THE CUSHION back onto the sofa. He turns round smartly, his shin connects with the edge of the centre table. He hobbles round the table, slumps backwards on the sofa. Leaning forward, he grabs the table by its leg; he overturns it. He thinks of dragging the table outside and ramming an axe through it. But Obiageli will think he is mad. *Hasn't she driven him mad already?*

Relief seeps through him as he rolls up his trouser leg: his flesh isn't scraped. As he looks up he notices some dust on the ceiling. Obiageli can't pretend that she hasn't seen it. Why doesn't she brush it clean? Every other Saturday she joins the other women to keep her church compound spotless.

Cracks in between the dust patches, Chux observes. The ceiling is giving. He gets angry with his landlord. *Where is my rent? I'll call thugs to throw you out!* – that's the only thing the *ewu* is interested in, not repairing the damages.

"I'm going to give it to him soon," Chux says.

As he glances away, Chux thinks the face in the framed picture on the wall is smirking. He scoffs at it. He rolls down his trouser leg and rights the table back on its legs. He has scattered the bedroom and sitting room. Overturned everything. Upside down. Yet, he can't find it anywhere.

Upside down. Chux remembers the woman on the radio show. That was how the crusade idea came to him. He was sitting squashed in a rickety bus, while on the radio a woman begged the preacher to pray for her because *"everything in her life is upside down"*. Right there Chux saw how best to solve his rent problems. A few hours later, he and Lemchi tied up all the details.

Chux gets up and goes to the backyard. He scans the grass. No ashes, nothing. Except the sound of Fela screaming, *Double Wahala for Dead Body*, on the other side of the wall. Feeling more frustrated than ever, Chux marches back into the sitting room, his fists clenched, as if ready to punch someone. He drops himself on the sofa, breathing hard. He grips his head with both hands, fingers clawing at his scalp.

15,890 naira can't just have vanished! Chux closes his eyes briefly. Three weeks before, he and Lemchi were sitting on the steps of the unfinished building behind his compound, both of them trying to learn the Bible by heart – not realising Obiageli would make a mess of their plan.

"*Nwanna*, we need to memorise everything."

"Receive it, receive your anointing!" Lemchi aped a voice.

"Have you discussed with the printer?" Chux asked.

"Ah, Jesus wept." Lemchi yawned. "Yes, we agreed on the price. One hundred copies will do."

Now, what would he tell Lemchi? All the money gone? Will Lemchi believe him? Chux ponders, as he recalls how both of them once posed as local government officials and sold fake stickers to drivers on MCC Road. A policeman appeared from nowhere, and they'd scampered off for fear of being caught. Later, he found out that a part of the money had slipped out of a hole in his pocket. But Lemchi shot him a suspicious stare, as if Chux was the person who'd cut the hole in his pocket.

"I'm dead." Chux slaps his head with both hands, picturing the livid expression on his friend's face. After all the trouble of planning the crusade, now this? He wishes he hadn't bothered. Lemchi never takes life seriously. While Chux was worrying about the crusade, Lemchi was busy hanging out with girls at bars and clubs. At least Lemchi brought some of those same girls to pose as ushers during the crusade.

Lemchi had also come up with the idea of Mt. Jericho Anointing Oil. Chux thought nobody would pay a kobo for such a tiny bottle, but his friend had pasted colourful stickers on each of the 800 bottles in the four cartons. That night, as Chux stomped across the podium rapping and reeling out a crazed language, the villagers jostled each other to grab a bottle.

Chux glares over at the picture of Christ as if it were responsible for his misfortune. Every week Obiageli would stroke its glassy surface, as though it were her own soft cheek. Suddenly Chux springs up from his seat and yanks the picture from the nail and hurls it against the wall. Shards fly. Eye for an eye! She will find her precious totem gone just like his money!

Chux jerks awake on the sofa at the sound of the door slamming. He didn't realise he'd drifted off, nor did he hear the door open. The outburst must have drained him. Now he stares at Obiageli as she walks past without even saying hello. She is humming, *Ebube Chineke*... It occurs to him that she must have seen the money where it was hidden in a nylon bag under the bed. Chux leaps from the sofa like a cat. In that brief second before he grabs her by the shoulders he wonders if she'd used the money for tithe or thanksgiving in her church.

"Where's the money?"

Obiageli twists her neck sideways. Chux wrenches her around to face him.

"What did you do with the money?" he asks.

Obigeli lifts her hand to her cheek, to wipe at the spit that trailed his question.

What has got into her? Obiageli has never defied him, Chux thinks. Lemchi doesn't have to put up with this kind of shit. Lemchi, beer and girls. Parties. A bachelor at 40.

Chux drops his hands from her shoulders. She shuffles off to the kitchen. Then Chux sights the black nylon bag in her hand and runs after her.

In the kitchen Chux makes a grab for the bag. Obiageli moves it out of reach. He swipes again; quietly, she hands the bag to him. He peers inside. Ukazi. Onions. Ede. Meat. Soup items. Chux drops the bag on the floor. She grins at him.

Anger scratches at his insides, and he snaps at her: "Woman, I'm not joking. Where's my money?!!"

"Your money?" she says. "Blood money, you mean." She bends over, picks up the bag, and lays it on the countertop. "I gave all to my church. The Apostle will hand it over to a charity home after he's done praying on it. After all, you and I decided not to keep it, didn't we?"

Chux remembers her threat two nights before: *"Return it or I pack my things and leave your house with my children. Which?"* He isn't sure he consented to either option, although he'd appeared cool – simply because he didn't want any fighting while the children sat huddled in front of the TV and because he was still giddy over the operation he and Lemchi had pulled off rather smoothly – and so she might have misconstrued it for acceptance. But for that parrot-mouthed church member of hers who showed her the poster!

"Prophet Jeremy?" Obiageli had spat out two days after the crusade in Ogbaku, waving a poster of him wielding a large Bible and gazing into the heavens.

Chux had stared disbelievingly at her, wondering how she got the poster. Then she narrated how Mama Atta Boy saw the poster at the gate of a school while waiting for a bus to return her to the city. She doubted the snitching woman at first, but to discredit her Obiageli went along to see the poster. As Lemchi had suggested, the print was a bit blurred – deliberately – so none of their friends or relatives would easily identify their faces. To further reduce their chances of getting recognised, they pasted the posters on the outskirts of Owerri.

"You've turned me into a professional liar," Obiageli accused him.

"How?" Chux stuttered.

Obiageli looked him up and down. "I lied," she blurted out. "I had to lie, to save myself from shame. Our family from shame; shame – something you no

163

longer have in you!"

Chux now remembers vividly the exact answer Obiageli had uttered, in order to crush Mama Atta Boy's curiosity. "Looks like him, but that's surely not my husband," his wife had said.

"You gave *that* man?" Chux says, gripping her wrist. He wishes he'd halved the money and given Lemchi his own share straightway.

"*That* man is more honourable than you," she replies.

Chux wants to yank the scarf off her head. The tatty scarf that gives her a stupid righteous look. Instead, he tightens his grip some more.

Obiageli pulls. "You're hurting me. Let go."

Chux shoves her aside and stamps off to the toilet. He flings the door open, swearing to get the money back from the Apostle, no matter what it takes. As he pulls down his fly and pees into the bowl, he hears the rumble of a car outside. Chux recognizes the sound as his landlord's Volvo. The old man always sounds his horn, whenever he appears at the compound. Chux feels the man wants the entire neighbourhood to know that he's arrived. Everybody should probably come out and kneel at his feet. Sometimes, he thinks the fool just wants to alarm his tenants. Still, he peeps out the window. He draws back at once, zips up fast. For an instant, Chux considers locking himself in the toilet.

In the kitchen, Obiageli is singing a song of Patty Obasi's and cutting the vegetables on a board, when Chux sneaks back. "It's him," he says, glancing over his shoulder as if the visitor had trailed him.

"*Onye?*" she asks.

"Landlord," he whispers. "Let him know I've travelled."

"I can't keep lying for you." Her voice is firm.

Chux thinks of shaking her shoulders till her teeth rattle. Frustration makes him feel like lashing out at her, pulling down the shelf of tableware. Alive in his mind is the threat of the old crook, his landlord. Barely a fortnight ago, Chux's cellphone had rung. He knew the ringtone: *Espionage*. He'd assigned it to his landlord's number; Obiageli, though, had beaten him to the phone where it lay vibrating on the table.

"Travel," he'd whispered.

She frowned, pressing the phone to her ear. "So sorry, sir," she said. "Baby was crying. My husband travelled." After she finished speaking to the landlord, she told Chux about his threats: by month's end, all their belongings would be thrown away.

Chux had always called it bluff. But now the threat is genuine. What is he going to do? Chux dashes back into the toilet, twisting the key in the lock. He leans his back against the door, panting. The landlord is already out there, ready to tear him to pieces. Any moment now, Lemchi will appear too.

Chux jumps up as fists pound on the front door. He hasn't paid his rent the last six months. It isn't his fault, though – the landlord is a Shylock. Just around last Christmas he came barking: "Mister, I've rearranged rent payments." Every tenant to pay in two instalments. The first instalment in January, the second in July. Six months' rent apiece. In Lemchi's compound, tenants pay rents on a monthly basis. Chux nearly blasted the old dog at the time. Perhaps he should step out and do it now.

Chux glares at the tiled wall and sees a reflection of himself dressed up in police uniform banging at someone else's door in Prefab – a man who had intimidated Lemchi's girlfriend. More images crowd into his head. The car dealer with connections across Seme border; the engineer who supervised a flow station in Egbema, and other spurious characters he and Lemchi had played over the course of six years – after Gibbs Enterprises laid him off for negligence.

His favourite scam was when Lemchi acted as a taxi driver and Chux disguised himself as a Gabonese businessman. "Sir, I can get you a translator, if you wish," Lemchi had told him, just at the point a man was sliding next to Chux in the backseat of the car.

"*Oui? Merci, merci,*" Chux replied, nodding. "*Mon ami,* you know, buyer, who I sell market for sodium hydroxide?"

Lemchi's eyes popped in the rear-view window. "You sell hydroxide?"

Chux reached for his briefcase. "Me, plenty in Gabon, Selenium plenty; plenty chemicals for printing money me sell to you, *c'est?*" He then slipped out a small bottle with 'Sodium Hydroxide' written in bold cursive lettering over it. The passenger, who had been pricking up his ears, immediately showed interest and lived to regret his greed.

The banging on the front door persists and resounds in the toilet window. A lizard drops out from nowhere. Chux hears Obiageli scream out, "I'm coming!"

Chux regrets not going to entreat the landlord beforehand, as she advised. But the last time Chux visited him, the bloody fool had turned up his nose, as though he stank. He leans over to spit and catches sight of a blob in the toilet bowl; Chux pulls back, wrinkling his nose. This is it? His life has been reduced to shit ready to be flushed down the drain? Chux becomes angry with his children's inattention. How many times must he drum it in their ears? He'd warned them to stop using the toilet, since the tap hardly runs. *Go behind the unfinished building and do your business.* Apparently nobody seems to take him seriously any longer, not even the woman whose life he is striving to improve!

The sound of Obiageli's scream jolts him back to reality. The old *nkita* must have hired a couple of touts to rough-handle him and his wife. Chux unbolts the door. He darts out. He sees Obiageli wrestling the TV set from the grasp of a shirtless young man. Two other men are forcing his sofa through the door, their biceps rippling. Chux turns as his wife thumps to the floor. The man scurries out through the door with the television, chuckling like a bush fowl.

Chux reaches out a hand to lift Obiageli to her feet, but she slaps it away.

"Do something!" she sobs.

For a moment, her teary face reminds him of all the people he has swindled, disappointed, quarrelled with; even the ones who threatened to send killers to him, who brought the police to handcuff him – although he got his bail without ado because some of the officers were his drinking buddies; even the ones who took his name to Okija and other shrines.

Chux realises he might have found a job if he'd tried hard enough, but then not every person is made for office jobs.

"Everything is in God's hands," he mutters, and trudges out of the sitting room into the yard.

"Ha, ha." The landlord swaggers over to him. The old dog looks smug with himself.

Chux's possessions are scattered about. He longs to swat at the chubby nose – but he imagines himself stretched out like a lizard on the ground, a thug's large foot crushing his spine.

The landlord smirks at him. Chux makes to leave, afraid that, if he doesn't restrain himself, he might deal the landlord a blow.

"I'm not through with you yet!"

Chux pauses, narrowing his eyes at him. He is about to spit out his own threats, when they both swing their heads in the direction of a Honda rocking towards them. The car pitches to a halt next to the Volvo. The landlord marches towards the car, probably to tell off the Honda driver for parking so close. The door opens slowly. Lemchi slides out, dapper in sleeves and chinos. He walks past the landlord, paying him no attention.

Chux wants to smile but panic seizes him. Lemchi would never forgive him when he discovers that the crusade money was gone.

"That's the car I was telling you –" Lemchi is saying.

"Do as I say," Chux cuts him short.

Lemchi cocks his head sideways. "What?"

"My landlord, you know him."

"What about the money?" Lemchi insists, looking impatient. "Jessica and I have some place to go; now."

Chux stiffens as the landlord moves towards them. "We're in trou…" His voice drifts off. The landlord is just behind him.

"Mister, it's time to say, how do you put it?" the landlord speaks aloud as though to impress Lemchi. "Good riddance to bad rubbish, right? Ha, ha."

Then the landlord heaves his bulk away, swaggering into the compound, to ensure his eviction orders have been thoroughly carried out.

Lemchi frowns. "I thought we were supposed to..."

"Sir!" Chux cries out.

The landlord turns round at the gate.

"May I introduce you to my lawyer," Chux says, patting Lemchi on the shoulder, hoping his friend will play along.

The landlord eyeballs him. "What rubbish are you talking about?"

Before Chux can reply, his children sprint into view. Their schoolbags dangle from their shoulders, swaying back and forth. Chux shivers.

"Daddy. Daddy, look!" Flocking behind him, the three kids point at the messy pile of cutlery and clothing and furniture strewn across the earth.

Chux hears Lemchi clear his throat. Fear grips him. In a flash he sees the disgrace that awaits him. Sweat pools in his armpits as Lemchi walks up to the landlord.

"Nobody is threatening anybody," his friend says. "But our judges, hmm, can be crazy. Women's rights, child abuse. Oh, you heard about Justice Ekezie's verdict – the one about the landlord who...? Oh, well, never mind. I assume you've nothing against children. Our judges, crazy bunch, hmm. I wonder why they get unnecessarily sentimental when it comes to cases involving poor kids young enough to be one's grandchildren, or assaulting – or, is it battering? The law is an ass, they say. You know what I think, Mr. Landlord?"

A shadow crosses the landlord face, and he frowns. Silence envelops everyone.

Chux tries to smile at Lemchi but his friend shoots him a stern look. Both of them turn to face the landlord, with professional calm.

"I'll be back!" the landlord threatens and storms past them into the compound, calling his heavies.

"We'll be waiting for you, sir!" Chux shouts after him, laughing.

As the two friends walk into the compound, Lemchi puts an arm over Chux's shoulders and says, "So where's my money, Prophet Jeremy?"

Uche Peter Umez won the *2008 Bath Spa University Creative Writing Competition* and was Highly Commended in the Commonwealth Short Story Competition (2006 & 2008). He was also finalist/runner-up for the *2007 Nigeria LNG Prize for Literature*. An alumnus of the *International Writing Program USA*, his short fiction, poems, children's stories, reviews and non-fiction have been published online and in print.

Bomb of Biafra

Uzor Maxim Uzoatu

HEAVY WERE THOSE DAYS. Women asked for bombs, kids begged for bullets, and a man's greatest need was the gun. The crowds bearing coffins in the street cried to be turned loose on the enemy. This was Biafra, and I was involved. I was a bomb, a primed bomb awaiting detonation.

I was without question the first human bomb in history, and the makers of the Guinness Book had better be alive to this world record. I was forged in the red heat of Biafra, and Father did not mince words when he turned toward me and said: "You are my bomb."

And thus I got my name: Bomb.

The wags of course called me a different name entirely: Bum! But that is another story. As a true Biafran I can only answer to my father's name for me.

Actually I was named Obumneme at birth but, like Pip in Dickens' *Great Expectations* who could not get on with Pirrip, I turned the name to Bumbum only for the wags to come up with Bum before my father handed down the clincher: Bomb. I thus became the ace in the war effort of Biafra against the old country Nigeria.

The war took nobody by surprise; not even the deaf. The first wave of headiness soon gave place to panic and there was war. Whole towns were transported to dire villages, and the airwaves broke out in singsong with the news: The Nigerian Civil War is here.

"I'm taking you to the village for safekeeping," Father announced that afternoon. "I'll unleash you on them when the time comes."

The village was home for rats and lizards. We killed and ate them. That was the Biafran way: killing rats for nourishment, eating lizards for protein. Up the struggle!

It's a terrible fate when a bomb is reduced to killing just lizards; and to think that the lizards most times prove more difficult to kill than humans!

The lizards of Biafra were a funny lot. On a certain Biafran morning this red-headed lizard danced on the red wall of Granny's hut – and grandly told me his name was Timothy! Enraged, I gave chase. The creature made to disappear into a fissure on the wall but I was too fast for him.

"Have mercy," said a voice across the compound wall.

I turned. The face of a girl showed above the palm-topped mud-wall.

"Please don't kill my brother," the girl said.

"And who is your brother?" I asked.

"Let him go," she said, pointing.

I looked at the lizard, and then at the girl. "How can a lizard be your brother?"

"This is Biafra." She smiled.

I affected a weary shrug of the shoulders, after a long pause. "What absurdity!"

"You have to understand these things," she said, jumping over the wall and into the compound. "Haven't you heard the Head of State? In this war the grasses and the sands and the animals are all fighting on our side. Hail Biafra."

I made some incoherent noises, thinking the girl was mad.

"My name is Nkechi," she said, patting me on the shoulder. "And what is yours?"

I was tongue-tied for moments on end before I could manage to blurt out: "Bomb".

"Bomb?" she screamed, breaking into merry laughter.

"But what's funny?"

"Who gave you that name?"

I sighed in disgust, making to walk away.

"At any rate, many thanks for not killing my brother, Mr. Bomb," she said, looking beyond me. "Let's go, Timothy."

I had heard of Biafran soldiers turning into tigers and lions in the war effort; I now saw a lizard turn into a young man. Timothy, smiling broadly, put a hand across the neck of Nkechi and they walked toward the rising sun.

I guess I fainted or something, for when next I found myself I was presiding over a steaming meal of agama lizards. I ran from the meal, screaming. I had made a terrifying entry into a world of nightmares.

It was after many moons that Father found me wandering deliriously amongst the talking grasses of Ndiorumbe. He let out a wild yelp, lifting me bodily upon a shoulder and took me straight to the lair of Ntioke the Witch-catcher. The wizened man of herbs did not ask any questions, did not utter any words. He laid me on my back on the torn brown mat, muttering throaty incantations. I saw and appreciated all his exertions, though I could not put out any words or respond to him in any perceptible manner. The room reeked of fowl ordure and blood mixed with the tang of multiform herbs. Ntioke picked up a red cockerel and dashed it on the wall, gasping with the exacting exercise. The cockerel fell dead at the head of the mat, a hand away from my head. Blood trickled out of its eyes and mouth. Ntioke scratched at the cockerel blood with his forefinger and pointed at the heavens before pushing the bloodied finger through my clenched teeth into my mouth. I felt sea saltiness spread from my tongue into the delta of my being. I also felt a stir in my loins and I could see Ntioke nod as though to answered prayers. He grabbed at some herbs on the rafters, flailed them on the heads of a handful of dark figurines and threw them into his mouth, chewing feverishly. The chewing lasted for moments on end with his eyes misting over and dribbles of water running down his nostrils. He suddenly coughed out the chewed herbs into his open right palm and threw the lot at my face with a quickness that had me gasping for breath.

"Ah Biafra!" Ntioke spoke at last, narrowing his squint eyes toward my father. "This war will take us to the end of the earth and back."

Father could not say a word, and no decipherable gesture was forthcoming from his blank mien.

Ntioke spoke some more, now looking fixedly at me. "He will soon come. You brought him in good time. He was not too far gone in the wilds of vagabond nightmares of our new order."

Silence stood in the air for some moments and I then heard a cock crow.

"The spirits are calling him to wake up," Ntioke said, patting my father on the jaw. He gave me a mild kick on my knee. "Wake up, son of our fortune!"

I stirred, struggling to say something but the words were beyond me.

"My son, are you all right?" I heard my father say, and he actually looked stupid with the effort.

"He is good," Ntioke assured him. "He is gathering together the armaments of this new dawn. We shall soon hear from him."

"It is only when a man hears the news that he wrings his hands in wonder," I muttered, and sat up.

Father was instantly exultant in triumph, throwing up his two fists into the air.

"Biafra has powers!" Father screamed, looking from me to the witch-catcher.

Ntioke cryptically assumed the aspect of a remote high priest, intoning: "Your boy will get to all sectors of this war. But he shall survive."

Father and I did not need to say any other words before it dawned on us that we stood dismissed from the presence of Ntioke. We literally fled.

We left in silence, me and my father, down the dwarf elephant grass-strewn pathway to Ogbana spring, and at the large clearing dominated by a huge cheleku tree we found hundreds of Biafrans running into the araba bush.

171

Father anxiously asked to know what was amiss from the first score or so of disappearing Biafrans, but mum was the word.

"Air raid!" cried a teenage boy who at last answered my father's repeated question.

Father looked at the sky but there was no plane in sight, and there was no harsh sound of an approaching jet bomber.

The sprightly teenage boy who had just hidden behind a lush thicket was still forthcoming with words for our benefit. "What are you looking for up in the air?" he asked with a hushed tone. "We are not running from any air raid from the sky. Air Raid of Biafra is on a conscription mission here. Hide before he gets you!"

Father quickly grabbed me by the throat and groin and hurled me into the bush. He just as quickly dived headlong to be by my side, cowering.

Who would not flee from the man nicknamed Air Raid, that quintessential maverick, feared by the Biafrans as much as the Nigerian enemies? He was not a soldier before the war but his intrepid feats at the war fronts had catapulted him in promotion to the post of almost the second-in-command to the Head of State. Born across the waters to a hyena father and a mad dog mother, he was boiled in a juju pot until he was 20. He walked through a hail of bullets to capture a battalion of Nigerian soldiers at Abagana. With a wave of the hand he brought down a jet fighter in Uga. The captured Russian pilot shat in his underpants, and spoke with gusto in Igbo: "*Anwuolam-o!*" Air Raid had no stomach for fright in the belly of any soldier of Biafra. He shot the soldier dead. He would rather have a Biafra with, say, only one brave soldier, maybe himself. Tutelage was not his forte; any person conscripted by him for the war effort was sent to the frontline straight away. The sight of him, in short, was sure death.

It was a good hour before we started emerging from the bush.

"This Air Raid fellow will kill all Biafrans before the Nigerians can manage to get here," said Otika, the Nigerian school principal turned Biafran palm wine tapper who had to scamper down from a tall palm tree when the name of Air Raid was mentioned. He had ample bruises on his chest and stomach to tell the story of his flight to safety.

"I am not here with you-o!" the man behind me screamed at Otika. "You are mentioning Air Raid's name in the open air, eh? I am sure Air Raid has heard you through the waves. You are finished. He will come for you today."

Nobody raised his voice again. We all walked in silence, like stricken mourners, until we ducked into our homes.

Professor Ntananke, a first cousin of Ntioke the Witch-catcher, was waiting for Father in the house. He was agitation in overdrive and would not let my father drink water and set down the cup before mouthing his many words.

"War without ideology!" hollered Professor Ntananke, stroking his whiting beards and pacing about the room. "Warfare without intellectual content! Brutish!"

"Sit down, Prof," Father said to his agitated friend, smiling. "I think I have palm wine somewhere."

"This nightmare calls for no wine, palm or coconut!" Professor retorted. "A war has to mean something. Look at this, your young son. What does he understand that we are up to?"

"Go and fetch me kola nuts, Bomb," Father said, swaying his right hand.

"Go nowhere, boy," Professor said to me. "You should be here to know what we are about."

I was confused. I sat where I sat and Father said nothing.

"We have to go into the books to understand this war," Professor continued, staring more at me than at my father. "Here, we scream: Ojukwu is the king of Biafra made in Aburi. Over there, they shout: Go on with one Nigeria! Gowon. But Tolstoy in *War and Peace* educates us that the so-called great heroes are only labels giving their names to the events without having any connection whatsoever with the events themselves. The Rostovs and Bolkonskis of Tolstoy's novel have a lot to teach the Ojukwus and the Gowons."

My father was laughing. "I can see that this war is affording you the opportunity to wax pedagogical!" Father laughed some more.

"You can afford to laugh for all I care in this tuppence republic," Professor said, still stroking his beards which, according to legend, he grew with Ojukwu at Oxford. "Every leader wants a nation to lead. But the world at large takes no notice, as was the fate of the Invisible Man of Ralph Ellison's novel of that name. Your nation is invisible!"

Father ran into the inner room and came back with a gourd of frothy palm wine. He helped himself to two gulps with a slit mini-calabash before setting down one for his friend.

"A war is won here," Professor was saying, touching his head, still pacing about and not looking at the drink presented by my father. "It is a brain job. How can a war come good when we waste our great minds? Our troika of fine minds is gone. Ah, that trinity of sublime creation! The poet was killed in action here. The fabulist's home was bombed and he now travels the world dodging sure death at every corner. And the dramatist, jailed in the old country, I hear is dead!"

"Bomb, drink to the health of the new nation," Father said, pouring me a generous dose of good wine.

Professor was unrelenting with his words. "I knew it would come to this, especially against the background of the venomous Northern orgies in which your good wife perished..."

It was like a thunderbolt. Father hurled the gourd and the remaining wine in it at Professor. The fast missile grazed the left side of Professor's head and exploded on the wall, splashing palm wine all about the room. Like a surprised rat, Professor Ntananke turned and ran. Father gave chase, maniacally. This touching of an unspeakable raw nerve, and then the pursuit and the disappearance all reminded me of the pirate Billy Bones' assault on Black Dog in Stevenson's *Treasure Island*. Father returned not much later, panting and mouthing dreadful oaths. We found no common words between us and could only share unbreakable silence.

And thus Biafra lingered, past days and deaths and weeks and wakes and months and monsters. I longed to set eyes on Nkechi and Timothy. Lizards were becoming a rarity. One had to make do with the infrequent broth of cassava leaves. Starvation and kwashiorkor had unleashed a bigger war on Biafra than the Nigerians. My head grew large and my stomach distended into an unwanted pregnancy.

"Bomb, the name of your disease is kwashiorkor," Cosmas my playmate said, wounding me forever.

I sneaked away from him to the refugee centre at the old mission school, hoping to scavenge some disused relief materials behind the padre's house. But the refugees beat me back with their protest, marching in their hundreds and singing:

Unu atachala okporoko
Unu erichala corn beef
Were mmili ofe gbanyere anyi
Red Cross gbakwaa oku!

You have chewed up the stockfish
You have eaten all the corned beef
Pouring only soup water for us
Red Cross, go to blazes!

I needed food badly, and only soldiers were fed. I asked to be conscripted into the Biafran Army. I met Cosmas at the Conscription Centre. I was turned down on account of age and ill-health.

"The age is not right," said the Conscripting Commander, dismissing me. "Here is Biafra. Hunger does not a soldier make."

Cosmas, who was a wee bit younger than me, was taken.

I thrashed about, grabbing at everything and nothing as I wept. The Commander took pity on me on account of my piercing sobs; he consoled me by giving me a wedding invitation card.

"You'll see the food you need there," he said, smiling knowingly.

"Nkechi weds Timothy," said the card.

I could hardly wait for the wedding day to dawn. And it was taking an eternity and eating me up. Days could no longer end while nights glided into other nights, world without end. I was brooding over the misfortune of the wedding date that apparently would never come, like Godot, when I saw the soldier. He was marching endlessly back and forth in his torn uniform, singing gibberish:

Lie lie lie lie
Lie lie lie ila laa
Soja bu ukpaka!

"*Atingbo!*" the assembled throng hailed him.

"He suffers from shell-shock," said a fellow nearby, hissing. "This war will leave us with no sanity anywhere."

The singing soldier paid no heed, marching as ever from one end to the other. His soft youthfulness could not be disguised by his gruff haggardness. There was something vaguely familiar about this soldier. I stared at him more intently, wondering. He kept marching and singing. Then something clicked in my head.

"Cosmas!" I shouted, jolting the surrounding throng.

The young soldier instantly turned and stared at the hailing voice, opening his large eyes wide to blaze like those of Ojukwu.

I could not stay with those staring eyes. And, even more woefully, all the eyes around were on me. In panic I ghosted away, and the marching soldier's voice resumed in earnest.

The intimate voice of that soldier kept me haunting company until the advent of the wedding of the war. Nkechi shimmered like an angel of the waves; Timothy the groom shone like the rising sun. We ate. We drank. Rice and stew very plenty in the time-tested RSVP mode! We ate some more. We drank some more. Assailed by the deadly sin of gluttony, many Biafrans fainted with food dropping from their mouths and anuses. Drunkenness put many of our countrymen and women to snoring siesta. Vomiting was all the rage and many urinated on themselves.

Father shat, screaming: "I don't know why Chinua did not put in the book that things fell apart when women started eating chicken anus!"

I romanced my vomit. Lizards and rats jumped out of many mouths. Biafra thus lapsed into a general hangover.

"Bomb, how come everybody ends up mad in this country?" a naked and

175

woozy Professor Ntananke was saying, swaying from one side to the other. "You are even madder than your friend Cosmas."

In dire pursuit of a headstrong black rat that invaded the party and ate up my vomit I got myself to the Uzuakoli sector of the war where Ojukwu's beards were sweeping the floor, gathering sand and tufts and dead leaves.

"Bomb!" Ojukwu shouted, turning to face me.

"The People's General!" I saluted, standing to rapt attention.

"Can't you see that this war is not going according to plan?" he asked me, his large eyes bearing down at me.

"What plan?" a voice from within me asked.

"You are a saboteur!" Ojukwu screamed, waving. "Execute him!"

"Nobody can execute a bomb," said a voice from inside the bush. "We can only detonate, not execute him."

A crocodile crawled out of the bush, commandeering all the attention. Ojukwu saluted the crocodile.

"Call me Ironside!" the crocodile shouted. "I cannot be killed by any man. Danjuma the Butcher wasted his bullets."

"Tell it to the world," Ojukwu was saying, smiling broadly. "Aguiyi-Ironsi is back. Biafra shall live forever."

I turned away, following the disco sounds ringing in my ears until I got to the cheleku clearing. Black Scorpion of Nigeria and Air Raid of Biafra were rollicking in a disco party, surrounded by a bevy of bewigged Biafran beauties.

"There is sweetness in Biafran womanhood," Black Scorpion said, boogying while resting his head on a heavy bosom. "Air Raid, my friend, only your babes can save you Biafrans from total annihilation!"

There were other sounds and noises and beats, and I found it hard to know which way to turn. I stood still, and then I retreated, not unlike Biafra.

"Happy survival!" The new music took everybody by surprise. Weighed down by hangover, Biafrans found it hard to believe that the war was over.

The appearance of a batch of Nigerian soldiers in the village was greeted with much trepidation. People ran. Timothy turned tail like the lizard he was and disappeared into the bush. Nkechi went to the Nigerian soldiers and later left with them.

When Timothy came out of the bush he was full of lament over the loss of his new bride.

"Do something, Bomb," he beseeched me. "They must not escape with her."

I was confused. "Who do you want back, your sister or your wife?"

"Give me back my life!" he pleaded, his legs slowly turning into a lizard's tail. "She is everything I have."

I looked into his pleading eyes, and I beheld my absurd destiny of killing lizards with the bomb. Then I saw my father, who promptly asked me to live up to his name for me. I could not but pick up a big stone and go after the man-lizard. I aimed at a phantom a stone meant for a lizard. I missed.

"The bomb of Biafra never fails!"

The voice was familiar in its vagueness. I looked. Nkechi was there beyond the wall of the compound, pleading that I spare the life of her brother and husband, as it was in the beginning.

"Who said that?" my father screamed, bounding out from the house as Timothy put a hand across the neck of Nkechi and they walked toward the setting sun.

"What?" I said ineffectually, and I stood stone still as I saw my father carrying a full calabash of palm wine and staggering from too much booze.

"You are still my Bomb," said my father, taking a swig and swaying. "I buried your mother, my wife, inside your soul. Some day for sure you'll explode and she'll come walking back here. It's not for nothing that our people say that I'd rather be missing than dead."

Just then the band of Nigerian soldiers returned, and their very dark and tall leader hollered: "Where is that disappearing witch woman of defunct Biafra?"

They were obviously looking for Nkechi. Before we could say a word they had rushed into the house upturning all things.

Father shook his head as he whispered to me: "Maybe if your mother were still here they would have seized her."

It was proving impossible for me to find words. I looked away from my father.

"You are still my Bomb," he continued. "But this new time calls for new tactics, clever ways. What can really matter is what is inside of us, not what we yell out..."

He was interrupted by the reappearance of the soldiers, and unaccountably Father hollered in the loudest voice I ever heard: "Bomb of Nigeria!"

It was as though the mere mention of "Nigeria" was magic, a drug maybe. The soldiers fell to Father's palm wine, swinging and dancing and screaming: "One Nigeria!"

"Bomb," Father said to me, "get me kola and alligator pepper for us to wash down the palm wine."

As I made to walk into the house, the leader of the soldiers patted me on the head, rolling with mouthfuls of palm wine my new alias "Bomb of Nigeria" or maybe the rave slogan of the moment "One Nigeria" – I cannot truly tell which phrases emerged from his mouth for he was too far gone in advanced drunkenness to make much meaning.

The party could not stop for days and nights on end as the leader on his own ordered more drinks from tapsters and brewers seen and unseen. And from the quondam rebel points, from the bushes and forests, the tall palm trees and the deeps of the caves, the erstwhile Biafrans who had turned into lower animals and insects took the cue that all it took to belong was to shout "One Nigeria", and thus the cockroaches, rats, lizards, worms, mosquitoes, ants, flies and chameleons all sang the new song and then donned their human toga to glorify the bacchanalia that became win-the-war Nigeria.

Uzor Maxim Uzoatu was born on 22 December 1960. He was educated at universities in Ife and Lagos in his native Nigeria. He is the author of the poetry collection, *God of Poetry*, and was nominated for the Caine Prize in 2008. Married with children, he lives in Lagos, Nigeria where he is the chair of the editorial board of the newspaper *News Star*.

Rules

The prize is awarded annually to a short story by an African writer published in English, whether in Africa or elsewhere. (Indicative length is between 3,000 and 10,000 words).

'An African writer' is normally taken to mean someone who was born in Africa, or who is a national of an African country, or whose parents are African, and whose work has reflected African sensibilities.

There is a cash prize of £10,000 for the winning author and a travel award for each of the short-listed candidates (up to five in all).

For practical reasons unpublished work and work in other languages is not eligible. Works translated into English from other languages are not excluded, provided they have been published in translation, and should such a work win, a proportion of the prize would be awarded to the translator.

The award is made in July each year, the deadline for submissions being 31 January. The short-list is selected from work published in the five years preceding the submissions deadline and not previously considered for a Caine Prize. Submissions should be made by publishers and will need to be accompanied by 12 original published copies of the work for consideration, sent to the address below. There is no application form.

Every effort is made to publicise the work of the short-listed authors through the broadcast as well as the printed media.

Winning and short-listed authors will be invited to participate in writers' workshops in Africa and elsewhere as resources permit.

The above rules were designed essentially to launch the Caine Prize and may be modified in the light of experience. Their objective is to establish the Caine Prize as a benchmark for excellence in African writing.

The Caine Prize
The Menier Gallery
Menier Chocolate Factory
51 Southwark Street
London, SE1 1RU
UK
Telephone: +44 (0)20 7378 6234
Fax: +44 (0)20 7378 6235
Website: www.caineprize.com

About the *New Internationalist*

The **New Internationalist** is an independent not-for-profit publishing co-operative. Our mission is to report on issues of world poverty and inequality; to focus attention on the unjust relationship between the powerful and the powerless worldwide; to debate and campaign for the radical changes necessary if the needs of all are to be met.

We publish informative current affairs titles and popular reference, like the *No-Nonsense Guides* series, complemented by world food, fiction, photography and alternative gift books, as well as calendars and diaries, maps and posters – all with a global justice world view.

We also publish the monthly **New Internationalist** magazine. Each month tackles a range of subjects, such as Afghanistan, Climate Justice, or the Economic Meltdown, exploring each issue in a concise way which is easy to understand. The main articles are packed full of photos, charts and graphs and each magazine also contains music, film and book reviews, country profiles, interviews and news.

To find out more about the **New Internationalist**, subscribe to the magazine, or buy any of our books take a look at: **www.newint.org**